"Jameson Currier knows men—app
Brimming with humor and gentle pa...., ...
book is a carnival of men's endlessly entertaining urges,
obsessions, tactics, and ploys." —Stephen Greco, *The
Sperm Engine*

"In his new collection, Jameson Currier reasserts himself as one of our preeminent masters of the short nar-
rative form. In these lapidary tales, he computes the
inscrutable calculus of desire with uncanny accuracy.
There is such precision in both the foreground and
background details of each tale that the effect is often
unnerving. This is not a microscope that Currier presents to you, dear reader; it is a mirror. And objects in
mirror are closer than they appear." —Thomas L. Long,
editor-in-chief, *Harrington Gay Men's Fiction Quarterly*

"Jameson Currier is a literary *rara avis,* a topflight
American short story writer who treads where he
pleases, and doesn't acknowledge genre boundaries. At
its best, his work—particularly his erotica—is filtered
through an exquisite poetic sensibility, and a prism of
humanity that lifts the story above and away from anything as pedestrian as a genre, and into the realm of fine
literature." —Michael Rowe, author of *Looking for
Brothers* and *Other Men's Sons*

"Jameson Currier's lyrical stories wake the heart as well
as the flesh—he understands the irrational complexities
of human desire, and moves beyond the simple mechan-
ics of sex to also explore the emotional and spiritual
aspects of two people connecting through love or lust
or any other passionate feeling." —Lawrence Schimel,
editor of *The Mammoth Book of Gay Erotica*; author of
Vacation in Ibiza

Desire
LUST
Passion
SEX

Desire
LUST
Passion
SEX

GReeN
CaNDY
PRess

Desire, Lust, Passion, Sex by Jameson Currier

ISBN 1-931160-25-2

Published by Green Candy Press,

www.greencandypress.com

Cover and interior design: Ian Phillips

Cover photo: Copyright © Jack Slomovits, www.jackny.com

All of the characters in this book are fictitious, and any resemblance to actual persons, living or dead, is purely coincidental.

Some of the stories in this work were originally published, some in different versions, in the following: "A Kiss" first appeared in *Gulf Stream Magazine*. "Alibis" first appeared in *Blithe House Quarterly*. "Buddies" first appeared in *Sex Buddies*. "Elvis Is Alive and Working on Eighth Avenue" first appeared in *Best Gay Erotica 1999*. "Fearless" first appeared in *Men on Men 5* and was excerpted in *Man of My Dreams*. "First Shave" first appeared in *Best Gay Erotica 1996* and was also published in *Rough and Ready* and *Best of the Best Gay Erotica*. An audio version of "Flash Gordon at the Exclusive Dating Service for Men" was recorded by the author for *marilynsroom.com*. "Lessons" first appeared in the anthology *Men Seeking Men* and was also published in *Overload*. "Snow" first appeared in *Velvetmafia.com* and was also published in *Best Gay Erotica 2003* and *Best American Erotica 2004*. "What Counts Most" first appeared in *Boyfriends from Hell*. "What Is Enough?" first appeared in *Best Gay Erotica 1998*; an earlier version was published in *The Great Lawn* as "What You Think." "What You Find" first appeared in *The Unmade Bed: Twentieth Century Erotica* and was also published in *Velvetmafia.com*. "What You Learn" first appeared in *Absinthe Literary Review* and *OutsiderInk.com* and was also published in *Best Gay Erotica 2004*.

Printed in Canada by Transcontinental Printing Inc.

Massively Distributed by P.G.W.

For all the dates, tricks,
buddies, friends, and lovers

Contents

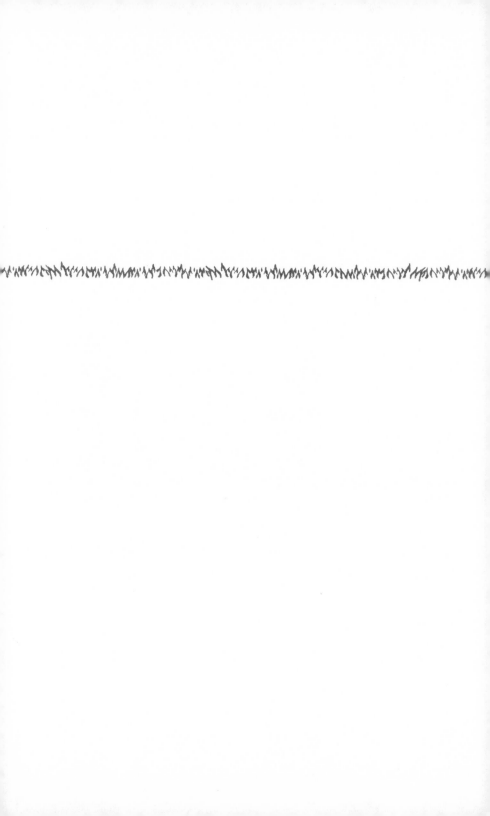

Lessons

There was a time in my life when I became a virgin again. It was during a period when a lot of things were going wrong, or, rather, a lot of people were disappearing without saying good-bye, and those who weren't disappearing were afraid that they would be disappearing soon themselves, and so, instead of waiting to see if I was going to vanish as well, I sequestered myself. I drew those willowy pink chenille curtains of mine closed, locked those over-painted louvered window gates up tighter than a chastity belt and decided to hide in the dark away from it all until it was safe to go back out in the sunlight again. It never really got safe again. Things never really got better but I learned how to adjust; I learned to peek through the slats, and to wear sunglasses and hats and whatever other protective gear I could get my body into when I went outside. Then one day I found myself no longer fretting about my self-imposed exile and back out in the sun again—in Sheep Meadow in Central Park carelessly sunbathing with my shirt off, without even putting on sunblock—and falling in love with a married man who was trying to fall out of love with his wife.

It was a complicated relationship for us both right from the start. Even though those gates of mine had been closed so long the locks were rusty, I was still standing outside my closet. He, alas, was hidden within his. But none of this hampered what happened between us in bed. In fact, that's how the relationship blossomed. Soon enough we began experimenting and I discovered that his greatest desire was for me to teach him how to become a bottom, or, in more technical terms, how to become "the passive partner who receives the penetration of a male's penis." And I became more than a willing coach, never one to shy away from the kind of muscular, beefcake ass he possessed. I spent hours getting that sphincter of his to relax, lubing up a small butt plug until he was comfortable with holding it inside his ass, then progressing to a slender dildo, then gradually moving up to a larger one, then a wider one, until one day we reached the point when he was ready to take my cock up his ass. I remember thinking at the time that if someone had given me that sort of time and attention, I would have no desire to find another boyfriend. I'd want to get married.

I should have realized this was too fun to last. Once my boyfriend had mastered my cock, it wasn't long before he wanted instead to play top to my bottom. The only problem was, he wasn't interested in giving me the same time and attention I had given him, nor was he interested in giving up being a bottom, either. Like I said, it was a complicated relationship—I was out and he was in and he wanted to be in and out with other guys. I never had the chance to switch from top to bottom with him, because we were too quickly switching between other partners and fighting too much about our positions. But he wasn't the only guy I had dated who, well, wanted to flip me over.

I should probably admit now that to many men I seem like the ideal bottom—boyish-looking and short, I don't even weigh in at 150 pounds—which is why I get such a delicious personal pleasure out of turning the tables and demanding that I be a top with all of these hunky macho guys who expect me to roll over and play bottom for them. But the truth is, even though I

looked boyish and my boyfriend wasn't really my boyfriend anymore, by this time I wasn't really boyish any longer. I suppose
this is a roundabout way of saying that I wasn't getting any
younger. And, as community folklore has it, after so much time
goes by, those closed gates soon look like a boarded-up wall; if
you want to open the window, you have to start over again and
knock out a hole to see the sun. So here I was a virgin again
after all these years of isolation and waiting for the right guy to
knock my window open.

And the real truth: I was a single and unattached aging gay
man yearning for love. What I wanted was to find a better man
than the kind I usually met, and one of the methods I thought
might help me in my personal quest would be to, well, make
myself more versatile in the bedroom department. Knock my
own gate down before someone else hit a brick wall.

Not long after I reached that insight I began perusing the
personals to meet my dream man, a habit I had gravitated to
for years and years and years, whenever I felt the dating pool
had grown too shallow. I picked up newspapers and magazines at the bars, the community center, the bookstore, the
newsstand—wherever I could find ones that carried men-for-
men personals. At home I would sit at my desk with a red felt-
tip pen poised in my hand, ready to circle the most desirable
ones. No matter how many personals I circled and notated in
the "Romance Only" or "Let's Date" sections, I always seemed
to gravitate to the "Raunch and Kink" or "Sex Only" sections,
fascinated by the obsessive nature of so many gay men and at
the same time frustrated that so many guys were looking for
such specific requirements, and knowing, really, that my
nature would most likely preclude any visits to the kinkier
sides of gay life. The only thing I had ever desired of a perfect sexual encounter was to give as much pleasure to my
partner as I wanted him to provide me. And that didn't necessarily include smelly jockstraps or foot worship, though it

also didn't rule them out.

And so one particularly lonely and forlorn day, this ad caught my eye:

BUTT PLAY 101

Let me teach you how to enjoy your ass and asshole.
I will show you how to experience ultimate pleasure
from the space between your legs.

I must confess now that I had never answered a sexual ad before. Yes, I read them and mulled them over, but I only circled and called the romantic, dream date ones. As for sex, because I'd always found enough action at the bars or the clubs or on the street—or from the dating ads—I hadn't ever needed to turn to the "Sex Only" personals as an outlet. My goal was to find a worthwhile long-term relationship or at least someone who would stick around after the third date, not someone who only wanted to stick his sticky fingers up my butt to get his rocks off. Nonetheless, I circled the ad, partly nostalgic over my lost boyfriend and partly curious about whether I should really consider a new method to snare a new one. A few days later, when I was leaving voice mail messages for all of my potential dream dates, I decided, *Oh, well, what the hell, let's respond to the butt player as well.*

None of my Perfect Husbands responded, but the butt player did. Our short, introductory phone conversation went something like this:

"So you're into butt play?" he asked.

"Not really," I replied.

"You ever had anything up your ass before?" he asked.

"Not in a while."

"I've helped a lot of beginners," he said.

"I'm not exactly a beginner," I stated, "just starting over."

"Boyfriend?" he asked.

"Not anymore."

"I can see you Sunday at nine," he said. His voice was cheerless and perfunctory, making it seem as if I had called to make a doctor's appointment for a shot of penicillin. Yet it was exactly this sexless, clinical exchange that made it so easy for me to accept his offer.

"Okay," I answered. We talked a few minutes more. He told me his address and that his name was Joey. He admitted that he was in his early fifties and had gray and black salt-and-pepper hair. As I hung up, I reminded myself that this was a learning experience—he was going to teach me to be a bottom, or at least teach me to be a *better* bottom. Henry Higgins wasn't exactly the perfect man for Eliza Doolittle when they met, either, you know.

⋀⋀⋀⋀

I arrived at Joey's apartment nervous and tipsy and more than fifteen minutes late, which (even on gay median time) is more than a rude way to begin an association. I had indulged in a glass of wine at the bar on the corner of Joey's street, a trendy little smoke-filled, artsy-fartsy place with skinny women in black dresses and guys in dark T-shirts and gold hoop earrings. As I gulped down the last third of my drink, I had reminded myself once again that this wasn't a date. This guy didn't advertise in the "Looking for Love" section, and I wasn't expecting Joey to be my Mr. Goodbar. He was only Mr. Chips, after all, and I could leave him as soon as he taught me, uh, well, how to enjoy the pleasure of a man's penetration.

"Want something to drink?" he asked as he ushered me into his apartment. My distress must have clearly shown on my face at that moment. Joey was more like sixty than fifty, and his salt-and-pepper hair was an unshaven beard. Otherwise, he was bald as a cue ball, with a puffy face that looked like a sandbag that had been punched and hadn't regained its shape. He was slightly shorter than me but more than three hundred pounds overweight, a fact he hadn't mentioned on the phone. He was dressed in the kind of light, blousy outfit that, when worn by street people, makes you immediately cross to the other side of the street. If he had not lived in one of those high-tech, luxury apartments that always seem to end up photographed in *Metropolitan Home* or the Thursday section of the *Times*, I would have turned around and left, because this potential dreamboat more closely resembled my worst nightmare.

I should probably add that the Sunday night I arrived at Joey's apartment, it was a warm, misty late spring evening that seemed to possess more humidity and mugginess than actual raindrops or heat. I stood in his doorway holding a moist umbrella, my split ends growing into an afro. I felt old and troll-like myself at that moment; I was conscious I was standing on a clean beige carpet, worried that I had brought with me all the urban dirt and soot and grime I had carefully tried to avoid out on the street. Joey's apartment was clearly more showplace than home. The smell from flowers in a crystal vase on a table near where I stood wafted up to my nose as I shook myself out of my damp jacket. The vestibule where I stood frozen like a rescued stray dog opened up into a living room entirely decorated in beige—a sofa and matching wing chairs were upholstered in a neutral, beige fabric; prints of blank beige-colored squares framed by beige wood were hung on a beige-painted wall; a shiny beige lamp rested on a shiny beige end table.

"Any wine?" I asked Joey as he led me to the sofa. I took a seat cautiously, resting my derriere lightly on the edge of a cushion as if I were going to leap out of the room at any instant, because I was embarrassed at shedding particles of dust into the immaculate surroundings. Beside me, a beige coffee table jutted out close to my knees, empty except for several *Playbills* arranged in the shape of a fan.

"Red or white?" he asked.

"Whatever's open," I answered.

During our entire greeting and exchange, Joey was beaming as if a Christmas gift had just walked through the door. I sat waiting for him to return, feeling like I had played this game a million times and was too old and tired to try it again tonight with an ancient schlumper.

"I loved this show," I said, trying to deflect my discomfort when Joey returned with a glass of wine that looked more beige than white. I reached over and plucked a *Playbill* out of the arrangement, the fan quickly disintegrating into an unorganized mess. As I lamely tried to straighten it up, the thought occurred to me: murderers don't like show tunes—do they? And wasn't Joey too old to be a murderer anyway? Isn't it usually the wealthy sixty-year-old man who is found with his throat slashed the next morning? Joey seemed unperturbed by the mess I had made on his coffee table. In fact, he seemed to be amused by my nervous stumbling about; when I looked up I noticed he was smiling, his mouth widening to reveal a set of conspicuously fake beige teeth.

"The dancing was terrific," he said, "but the music was abysmal." He waved his hand in the air on his last word, as if shooing away a fly, but then he started telling me about a theatrical wig maker he knew who worked backstage and as the gossip flew from his mouth, his hand waved back and forth like a flag flapping in the wind on Independence Day.

I didn't really mind all the talk about the theater; I was grateful for any distraction from the matter at hand. We sat and kibitzed about a lighting designer stepping out of his boundaries to become a director and a composer known for his S&M tendencies. In fact, we talked so long about the theater that I completely forgot the reason why I was there in the first place. Joey was becoming a friend, not a potential teacher, and his fuzzy potato head no longer looked as if it belonged to a derelict. I could see the honesty in his face even if I couldn't imagine him successfully pleasuring my ass. But then Joey abruptly ended the conversation, leaning over and saying, "Well, shall we get started?" Suddenly his wrists were no longer limp; one hand was firmly placed against my shoulder, the other reaching around to remove my empty glass from the coffee table.

"Uh, sure," I answered, not really certain I wanted to go through with it.

"You can leave your clothes on the chair," he said, as a doctor might before leaving a patient alone in an examining room. In fact, Joey did leave me alone in the room while he carried away the empty glass, but he returned by the time I had managed to rise from the couch and fumble with the buttons on my shirt. Joey walked to a set of louvered doors that I had thought was a closet, but opened, they revealed a full-size bed built into a small nook that must have once been a laundry room. Along the bottom of the bed was a row of drawers built into the frame and Joey opened the middle drawer and began pulling out an assortment of items: a pair of latex gloves, a box of condoms, an industrial-sized bottle of lubricant, four or five different-sized dildos, none of which, I felt certain, I could possibly accommodate, a box of baby wipes and a plastic mat, which he unfolded and placed on top of the beige bedspread. I was deliberately taking my time with my clothes, folding and refolding them as he moved swiftly about his little alcove. Finally, he turned and looked at me standing sheepishly in my underwear and T-shirt.

"I sterilize all the dildos in the dishwasher," he said, as if that were my most crucial concern about sticking a giant object up my ass.

"The dishwasher?" I responded, flabbergasted by a mental image of a row of dildos sitting straight up in a car wash. The next thing I knew I was standing behind him staring at the paraphernalia spread out on the bed, all of it for the sole purpose of entertaining my ass. Things had never seemed this complicated when I played the same game with my ex-boyfriend. But that was the difference, wasn't it? I reminded myself. It had been a game with my boyfriend. This was a lesson.

"And I always use condoms on the dildos," he said, patting the plastic mat. "Take your shorts off and sit up here." Joey seemed to realize as he said this that there was hardly room for me to sit on the bed because of all his equipment, and he started rearranging things to make a space for me, or, worse, for *us*. I realized the moment I dropped my briefs that I should have thought twice before agreeing to all of this. Was I that desperate to learn how to enjoy my ass? Shouldn't I have really concentrated on finding a boyfriend *first*? I looked down at my cock and noticed it appeared smaller and more frightened than I had seen it in years.

"Have you had many responses to your ad?" I asked when I was seated on the edge of the bed, shifting myself onto the mat. Somehow Joey was already completely undressed and I was amazed to see that his body looked no different than when he had been wearing his billowy outfit: it was as lumpy and wavy as beige fabric that had been sat on all day. The only difference between his body and his clothing was the gold Hebrew symbol dangling from a chain around his neck now visible against the sparse, gray fluff of his chest. And his erection, of course: his small, slender dick popped straight out at me like a breadstick misplaced in an Easter basket.

"Nope," he said. "You're my first. I just placed the ad last week."

Great, I thought, *a virgin again. And a guinea pig.*

꧁꧂

But it was then that the lesson began. Or life unfolded. Isn't that what teaching is all about? The passing of knowledge gained not so much on one subject but after the cumulative experiences of many years.

"When I first met my lover I was strictly a top," Joey said. I was on my back with my legs bent and my knees pulled to my chest. "I wasn't interested in somebody sticking something inside me, because all I wanted to do was to stick something myself, you know? Then, after we were together for about four years, we started changing roles. He didn't always want to be the bottom so I experimented with it some and decided I liked it, and we changed roles. He was the top and I was the bottom. That lasted for a few more years and then he decided he wanted to be the bottom again. That's when we started getting all this stuff," he said, waving his hand at his assortment of dildos.

"I think that's more than I can handle," I said, twisting my body to look at the smallest dildo, which in my estimation was about twelve inches long and eight inches wide.

"You think so? We'll see."

Joey had positioned himself at the end of the bed, a plump round period to my wavy exclamation point. He lifted one of my legs and rested it against his shoulder. The next thing I knew, his wet gloved finger was in my rectum and I could feel him twiddling my prostate gland. I leaned up to watch his hand inside me, expecting him to say at any point, "Scalpel," or "Sutures," but instead he said, "You're very tight."

I nodded, wishing there were some music playing or somebody kissing me or a video being shown or, better yet, that I had another glass of beige wine in my hand. Instead, all I heard was Joey beginning to breathe harder, like someone with asthma. I lay back down, the mat crinkling as my skin pressed against it. I closed my eyes and tried to imagine myself a thousand miles away, but instead heard the *slumpf, slumpf, slumpf* of Joey pumping more lubricant out of a bottle and into his hand and then into my ass.

"It's the small ones that are the hardest, you know," he said.

I leaned my head up again and looked at him in surprise. "It's the truth. It's all about stretching. The walls don't stretch that much with the tiny ones. The big ones force you to relax in order to accommodate them. Give me a big, fat dick any day. It's so much easier to manage and it's a lot more fun." He started laughing, a high-pitched hiccup that started in the back of his throat and ended with the quivering of his shoulders and saggy chest.

It was such an odd moment from someone I had heretofore regarded as a clinical, professional worker. "It's all about relaxing, you know," he said, still chuckling. "Once you learn how to relax those muscles down there you can take a football."

The thought of a football up my ass was definitely unappealing, and I pumped a swipe of lube from the bottle and wrapped the oily palm of my hand around my cock, trying to force myself to become harder. Above me, I heard Joey gasp.

"What's wrong?" I asked.

"Ahh, why did you do that?" he asked.

"Do what?" I asked, shocked.

"I wanted to suck your dick. Now I can't take it in my mouth. And you have such a beautiful dick."

"Ohhh," I said, sorry, really sorry, that he hadn't acted quicker. "Thank you," I added, feeling like the moronic pupil who has disappointed the teacher.

Next, he took a slender dildo I hadn't noticed before, the kind I had once used on my ex-boyfriend, lubed it up, and inserted it into my ass. It went in easily, though I could feel the walls of my ass caving into the dildo instead of it stretching them further. "You've been practicing," he said.

"Not really. Those Kegel exercises don't work for me."

"Oh sure they do," he said. "You're just uptight. What're

you so nervous about?"

Life, I thought. I'm nervous because I'm still alive after all these years. The only thing that worked out for me was that I didn't die when everyone else did.

"Open your eyes," he said and lightly slapped my chest.

I could feel the residue of lube where his hand had grazed my skin.

"I'm not going to hurt you," he said. "I won't do anything you don't want me to do. You can trust me. After a few lessons, you'll be able to take King Dong over there."

"King Dong?"

"The super-deluxe double-headed one," he said, nodding at the giant dildo with a cock head on each end. "My boyfriend and I used to play with that one a lot. There was a time when we were both bottoms. Come to think of it, there was a time when everyone in the city was a bottom. It sure was difficult to find a top some nights."

I gave him a smile and leaned back and started pumping my cock again. I felt myself growing thicker and he took the slender dildo out of my ass and lubed up a wider and longer one. Before I knew it, it was inside my ass, and I was rock hard, pumping my cock and arching my back away from the mat. And then I suddenly felt a decade younger, and a memory washed over me of a man I had dated on Fire Island. Joey bent my legs and rubbed my thighs just as the man had. He kept the dildo far up inside me and cupped my balls and rubbed them with his slippery hands. Then he reached up and twisted my left nipple.

"The first time I was fucked, my boyfriend was so impatient that he made me bleed," Joey said. "I turned him into a great lover, though. Then he left me. Then he came back. Said he couldn't find anyone better in bed. Oh, he could find others to have sex with, don't get me wrong. But none of them had my touch. It worked for both of us though. He made me feel so beautiful."

Joey was breathing hard through his mouth by now, and he moaned and moved one hand to my cock and stroked it as he returned to lightly pushing the dildo in and out of my ass. "That okay?" he asked.

I nodded back at him.

"I miss him," Joey said. "He died about three years ago."

He stopped pushing the dildo in and out of me and pulled himself up out of his hunched over position. "That doesn't bother you, does it? Everything we're doing is safe."

I nodded again that it was all right to continue. I was aware that we hadn't kissed each other, aware that not a single drop of body fluid had been exchanged between us. No tears. No sweat. As I looked at Joey's face as he worked over my ass and cock, alternating one hand between stroking his cock and my own, I realized he had survived, as I had, but his road might have been more difficult than my own. I sensed that the puffiness bloating his face was not entirely due to the ravages of aging but likely came from medication or the overuse of alcohol.

But I also realized he was enjoying his task. Obviously, he had taken out the ad because he enjoyed sticking something up a guy's butt, enjoyed giving a guy pleasure this way; perhaps this was his fantasy, his fetish, the scene he wanted to play—older teacher instructing the younger pupil. The thought of it made me smile and the delight surged through me like a jolt of electricity. I felt my body finally become sensitive to his touch. My first shot came with a wave of release, replaced almost immediately by a flood of tension and pressure and then a second shot into Joey's waiting palm.

Before he had a chance to remove the dildo from my ass or wipe my come from his hand, I reached up and gave his cock a few quick pumps with my slick, hollowed fist. He came instantly, his come spurting over my wrist and onto the mat with a plop, plop, plop. He laughed as he caught his breath. "Thank you," he said.

Thank you, I repeated in my mind, embarrassed that he had thanked me for letting him fuck me with a dildo and quickly jerking him off. As I dried myself off with the baby wipes and paper towels, it occurred to me that teaching was such a selfless act. In that way it bore a striking resemblance to being in love—wanting to do something for someone else without the expectation or need of anything being returned. You don't expect someone to thank you. Lovers can be the best teachers. And teachers can be the best lovers, too. But I was aware that my encounter with Joey had not been without a certain level of self-absorption and self-need. His. And mine. Joey had knocked a window out in my wall for me. And I liked to think I might have brought in a little sunlight for him.

When I was dressed and standing at the door in my still damp jacket, Joey held his hand out for me to shake. Instead of taking it, I leaned over and kissed him on his fuzzy cheek. He smiled and held the door open for me. As I stepped outside, I realized that I had revealed little of myself other than the intimacy of my body. I hadn't even told him about *my* ex-boyfriend. But it was already too late; I felt myself headed back into my shuttered, private little world. Before he closed the door behind me, I turned back and said, "Thank you. It was fun."

And then I was back out on the street again, slapping my tennis shoes against the puddles of water like a teenager, eager to be a teacher again.

.

Snow

Outside the window, the snow obliterated the view of the highway, but since Tyler was less than a mile from the airport there wasn't much to see except ramps and lanes and traffic. The snow had started the previous morning when he had landed in the city for his meeting: small, enchanting, romantic flurries. By the time he had hailed a cab in the afternoon, four inches were already on the ground and flights were being delayed. He'd gotten one of the last rooms at the hotel, just as everyone—the receptionist, the cab driver, the airline reservations clerk—had started to mouth the word *blizzard* to him, or, rather, started to mouth *two* words, *big blizzard,* as if the description *blizzard* was not an adequate enough weather forecast to instill a sense of urgency to get some place and stay there for a while. Now, in Tyler's fourth floor hotel room, the snow outside was so fierce it drained the color from everything: the dark green bedspread, the hunting print above the bed, the cherry wood of the desk and chair. Even the air in the room seemed as if it had been washed away, or, rather, had been sucked into a clear bottle and frozen, waiting to be thawed. Tyler, stripped of all his clothes, pressed himself close to the windowpane, the stale coolness seeping through the glass like an undetected gas leak. His shoulder felt sore so he rotated his arm, then rubbed his dry

hand across his drier skin. Winter, he thought. Aches.
Arthritis.

Tyler stood at the window with his back to a young
man named Brad or Chad or Tad or something like that.
Tyler didn't care anymore what the guy called himself. He
had cared the night before, when Tad had arrived, but for the
last twelve hours he hadn't cared at all. Any sense of intimacy
Tyler had felt for Brad or Chad had evaporated long ago.
Tyler was bothered by his growing callousness—wasn't this
what he had always wanted? Time alone with a young man?
They had stayed up late drinking a bottle of wine, snuggling
against each other, and watching television till Tad, or Brad, fell
asleep. Tyler had absorbed the alcohol quickly, the wine fading into a headache and insomnia. Tyler had held whatever-
his-name-was in his arms until he felt himself sweating, then
pushed the young man away so that he slept on his side.

But by morning Tyler had been seized by a weighty rest-
lessness. At the window, Tyler rubbed his hand along the fine
hair of his own chest and realized he might be attracted to
Brad if he had been someone else. *Another* Brad. Maybe a
Chad, he said to himself with a laugh. I've had Brad, he
thought. Now give me Chad. Glancing down, Tyler watched
with bored interest as his testicles shrank the closer he
moved to the window. If anyone were in the parking lot
looking up at his window, Tyler knew they would be unable
to see him, striped by the blinds, with freezing nuts and a
painful shoulder.

Todd—it was Todd, Tyler decided—lay on the floor wearing only his red flannel boxer shorts, an item of clothing he
had sexily revealed with a flourish the evening before. Todd
was young and lean, a handsome brunet with a nose too big
for his face. Now he was busy touching his knee to his nose
doing stomach exercises and shooting annoying breaths out
of his mouth as if he were about to hurl a spitball. He'd been

doing this senseless thing for almost an hour.

"Let's go down to the fitness room," Todd said. "Mr. Tyler?"

His voice, in this air, stayed even after the meaning was gone from his words. The room remained full of his voice— dropped into corners like packed snow on the roadside in spring. "I'm sure the fitness room is more like a fitness *closet,*" Tyler said. The edge in his voice was easily detectable. "And it's not 'Mr. Tyler.' It's just 'Tyler.'" He didn't bother to look back at Todd. He had studied and studied the body till it no longer excited him. Todd had finely carved abs like the cuts of a diamond, and it was a magnificent display watching them flex and twist and breathe. But what was the purpose, Tyler wondered? He had seen them and now they were ancient history. He wanted something else. But even more, he wanted to be *somewhere* else.

"At least the electricity works," Todd said. "Last year we lost power."

"How long did it last?" Tyler asked.

"Three days," Todd said. He held his knee to his nose. "Can you see anything?" he asked.

Tyler didn't respond. He couldn't see anything beyond the white wall of snow. When he arrived at the airport yesterday he had been delighted to hear that the flight had been canceled, not from the snow—snow was always expected in this region—but because of the wind gusts. The airport closing gave him a legitimate reason to stay overnight, a bona fide expense report item to submit, a chance to have some fun before returning back to the closeted grind of corporate meetings and lunches and lectures and conference calls. Tyler had seized the opportunity to order room service and a hustler. Todd had arrived quicker than the food. By the time they had finished, though, there were already four more inches of snow, frozen granules mixed in with the lighter stuff—and the television said bus service had been suspended until the

roads could be cleared and sanded. And Tyler hadn't been so
eager to see Todd disappear.

"Everybody's always in a hurry to get somewhere,"
Todd said.

Tyler didn't answer.

"Do you like my stomach?" Todd asked.

It was only the thousandth time he had asked Tyler that
question. He heard the insecurity creeping into Todd's voice
and if he could placate Todd without using too much energy,
he decided he would. So he nodded. He could have easily
turned Todd out into the snow last night. Wham, bang, here's
your money, so long, don't hurry back even though you are
gorgeous and it was incredible sex. But it was late and dangerous outside and early on Todd had tapped into that warm
fuzzy paternal spot Tyler always felt for the young and pretty
boys who looked put upon. Now, Todd's company had worn
thin. Tyler turned and took a long look at Todd's stomach and
managed to work up a grin, trying not to be one of those
sour old businessmen, who, well, float into town and hire hus-
tlers. "What's not to like? You should do movies."

Todd stretched both legs out in front of him and pointed
his toes, then sat up straight at the waist, a perfect right angle,
sure of himself. "I guess," he said, then smiled at himself.
"Best abs in Hollywood."

Tyler started to turn back to the window, wondering
why he was the one now doing the pampering. Wasn't Todd
supposed to be indulging *him?*

"I was in a commercial once," Todd said. "I did an intern-
ship at a television station my sophomore year. One of the
camera guys was filming a diet commercial. I got to be the
'after' guy. Did you know that it's not the same person? I
always believed that they could lose the weight."

Tyler did not react. Too much chatter, he thought, and he
tried to tune Todd out.

Snow

"Wanna play around?" Todd said, dropping his voice into that low whispery octave that had so excited Tyler last night. "No charge since you're letting me stay."

"Too beat," Tyler said, and looked back at the window, weary and bored.

"I'm going to go downstairs," Todd said, making it sound like a threat, though Tyler couldn't imagine what kind of threat it could be.

"Better put something on first," Tyler replied.

Todd didn't move from the rigid shape he'd got himself into. With the lamp on inside the room, Tyler could see Todd's reflection in the window and he studied that—the reflection—squinting to see if he could detect the definition of Todd's abs in the snow.

Then he looked beyond the reflection, back into the snow. It swirled and curled and danced in front of his eyes like a busy computer screen saver. The warmth of the room was pulled up through the window and sucked off into the snow. He looked down at the parking lot and thought he could detect someone racing into the snow, his hands pumping together as if clapping, probably to keep the circulation going.

At the window he looked deeper into the snow, believing for a minute he saw thousands of men clapping their mittened hands together. They were sure they were going to freeze if they remained motionless, never to arrive someplace warm. Then they disappeared.

"Tyler?" Todd asked.

Tyler ran his hand down to his groin and across his cock. He was aware of Todd looking at him.

"Is it still hard?"

"Sure," Tyler answered, playing the suggestive innuendo game but unable to mask the cynical tone in his voice.

"How much longer?" Todd asked. That raspy voice again.

Desire, Lust, Passion, Sex

How much longer snowing? Tyler thought, or in this room? Or in this room *with him?*

"What's your hurry? Am I such unpleasant company?"

"Of course not," Todd said. He pouted in a boyishly self-absorbed manner.

"It's just the snow's making me cranky," Tyler said.

"Let's play some more," Todd said. He stretched out his body and cupped his balls.

"Aren't you worn out?" Tyler asked.

"No," Todd said, his grin taking on a fake, impish quality. "Are you?"

"Yes," Tyler said. "You're too much for me."

"So let's just neck some more."

Tyler didn't really want to be unkind to him, though he knew he was being hustled now. "Neither of us has shaved."

"Want me to shave you?"

Years ago he would have been delighted with the offer. *Hours* ago he would have been delighted. "I'm not twenty anymore, though I wish I were, sometimes." Tyler turned and looked at Todd. "Or I wish I were twenty and knew what I know now."

Todd smirked. Tyler turned and faced the window again. As he did he caught sight of his own reflection this time, his white hair crossing against the currents of snow. Everything would be all right again soon. All he had to do was wait.

"Tyler?"

"Huh?"

"Wanna shower together?"

"Hmmm."

"Or soak in a bath?"

"My joints are damp enough," Tyler said.

Todd went into the bathroom. Tyler heard him take a leak and flush the toilet. Then he turned the water on. Then he heard the shower begin and the sound of the water change as Todd stepped into the flow. Tyler stayed at the window and ran a hand over his chest and pinched the slackness at his hips. He was still there when Todd came back into the room, dripping onto the carpet.

"Tyler?"

"Huh?"

"I'm going crazy in this room."

"Put something on. You're going to get a cold."

Todd put his boxers back on and a T-shirt and ran the towel through his hair. Tyler watched the process in the reflections of the window, momentarily imagining Todd was a soccer player, toweling off after a game. The image burst apart in another flurry of snow and Tyler again felt old and vulnerable in his sagging flesh.

"Wanna get something to eat?" Todd asked.

"If you want."

"Room service?" Todd asked.

"Sure."

Behind him, Tyler heard Todd pad across the carpeted floor and sit at the desk, thumbing through the hotel journal till he reached the room service menu.

"What do you want?" Todd asked.

Tyler smirked at the loaded irony of the question. I want to be out of this room, in an airport, on my way home, away from *you,* on my way to someone else. For a moment he thought about running out like a lunatic—racing down the hall and into the lobby with nothing on. At least he might be arrested. At least it would take him to jail. *Somewhere else.*

"Nothing heavy," he answered.

"How about some ice cream?" Todd asked. "Or a milkshake?"

"Coffee," Tyler said. "I'd like something warmer."

The ice cream and the coffee came ten minutes later. Todd's spoon clinked against the glass at an annoying speed.

Tyler sat in a chair facing the window, a cup in his hands.

"That killed a half hour," Tyler said when he had finished his coffee. Tyler finally pulled himself away from the window and sat on the edge of the bed and turned on the television. Todd curled up into a fetal position on the bed, a pillow crammed between his legs, as if waiting to be petted.

"Wanna watch a movie?" Todd asked. "They have a movie selection here."

"Let's check the news first," Tyler replied. He flipped the channel, wondering if God would give him a respite with the snow. Even a little one. He shook his head to clear it.

"Something the matter?" Todd asked.

Tyler shook his head to indicate *no*. The moving images on the screen made his vision blur. He lay down, exhausted from the anxiety of trying to decide how long he might have to stay. He thought that maybe he couldn't last—that maybe he'd have to cancel his appointments for tomorrow as well. The snow had become his business now. Something tugged at his inner ear. A rumble that seemed to shake the foundation of the building. He lay still and quiet and then felt it again. "What?" he asked.

"I didn't say anything."

"Are you sure?"

"Yes."

Maybe it was Todd's voice again, stirring in the room from some dead sentence. It tugged again, and Tyler realized it was a sound outside the room, far off. "Hear that?"

"I don't hear anything."

"It was the parking lot. Someone's leaving." Tyler felt his pulse quicken and, as he lifted himself off the bed, he struggled to overcome a dizziness. He padded across the carpet and looked out of the window again.

"Maybe they're salting the highway."

"No, listen," Tyler said. In another minute he heard it

again, barely above the blood beating in his ears. Todd joined him at the window. Tyler smelled the soap Todd had used. He was aware of Todd's heat and the hairs on his leg stood up, warning him.

"It's lighter," Tyler said, looking out through the snow, the tone of his voice brighter, breezier.

"Sure is," Todd added.

While they were watching the snow, a man walked through the parking lot beneath them. Tyler's eyes followed him, watching the man's mittened hands clap together. The snow swirled in thinner gusts now, flaking against the window before melting.

Tyler walked to the phone and dialed. "Are they back on schedule?" he asked. As the receptionist explained that flights were now leaving, Tyler thought that his giddiness would give him a heart attack, his blood now a roar in his ears. He hung up the phone, smiling.

Tyler packed hurriedly and with a determination he had not possessed since he had arrived in the city. He kept looking outside as he packed, watching the flurries thin out. He could now see the sharp line on the horizon where the highway was.

Todd was dressed in his jeans and coat in a matter of seconds. Tyler waited for him to ask for more money, but as Tyler lifted his suitcase off the bed and moved toward the door there was nothing. Impulsively Tyler stopped and kissed Todd abruptly on the lips with a passion he hadn't shown the boy since he'd first arrived in the room. Todd slipped his arms under Tyler's jacket and returned the kiss. Suddenly they were all hot and bothered at the idea of losing each other. "I'm here often," Tyler said. "Could I see you again?"

Todd nodded and Tyler knew that if he wanted more he would have to pay the price of it. In the elevator he felt relaxed. Peace, he thought, and studied Todd with his clothes on, finding himself mentally undressing him and growing hard at the thought of the young man.

By the time Tyler reached the airport he was as exuberant as the sun, the light bouncing so brightly off the snowdrifts he paused only to search for his sunglasses.

What Is Enough?

He thinks you have incredible buns.

You like the tight flatness of his stomach.

He cups his mouth around your chin and you feel his tongue wet the morning stubble of your beard. He is lying on top of you. You run your hands down his back, tapping the knots of his spine like the keys of a piano. You press your face against his neck, detecting scents of grass and tarragon and Perry Ellis cologne buried beneath the dark, wiry hairs of his chest. He brushes his cheek against yours and you smell his breath, sour and bitter as burnt chocolate, but surprisingly fragrant and arousing to you because you know it as one of his morning smells. He shifts his body a fraction lower so that his sternum presses against yours, and the abrasion and then sudden stillness of skin against skin makes your chest become moist with sweat and your armpits and brow itch as the heat of him, the fever of his flesh, engulfs you. He lifts himself up and rolls over on his back. The bedsheet follows him and twists around your left leg so that you are pinned in an awkward position. As you turn over to wrap your arms around his waist and kick your leg free the sun catches in your eyes and you squint. He pushes you back on your back and uses your body as a pillow, folding one arm beneath your neck and stretching the other across your thigh, curling his body so that it bends around you. You comb your fingers through the short black strands of his hair and then stroke the back of his neck while looking up at the ceiling—dark timbers slanting skyward to make a frame which cracks and creaks like the joints of an old man. You think you might love this man, this one feels different than the others: more magnetic, seductive, sensual. The one just before him, the one you loved not too long ago, annoyed you, irritated you, baffled and confused you. Your body becomes rigid for a moment as you wonder if this one will someday say he loves you.

Looking at him, you notice he has closed his eyes. You think he wants to go back to sleep so you wedge yourself from underneath him. When you reach the edge of the bed he grabs you from behind and begins to kiss the back of your neck. You arch your back as he works his lips around your right shoulder. He slips his hand through the hairs of your chest, rubbing your skin, finally settling two fingers against a nipple and dialing as though fine-tuning a radio. He rubs your chest again, harder, and you feel a lightness, like a startled bird, flush up into your lungs. You slide around in his grasp and kiss him lightly on the forehead; as you do, your bodies slowly bend back to the bed. Now you are on top of him and you kiss, in sequence, his eyebrows, eyelashes, nose, cheeks, and chin before your lips meet his. Again you notice his breath is warm and bitter and when your tongue enters his mouth you feel it slide against his upper teeth. You relax your body even more, stretching out on top of his.

He places his hands on your shoulders and gently begins to massage the muscles of your back. Again you notice the solidity of his actions. He works his fingers deeply, separating and manipulating each tendon. As you lean your head against his shoulder, your eyes buried into the pillow, you think again about Bryan, the man before this one. Bryan was always hesitant, his glances unsure, uncertain if he even wanted to be with you. He never liked being touched, never enjoyed being embraced. This man, Ross, has no such confusions. He seems to you to be the type of man who never sleeps alone; if he weren't with you, there would be another. You think about your life before Ross, before Bryan, what it was like sleeping alone, waking up in the morning in a bed by yourself. You were not unhappy then, but you were not content, either. You had created your own little world in which to think and live; you were self-sufficient with friends and fantasies. Yet you believed there was a man out there for you somewhere, one who wanted to be with you as much as you wanted to be with him. You never considered yourself particular, all you asked is that the right man be loving and committed. You didn't care if he was taller or shorter, blond or brunet. But you had built bridges across your heart in case you never found him; you had hidden your emotions beneath a functional, businesslike personality so you couldn't be hurt. The last thing that you, a man in his thirties, needed was to have your heart broken. You had enough anxieties from potential viruses and escalating interest rates.

When you first started dating Bryan, you were relieved when you discovered that you shared similarities. You were both from large, religious families, had come out in your early twenties, had an appreciation for music and a desire to travel. You were excited to have met someone you liked and who liked you as much in return. In fact, he became your friend before you had sex together. When he began to stay overnight at your apartment you were wildly alert, unable to sleep. You were not used to another body beside you in bed. You were not used to sharing blankets, sheets, pillows, and a limited cubic space. You worried whether your tossing and turning prevented him from sleeping. In the mornings you were exhausted, squeezed into positions you would never have found yourself in if you were alone. Later, when you became used to him, used to his smells and sounds and habits, even the way he would turn over on his side and cough to clear his throat, you still could not sleep. You were always disoriented and restless when you slept over at his apartment. At yours, you didn't understand why he seldom held you in bed, were confused why he never made the first advances for sex. You worried he would leave you, if he had met someone else. You wondered if he was attracted to you, had decided he no longer wanted to be with you. You ached for him just to touch you. Now, as Ross's hands work their way down your back and knead your buttocks you understand what a friend once told you was so special about sex, how the human skin needs to be touched. You remember the reason why you decided to be gay: you enjoyed sex with men more than women. Now, though you have only known Ross a few weeks, you are aware you are used to all of him: the bulkiness of his frame, the muskiness of his underarms, his method of nuzzling his unshaven face into the crook of your neck, the way he tries to lift your body away from his and pull you back again, as though doing push-ups in space.

This is the time you think Ross likes you best. It is Sunday morning and he is relaxed, rested, ready for sex. His thoughts are focused entirely on you. When you first began dating Bryan, sex was an issue. You were frightened, had not been with a man in a long time. You set the rules right up front: everything safe. He agreed but his caution was different. He wanted to wait before sleeping with you. He felt it should be "making love" not "having sex." You said you felt it should be spontaneous, something both of you wanted, not something planned. Sex with Bryan was awkward, abrupt, unfulfilling. You feel vibrant just being with Ross. Ross tells you you are handsome, whispers that you are the best sex he has had. And he makes you feel special, like now as he sweeps his face across your stomach. Your feet are tucked between his. He runs his hand up and down your thighs and you feel the roughness of it, thick and dry from working outdoors, and yet when you touch his waist you notice the softness of this part of his skin, supple and tender as a woman's flesh.

Bryan told you his caution, his hesitancy to commit to a relationship, was his way of planting a seed in your heart, weeding and watering it and watching it grow. You told him you were the type that fell in love instantly. You were ruled by instinct, and your instinct was usually right. Once, when Bryan was drunk, he said he didn't love you and maybe never would and you walked out on him, telling yourself you didn't need all this in the first place: you didn't need a one-sided relationship, you didn't need all this frustration and confusion, and you felt sure that by being alone you could now be happy. But he came after you and apologized and was more attentive than before. He called every day and cooked dinner for you, sometimes showing up unannounced at your apartment, unexpectedly taking you out to a movie or to try a new restaurant. He wanted to know everything about you: your past, your personality, your passions. He wanted to spend time with you, get to know you better. It was then that you decided if this was a man who would never be able to say I love you, you would at least find a way to make him need to be with you.

Ross pokes his fingers beneath your arm and tickles you. He knows this drives you crazy. Somewhere between Bryan and Ross you became touch sensitive. You twist yourself away from his hand and push your finger back and forth where his skin touches his pelvis. He wiggles and laughs. This is one of the most sensitive areas of his body. He holds you tighter and your fingers slip to his ribs and again you find another tender, ticklish spot. He jerks away from you and grasps both of your hands by the wrists and pins them against the mattress. Sometimes this playfulness will lead to a wrestling match, one trying to tickle till the other gives in.

But this morning he kisses you lightly around the neck, till he works his way up to your lips.

You know his body by heart: his hair, thick, dark waves cascading around a pronounced widow's peak; his shoulders, broad and bony and lightly freckled; his chest, covered with a thick coating of fine black hairs, nipples large and round as quarters; his arms, long and hard, rigid with muscles; his legs, lean and coarse with thicker, tighter strands of hair. Though Ross is five years older than Bryan, in surprisingly better physical shape than Bryan, he has the same difficulty as Bryan in articulating his emotions. But it is easier for you to know what Ross is feeling. You can tell by looking at his face: the sharp, striking cheekbones that lift when he's happy; the almond-shaped eyes that become fine lines when he worries; the slender lips that dimple at the ends when he smiles; the solid line of his jaw when he flexes with anger. He is always in motion, expressing himself physically—gardening, swimming, cleaning, or just eating a piece of fruit. And Ross is always touching you, holding you, draping his arm around your shoulder or your waist, whether alone or in public. And you can remember every time you have had sex together, though you would never tell him you could do so; if you did you would worry whether it would scare him—make him back away from you. With Ross, sex is easy and natural, whether in bed, on the kitchen floor, or in the shower. Sex is the tool he uses to unlock your thoughts, make you throw away your worries. That was not the case with Bryan.

When you first started dating Bryan you gave each other little gifts to express your affection: flowers, a bottle of wine, a deck of playing cards, or a book. You began to collect things that reminded you of the times you spent together: a shell from a beach, a tiny plastic swizzle stick from a cocktail he ordered, a candlestick you pointed to at a flea market. After your third date he asked you if you wanted to date someone else. You said no. He said he liked you because you seemed to be the type of guy who was willing to make a commitment. Since he said that, you have often wondered what it was you tried to commit to; your relationship seemed superficial and shallow, all he wanted was a string of wonderful dates, good times, and nice trips out of town. He wanted to take things slowly; you did not have sex with him until the fifth or sixth date. You slept with Ross the night you met him at a friend's party. All the chemistry and electricity was there with Ross, right at the start.

It still is, but sometimes you feel you know so little about Ross. You don't know what he talks about with his friends. You don't know how he spends his day at work. And Ross knows so little about you. He doesn't know how you got the tiny scar beneath your left eye, doesn't know how many friends you've lost. The first dates you had with Bryan were full of questions; he asked about your family, your job, your earlier boyfriends, your likes and dislikes. And you asked questions of him. Bryan set a standard, both good and bad, you can't ignore. You can't shake off your comparisons; Bryan was much more the romantic—he could spend an evening talking about the future you would share together.

Sometimes you wonder what he is doing now, who Bryan is dating, where he is eating, what he's watching on TV. Sometimes you think you bounced from one man to another too quickly. You were right up front with Ross the night you met him. You told him that you had just split up with a guy and weren't emotionally in any sort of state to start dating. You explained to Ross that night, as you lay in bed together, that Bryan was hesitant about opening up his life to accommodate you. He was protective of his friends, his possessions, his feelings. You became jealous of everything in his life—even of the affection he gave to his cats. But in the end, the reason why you told Bryan that you would never see him again, could not be friends with him, in fact, could never even talk to him again, was because he told you he wanted to see other men. You told him he could date other men but not you at the same time. You told him he had to make a choice, a commitment, one way or the other. He said he liked you, loved you, in fact, but there was no spark, and he needed to see if he could find it with someone else. You grew angry and said you did not find him sexy. He said he was not attracted to you, that you were not his type anyway. There was not a fight. Nothing was left to be said, but the words spoken were too true not to hurt. You were both aggravated because each of you had been desperate to make the relationship work in your own, separate, individual ways.

Ross said you were not the only man with a broken heart. He has had boyfriends and lovers come and go. Some have died. Once, late at night, when he noticed you had been crying, Ross told you he felt your emotions were too large. You told him it was unhealthy to keep everything bottled inside. When you lived alone you worried about bills and how and where to meet a man. When you started dating you worried about bills and how to keep hold of a man. Later, you worried about bills and where that man was when he wasn't with you. Now, Ross thinks you think too much, that too many thoughts are circulating behind your eyes. And he can tell when you are upset, when the thoughts are turning sour. He doesn't have to read your expression or feel for the tension in your body. He knows it intuitively. And when he sees it he smothers you, holding you in his arms till it doesn't matter anymore. He leads you to a subconscious state, a place where no language, questions, or problems exist, till there's not a thought left to think about.

His eyes are open now, as large as dark brown plates before your face. Just when you thought he had moved somewhere inside himself, here he is, looking at you, thinking of you.

What Is Enough?

You slip a hand down his stomach and cup his balls, squeezing them a few times before you start to rub the inside of his thigh. His breath quickens and he begins to kiss you harder; you know he has reached the point where his passion ignites. He buries his head against your chest and begins to lick your left nipple while fingering the indentation of your triceps and twisting his legs around yours. You know he likes your body. You can tell by the way he touches it, strokes it, holds it. You can tell he likes the way your body fits neatly against his, two hard knots of muscle against each other. This is why you continue to do your sit-ups every day, why you go biking and make three trips to the gym every week. He reaches your navel and slides his tongue down to the soft, springy hairs of your groin. You arch your back and twist your hands through his hair. You feel bristly and intense, as though walking through fire. You move by instinct now, your skin feels both pliant and thickened, you can hear your heart pumping violently in your chest. He moves as though weightless, swimming underwater, his body now feels polished and leathery. First he is on top of you, stroking you, then you on him, forcing his arms against the pillow with the palms of your hands as you rock your hips together, the friction making him both smile and moan. Just when you sense he is about to come you back away, teasing him. He gasps and lunges for you and you both roll over onto your sides. You push him onto his back again and when you hold his cock you feel as powerful as a magician suspending a willing victim in midair. He squirms as you move your fist up and down, stops, tenses his body, and holds his breath. You know he has disconnected entirely from you. A warm, pearly-white liquid spills over your fingers. He exhales heavily several times and you rub your hand against his stomach. There's a moment in which you are both silent and still, then he rolls over and is on top of you, his knees straddling your hips. He reaches for your cock and slowly strokes it. You drift in and out of a dream-like state. He starts moving his hand faster; you begin breathing through your mouth. Finally, the motion is so overpowering, you tilt your neck and thrust the back of your head against the bed. He relaxes his grip and you go simultaneously blind and deaf, your thoughts disappear as he lifts you into an orgasm.

You hear him turn on the water for the shower. You roll over and clutch a pillow, sliding it beneath your chest. You take a deep breath and you smell him still beside you. As you shift your weight you feel relaxed but empty, your stomach suddenly cold and wet, your body detached from your mind. You slip your feet beneath the sheet and twist them together, searching for some lingering warmth of him. You think a moment about being all that someone wants. Is Ross enough for you? Could it happen this time? Is this what you *want* or what you *need*?

And then you roll over and close your eyes, wondering if you could convince yourself you could be enough for Ross.

First Shave

Gary lies on the bed diagonally and I pull his body closer toward me so that his legs dangle over the edge. His erection stretches up toward his navel and I grasp his cock and give it a few pumps with my fist. The water is in a large pot on the night stand beside the bed, and I lean back from where I am standing and dip the tips of my fingers in the pot to wet them, then dip my hand all the way in, clutching a grip of the warm water in my palm. I lean back toward Gary and drip the water over his waiting balls and cock, his skin soaking in the water, then run my hand over his balls, the liquid a slick lubricant as I reach up and play with the shaft of his cock. Gary's eyes are closed, but he smiles as I run my fist back and forth along the head of his dick. I cup his balls with the palm of my other hand, feeling the warmth and wetness of them now, then move my own dick, stiff and needy, so that it falls against his balls.

I reach over and get the shaving creme from the night stand, squirt a handful of it into my palm, and rub it on Gary's balls. I let the skin soak this up, and while waiting I use the creme as a lubricant to play some more with his cock. Gary smiles again, wider, till his lips seem to stretch almost to his ears, and then he opens his eyes and looks down at my hand, the shank of his neck flushed red from where my movements have excited him. I take my free hand and lightly squeeze his left nipple, and he shoves his head back against the bed, lifting his ass up slightly so that his dick slips in and out of my closed fist with the rocking motion he makes.

When he relaxes again, I reach for the razor from the night stand, do a fast check of the shaving creme on his balls, and decide to squirt some more on them. I use one hand to pin his dick against his stomach, then point the razor right beneath the shaft of his cock. I bring the razor down slowly against his skin, feeling the hair on his sack pull a little as I work on him, shaving him in short, firm strokes. Overcome slightly by the reality of my own shyness, I lean back and rinse the razor in the pot of water, even though I could have shaved some more of him. This is my first time shaving Gary, and I feel the tenseness in the arch of my back. After eight months of our irregularly dating each other, Gary finally trusts me enough to let me hold a razor to his balls.

Not that he should, of course. We're not lovers; we're not roommates—nor friends, either, really. Merely two men who date each other, something a little more complex than fuck buddies. Gary already *has* a lover. *Isn't that always the story? The way it goes? The good ones always taken? Or at least the sexy ones?* Gary's been with Eric for almost twenty years now, and he tells me every time I see him that he and Eric haven't had sex in years. Every time he mentions Eric, however, I feel both jealous and envious; Eric has a daily intimacy with Gary I know I will never possess.

Now, using my thumb and fourth finger, I stretch some of the skin of Gary's balls, and shave the skin I have pulled taut. Then I push one of the sides of his scrotum tight against the other, shaving it and continuing slightly underneath. I do the same with the other side of his sack, dip the razor clean, and then play with his cock to make sure he is enjoying all this attention.

Gary first shaved his balls when he started dating a guy

who had shaved *his* balls and ass. Not Eric, of course; Gary has been seeing other guys since his relationship with Eric began, when they were college roommates. They didn't even start out monogamous, Gary told me the night he first slept over at my apartment, but they made a rule, right up front, of never discussing their other lovers, dates, or tricks with each other. How Gary explains his clean-shaven balls to Eric now, I have no idea, though I think it might have something to do with the absence of sex between them. But if I try to understand the complexity of *their* relationship, I only become frustrated with the inadequacy of *ours*.

I want more than this, of course; or, rather, I want more than what Gary is willing to give me. He likes our arrangement the way it is—once or twice a week for a movie, some dinner, and, inevitably, a lot of sex. When Eric is out of town, one of us sleeps over at the other's apartment.

At first, all Gary wanted us to be was fuck buddies, an arrangement I was perfectly capable of accepting, though not happily. But Gary wouldn't stop calling me—first for sex, then later, to complain about Eric. He called from the office, from the car, from the lobby of the theater, till sometimes we spoke to each other four or five times a day. Then he would disappear for a long stretch of time, only to turn up and start calling repeatedly again. I always expected that Gary would have used me up by now, but instead he arrives with little gifts—toys which we will use later, together, in bed—handcuffs, rings, clamps, dildos, flavored lube. That's how the shaving came about. Gary arrived tonight with a disposable razor and shaving creme.

I continue to talk to Gary's body with my hands. His dick is rock-solid hard, thick and pumped like his morning erections always are, and I sneak a look at the whole package of him, the hefty, well-fed physique of a well-groomed middle-aged theatrical producer. What is this thing I have for older men, anyway? Gary is effortlessly a man, natural and unrattled as a father, with full round biceps and a chest and stomach covered with flat brown hair, the ends of which are tipped with gray. There is a good twenty years difference between us; Gary says, more often than not, that I look like Eric did when they first met. In spite of his comparisons, in spite of knowing I'm being compared, I also find Gary inherently sexy. I play with myself for a moment, stroking my cock as I look him over, then tell him first to turn over on his stomach, then push himself up and support himself on his knees and elbows.

His ass—the white, creamy complexion of it—is now pitched heavenly into the air, and I cup his cheeks with my wet hands, kneading them first and then giving them light slaps. His skin is baby soft but firm beneath the flesh, and I slap and knead, slap and knead, as Gary shifts himself beneath me to accommodate my grips, his ass pushing itself even higher into the air above him, as if trying to drink in the air through his asshole.

Not long after I had met Gary, he told me that he liked the slick feel of his cleanly-shaved balls, and that he would go wild when someone just touched him there, cupping them completely into his warm palms. Now Gary shaves the evening before he sees me, he tells me, in order to give the skin time to heal if he nicks himself. I worry a moment about nicking him now, imagine how I would handle the blood if that should happen. But I shake off the thought, mentally chant it out of the room. *That will not happen*, I tell myself over and over, *because he trusts me. No blood. No blood. No blood.*

I run a finger from the base of Gary's spine, down through the crack of his ass, back down to his balls. I cup them with one hand, then take my other hand and rub my fingers against his asshole. The hole is red and almost angry-looking, and I study the hairs along the puckered surface. I reach over to the still-warm water, wet my fingertips, then run them into the crack of his ass, digging a damp finger slightly into his asshole. I play with the water some more against his ass, then squirt shaving creme into my hand and rub it along the crack.

I tell him to spread his knees even further, widening my view of his asshole. I slap the skin some more, then take the razor in one hand and with my other hand spread the skin of his other cheek—first for support, and then, when I am sure of the flesh, to stretch the skin even further apart.

I shave the base of his spine first, then, in short quick strokes work my way down the crack to his asshole, watching the warm creamy liquid drip down onto his balls. When I reach the more furrowed surface of his asshole, I slow down, almost tapping the razor against his skin. I can tell he is even more aroused now, imagine my quick, light movements must feel as if he is being tickled there, and I smile at the thought of it, and continue shaving him.

When I first started dating Gary, I wanted desperately to fall in love with someone, having just emerged from a string of very bad and fruitless blind dates. The moment Gary told me about Eric, I was ready to end it between us. *Who wants to be the other woman, after all?* Had the sex not been so good, so comfortable, so hot and inventive between us, he could never have convinced me to continue.

I rinse the razor and continue shaving his asshole, using the razor a little harder now to get a closer shave. I run a finger along the clean, finished surface of the skin, testing the smoothness. I decide I want it to feel even smoother, and repeat my strokes along his ass. I stop midway, however, reach underneath him and pump his cock. He groans and shifts his body. I knead his cheeks, then finish with the remainder of his ass.

The shave is done now, but I touch up the underside of his balls to get a closer shave from this angle. The creme, water, and shave only take a moment, and I use the excess liquid to lube his dick, feeling as I do the damp sensation of his pre-come wetting his cock. I place the razor back on the night stand, wet my hand again in the pot, and then begin to finger his asshole. One finger slips easily in, and I wiggle it around inside him, feeling for his prostate. I find it—a hard little nodule beneath the tip of my finger—and massage it. He groans again, and I wedge a second finger into his ass, move it in and out, in and out, listening to his moans to make sure that they emanate more from pleasure than from pain.

Gary told me that Eric hadn't fucked him since Eric tested positive, almost five years ago. Gary is negative and the difference in their serostatuses, he said, not only pushed them further apart sexually, but bound them closer together emotionally. How could he walk out on Eric now, not knowing what the future could mean for either of them? Of course it upset me when I heard it; it still does when I think about it. Eric is asymptomatic and Gary, I know, does not *want* to leave him. *This is what I have*, I remind myself, and continue fingering Gary's ass. *This is what I get.* If I want more or something else, I know I have to get out and look elsewhere.

I take a condom from the night stand, unwrap it, and slip it over my cock. I lean over Gary's ass and push my dick slowly in. Gary takes a deep breath, and I wrap my arm around his waist as I fuck him from behind, my movements slow and thoughtful, in and out, in and out, so that he feels every inch of my dick and my swinging balls against his now-hairless ass.

He groans louder as I go in deeper and faster, and my thoughts change now from erotic to frustrated. Gary's sexual appetite is insatiable—I'm not his only companion-slash-fuck buddy. My friend Martin's seen Gary at the bar picking up tricks; my neighbor, Jon, saw him and a date at a premiere at the Ziegfeld. Gary's even taken me to the bar with him a couple of times when he's been in search of fresh meat. Now, instead of pushing myself harder into Gary, I take deep

First Shave

breaths, rapidly and loudly, wanting to believe, as I do, that Gary is not just another jerk fucking me over, using me like a sex toy. Beneath me, beneath Gary's ass, I reach down and pump his cock as I fuck him. Gary suddenly comes into my fist and I rub his hot cream back up against the shaft of his cock, around the base, and onto his slippery balls.

I pull out of him and watch myself come into the tip of the condom, my dick suspended above Gary's milky ass. Gary twists his body beneath me, twirls around so that his ass rests again on the bed. His eyes look up at me, searching for my own. I meet his gaze and watch his lips purse together as if to speak. For an instant, I think he will say something romantic, caring, but I lean down into him, wanting to cut him off, not wanting to hear some sort of halfhearted remark about how nice he thinks I am. Instead, he stops my face right above his own by shoving his hands against the side of my skull. In a moment, the power between us shifts. Gary is twice as big as I am, and he could easily crush my skull in his hands. Instead, he twists my head so that my ear is right above his lips. "Show me you care," he says lightly into my ear. "Come on. I want you to do it again."

Alibis

"I'm supposed to be in Vegas this weekend," Hal said. He was in bed, his body spooning Jake's, eyes gazing out to the gray winter view of the river.

"Vegas?" Jake echoed back, feeling his voice travel through his chest and into Hal's.

"I'm an alibi," Hal said. "My friend Richard doesn't want his lover to know that he really went to Arkansas to see his other boyfriend."

Jake turned his body so that he faced Hal. "That's pretty rotten," Jake said, his hand searching out Hal's and weaving their fingers together.

"Not really," Hal answered. "Everybody does it."

"Really?" Jake asked, feeling Hal twist the skin against the joint of his third finger. "*Everybody?*"

"Sure. They just started living together a few months ago—Richard and John," Hal added. "The day they were moving in with each other, John found a letter in Richard's trash. Richard was moving into John's apartment and John was helping Richard move. John found the draft of a letter Richard had written to a guy named Tom telling him that they had to end their affair because Richard was moving in with John. John knew nothing about Tom, of course—didn't even think that there could be a Tom. But he played it real cool and didn't mention anything to Richard after he discovered the letter. Since they were moving in with each other and everything, Richard was writing to end the affair. John was always so easygoing when they were dating, but once they were living together John starts asking Richard about where he's been at night, why he gets home so late, where he's going in the middle of the day, and it started to drive Richard crazy because he hates to have to account for his time. But get this—by then Richard was trying to be faithful. He was avoiding Tom. But he had no idea why John was being so nosy. He was never that way when they were dating and living in different parts of the city."

"Uptown, downtown?" Jake asked.

"East, west," Hal answered. "John had one of those rambling old apartments that Richard loved while he was dating John but hated the moment he moved in. Anyway, so one day John checks the mail and there's a postcard from Tom to Richard and it was signed with *X*s and *O*s and 'Love, Tom.' So, of course, John's mind goes racing with all these crazy thoughts. When Richard gets home that night he sees the mail and the postcard and John on the treadmill—John's so pissed off he won't even look at Richard. So the rest of the night he stays in one room and Richard is in the other. Finally, when they both have to end up in the bedroom, Richard tells John that it's over with Tom and he has no intention of seeing him anymore."

"So why did Tom send the postcard, then?" Jake asked.

"I'm sure that's just what John wanted to know but was too polite to ask," Hal said. "It seems that Richard never *sent* the letter to Tom. John only found the *draft* of it. And Tom didn't know that John and Richard had moved in together; he only thought that Richard had moved to a new apartment. They only saw each other once every couple of months when Tom came to the city—he lives in Arkansas and was always staying at one of those pricey midtown hotels."

Hal lifted himself up and rolled over, shifting their position so that he was on top of Jake, his knees straddling Jake's waist.

"So this is where it gets sticky," Hal said, running his fingers up and down the indentations of Jake's rib cage. "Richard called Tom to tell him he wasn't going to make it to Arkansas to celebrate Tom's thirtieth birthday because he had to go to his brother's fortieth birthday party in Boston and Tom got so upset because they'd been seeing each other for almost four years and Richard had never come to Arkansas. Tom was always coming into the city to see Richard. So, of course, Richard, who is not exactly loaded with charm all the time, said, in his most condescending manner, 'But I have no desire to go to Arkansas,' which really pissed Tom off and he called Richard selfish and egotistical and hung up on him. Well, you know the worst thing you can do to a guy is to dump him and Richard went ballistic because he thought *he* should have dumped *Tom*. So Richard gets all upset and calls Tom back and apologizes and says he'll come to Arkansas the following week. Which is why I'm in Vegas this weekend."

"I thought you said Richard went to Arkansas," Jake said.

"He did," Hal answered. "He went to Arkansas but he told John that he went to Vegas. It's the one place John trusts him."

"*Trusts him?*" Jake responded, surprised. "In *Vegas?*"

"Money is the one thing Richard is more obsessed with than sex. John knows that Richard would be more absorbed with winning than scoring, if you catch my drift."

"And you're there to chaperone, I take it?"

"Yep. The thing is," Hal said. "They've been there before—Richard and Tom. That's where they met. John doesn't know that. Richard met Tom before he met John. I think Tom's never wanting to leave Arkansas is why they're not together instead of Richard and John." Hal's fingers had now found their way to Jake's groin, and he worked his fingers through the stiff pubic hair matted together where Jake's come had dried. "Well, no, the truth is, they really met in Palm Springs but they drove up to Las Vegas together because Tom wanted to get a tattoo."

"He couldn't get one in Palm Springs?" Jake asked.

"I think Tom wanted to go to Vegas," Hal said. "There's only so much you can do in Palm Springs anyway unless you want to chase boys or hunt for money and Tom already had money and he was just out of college then. So they drove to Vegas and get this—Tom gets this tattoo of an angel on his shoulder. Angel on my shoulder, get it? Well, Richard likes it and he decides he wants to get a matching one on his ass, only he's too chicken to do it."

Jake placed one of his hands behind his head. With his other he massaged Hal's cock till he felt it begin to thicken.

"A couple of years go by and Richard meets John," Hal continued, leaning down and pressing a palm against Jake's chest. "After they've been hot and heavy for a while and it looks like they might last as a couple, they start talking about living together. Only Richard doesn't want to do rings or anything because he doesn't want to get that serious, so he says why don't they get matching tattoos?"

"Oh, no," Jake laughed.

"You got it," Hal laughed back, his hand clutching Jake's pectoral muscle. "Richard suggests that John get a tattoo of an angel on his shoulder and Richard gets one on his ass. So a few months later, when Tom finally sees Richard's tattoo, Tom's ecstatic because he thinks Richard did it for him, he finally made a commitment to *Tom*."

Jake stretched himself and tensed his body beneath Hal. Hal shifted himself again so that they were lying side by side, their hands still fingering each other's stiffening cocks. "So neither one knows about the other's tattoos?" Jake asked.

"Nope."

There was a silence, then, between them till Hal leaned

into Jake and kissed him. "I've never been to Vegas," Jake whispered when they parted for air.

"Neither have I," Hal said, nibbling at Jake's earlobe.

"Aren't you worried if John asks you about it?" Jake asked, shifting their positions now so that he straddled Hal's waist.

"I've been to Atlantic City," Hal answered. "I'm sure it's similar."

"Where are you staying?" Jake asked, weaving their fingers together again and pushing Hal's hands against the pillows.

"Huh?" Hal asked.

"Where in Vegas?"

"Caesar's."

"I hear it's similar," Jake said, and clutched Hal's cock together with his own in his fist, rubbing them together. He shifted his eyes out into Hal's darkened bedroom, casting his gaze about to find where they had discarded their clothes earlier in the evening. Beyond where his underwear had landed Jake noticed the door of Hal's closet cracked open from when Hal had gotten up to get lubricant earlier in the evening. He squinted his eyes and tried to see inside, noticing only a row of shoes on the floor. "What if you had gotten him on the line tonight instead of me?" Jake asked.

"That's not his style," Hal said, propping one arm behind his head now. "He's the one guy in the city who isn't happy that he's in an open relationship."

"How do you know that?" Jake asked.

"John's the quiet type," Hal said. "But he opens up after a few drinks."

Jake continued to study the inside of the closet, till his eyes distinctly made out a row of sneakers at the edge of the closet door. From his angle it looked as if the shoes belonged to two different-sized feet. "Why doesn't he just get out of it then?" he asked.

"It's one of those messy real estate relationships," Hal

said. "Richard has the money but John had the co-op. Only thing is, Richard complains that John is draining them dry. They took out a joint checking account and John keeps writing checks without telling Richard and they're fighting like crazy over little things that John is buying for Richard's stuff— like Halogen lightbulbs and laser printer cartridges. But then I heard that John had taken money out to renew his gym membership which was why Richard decided to use the joint money to take his trip to Arkansas."

"Sounds like they're not going to last long, anyway," Jake said. He moved his eyes once again through the room, this time to where his watch rested on the night stand beside the bed. He looked at the clock behind the watch, then noticed there was another clock on the night stand on the opposite side of the bed. "There's got to be some level of trust tucked away in all the dishonesty."

"And where are you supposed to be tonight?" Hal asked, smiling.

"Not here," Jake answered. "But everybody does it," he added and leaned down and kissed Hal on the eyebrows. "So do you know anyone who went to Vegas this weekend?" Jake asked when he broke away.

"Nope," Hal answered, his eyebrows thickening with thought.

"And you trust him?" Jake asked, titling his head to the clock on the night stand.

Hal cocked his head back and smiled. "Sure," he answered. "Everybody does it."

⁂

"Nice watch," Jake said to the man seated next to him at the bar. "I used to have one like it."

The guy looked over and met Jake's stare and nodded.

Alibis

They were seated in the empty downstairs bar, away from the piano and the sing-along show tunes. An overhead pinspot highlighted the portrait of a nude man on the back wall. Cigarette smoke and stale beer wafted through the air vents.

"I was robbed a few months ago," Jake said, aware of a nervous edge to his voice. "Well, not robbed, you know. I told my insurance company I was robbed so I could replace it. I filed a police report and everything."

The man nodded again, taking in Jake and his nervousness and his story. "I don't usually wear one this expensive," the guy said. "My other one stopped. This was a gift."

"Mine, too," Jake replied. He tried not to show his pleasure that the man had responded. Jake had liked the man's hard edge when he had sat next to him at the bar. There was a solid toughness to him that wasn't usually found among the business suit crowd that frequented this place. "A boyfriend gave it to me," Jake added. "But I'm not seeing him anymore."

"Was he still your boyfriend when your watch was stolen?"

"He knew I *lost* my watch," Jake said, moving in closer to the man, wanting to rub his tongue over the day-old stubble on the man's jaw. "One of those complicated things, you know. I left it some place I couldn't get back to," Jake said. "No number. No last name."

"There's always a price," the guy said, his eyes squinting as he smiled back at Jake.

Their eyes met again. Jake liked the dark country drawl of the man's voice. "Usually," Jake answered back with a light laugh.

Jake offered to buy the man another drink but when the bartender brought the glasses to their spot the man paid for both drinks.

"Thanks," Jake said and tipped his glass against the man's as a toast. The rest of the time was easy. They introduced themselves. The man placed a hand against Jake's thigh; Jake leaned in closer and closer until he succeeded in running his tongue against the man's stubbly chin.

They left the bar not long after that, ending up at the man's apartment uptown. Jake played the aggressor, kissing the man over and over, his tongue searching out the caverns and canyons of the man's mouth and face. He undressed the man in the dimly lit hallway, a light spilling out from the hood of a kitchen appliance. Jake unbuttoned the man's shirt, unzipped his pants, till the man reacted by leading him down a long corridor of rooms, past a door of a bathroom where another night light was on, and into the darkened bedroom beside it.

The man easily outsized Jake. Undressed, the tough edge of his face was echoed in his body. It was a hard, serious body, hairy and muscular, the kind which seemed to Jake impenetrable, distant, masculine. He had a thick cock of average length, his pubic hair trimmed close to the skin, throwing the focus of his genitals onto his large, weighty balls. The man took off his watch and placed it on a night stand beside the bed. On the bed, Jake took the man's penis in his mouth and sucked on it, feeling it grow stiffer inside him. In a moment the man squirmed and pushed Jake back against the bed and his lips were moving over the top of Jake's cock. Jake groaned and the man lifted Jake's legs up and kneaded his asshole.

They broke apart when the man fumbled through the drawer of the night table and withdrew lubricant and condoms. Soon he was back, working two wet fingers into Jake's ass.

"Is this okay?" the man asked.

Jake was touched by the concern. "Do it," Jake said.

The man took a palm full of liquid and rubbed it up and down the shaft of Jake's cock and then onto his own. He wet Jake's ass again. Then he pressed himself inside.

Jake moaned and began rocking his hips. Before long the man was on his back and Jake was seated on his cock. Jake easily came in this position, shooting onto the guy's chest. Jake moved to the side and the man removed his condom. In a few seconds he reached an orgasm too, his release thick and white, soaking in what light had made its way into the room.

While he was drying himself off with a towel the man said, "You can stay over if you want."

"Sure," Jake easily answered. "For a while."

The man stood and walked to the doorway of the bedroom. "Want a beer?" he asked.

"Sure," Jake looked up and answered. The man's frame was silhouetted in the light. It reminded Jake of one of those perfect physique logos. The man turned and walked into the hallway. It was then, when the man moved into the light, that Jake first noticed a tattoo on the man's shoulder.

The man returned with two bottles of beer. Jake sat up and took a bottle from the man. They clinked bottles and each took a long sip. "This is a big place to have all to yourself," Jake said.

"I had a roommate for a while," the man said, "but it didn't work out."

"It's difficult to make a commitment in this city," Jake said. "I know."

"No one really tries to make it work," the man said. "They try to work around it." He took another sip of his beer. "I know," he added.

Jake nodded and took a sip of beer. The man leaned against the headboard. "He accused me of seeing someone else," the man said, "so he moved out."

"Were you?" Jake asked. "Seeing someone else?"

"Nobody's a saint," the man answered. "I'd meet somebody in a bar once in a while. Nothing that amounted to an affair. I never brought anyone back here when he was living here. I played by the rules."

"There are rules?" Jake laughed. "Tell me."

"*His* rules," the man answered. "But we weren't playing

the same game." The man drank the last of his beer and sat the bottle on the night table beside his watch. "He kept telling me it was over with this other guy he was seeing long before he met me. But it wasn't. I know it wasn't. He said he was moving out because I was always cheating around on him. That I was unfaithful. He really moved out because his other boyfriend moved into town. He didn't tell me that. A friend of his told me about it. I was so mad when I found out he lied to me I was drunk for three days straight."

Jake rolled over and placed his bottle on the night stand next to the watch and the other empty bottle. He turned back into the bed and gave the man a long, wet kiss. When they parted, Jake shifted the man so that he lay on his stomach. Jake straddled the man's ass and massaged his shoulders, conscious of trying to make out the outline of the man's tattoo. "Where was the other boyfriend from?" Jake asked.

"Arkansas," the man answered.

There it was, Jake saw. An angel on his shoulder. He worked his fingers back and forth against the tense muscles of the man's back.

"It wasn't really the thing that broke us up, though," the man said. "I set up a joint account for us to use for expenses. He was always struggling with money. Everybody always thought he was well-off because his family had been well-off, but he could barely pay his rent every month. I knew when he moved up here that things were going to be more expensive for him and I was lenient at first about him contributing to food and expenses and stuff. He borrowed money to pay the movers, he borrowed money to put some of his stuff in storage. But he never put any money into the account. We'd go out to the theater and he would take money out of the account to pay for tickets. The thing that ended it was when he bought his other boyfriend a birthday present from the account."

"How do you know that?" Jake said.

"He wrote out a large check from the account. He said he was going to Las Vegas with his best friend. His best friend's lover—this guy named Dave—works for one of my clients. I happen to see him from time to time at the gym. Dave went to Florida on business that weekend. He told me his lover never went to Vegas that weekend. He said there were over a hundred dollars of phone charges from that weekend on their phone bill. Of course Dave didn't go away on business either. He was in Boston with one of his boyfriends."

"Looks like everybody does it."

"I guess so," the man replied. "Dave knew I was upset when he told me. So he took me to one of those clubs downtown. I got smashed quickly and Dave took me back to his place and we fooled around some before I really fell off the deep end. Dave's boyfriend was away on business, or so he said. He gave me the watch to cheer me up. Dave said his boyfriend had found it on the street."

"*On the street?*" Jake asked. He reached over and studied the watch, holding the band between his fingers. The man rolled over beneath Jake and lifted himself up on his elbows and kissed Jake deeply.

"Did you love him?" Jake asked, still dangling the watch from his fingers.

"Who?" the man asked.

"Your boyfriend," Jake answered, teasing the man with the watch, dangling it in front of his eyes. "Your ex-boyfriend."

"No," the man answered. He reached up and clutched both the watch and Jake's hand. He slipped his fingers inside the band and Jake let the watch slip away from his grasp. "I loved our sex though."

"What about Dave?" Jake asked. "Did you love *him?*"

The man took the watch and slipped it onto Jake's wrist. It was a perfect fit. "No," the man answered. "Of course not.

Desire, Lust, Passion, Sex

But I always love sex."

Jake lifted his arm toward the ceiling, trying to get the face of the watch to catch the light that spilled in from the doorway. When it failed to catch the light he moved his wrist to his ear till he heard the familiar ticking sound. Jake moved the arm with the watch toward his other hand. The man stopped him when he tried to remove the watch. "Keep it on for a while," the man said. "It looks good on you."

Jake lifted his arm again toward the ceiling. "It's never about love, you know," he said. "It's always about sex. Sex, sex, and more sex. Sex always uncovers the things love hides. Everybody does it, John. Everybody loves sex more than love."

Fearless

Though he harbored a virus within his body that frightened so many people and that so many more misunderstood, Barry did not think of himself as diseased or infected. He liked to consider that they, he and his virus, coexisted with each other, as many members of his support group preferred to define the relationship. So it always came as a surprise to Barry when someone found out he was HIV-positive and asked if he had any symptoms. "None," he always answered, though he would never vocally complete his thought, *none of your damn business*. And then he would feel the intensity of his interrogator's stare, scrutinizing him as if to prove he was lying, possibly even thinking that the red bump on his cheek was something more than a blemish, something far, far more frightening. Or if nothing physical was detected, nothing, nothing, nothing at all, his interrogator would look deeper, right into his soul, hoping to discover the roots of depression by the way he carried his body. After years of questions, frowning eyes, and too-sincere embraces, Barry was still learning how to channel his anger. In his support group he was always yelling at everyone, "Don't you realize how much stronger you are than this virus?"

David, however, could not shake off his years and years of loss. For him the epidemic had been going on far too long.

Desire, Lust, Passion, Sex

He had lost most of his friends, his coworkers, the men he knew at the gym or the bars or the clubs or the baths. He had even lost his job and his health benefits when his boss died and the company closed, a greeting card company that operated out of a Greenwich Village brownstone. In the early days of the epidemic David had volunteered, done fundraising, worked as a buddy; later, he marched in demonstrations and buried even more friends. Things had changed for David. When he had first moved to the city he was light and campy; now he felt he was entirely too serious, solemn, and glum. He approached everything now with anxiety.

⋀⋀⋀⋀⋀

They met in the rain.

The night before the AIDS Walk had been a restless one for David. Two years ago he had walked with a group of twelve friends. Now, four were dead, one had gone to live with his parents, two had moved away from the city, two others were diagnosed. This year, everyone he knew who might walk was tired and burned out, bowing out graciously by explaining they would be out of town for the weekend. This year, the weatherman had predicted rain. In the morning when David got out of bed the rain fell so hard on the roof of his fifth-floor apartment it sounded like a subway car approaching but never arriving. It left him feeling impatient and uneasy, eager to settle on some sort of destination. Should he walk today? Would anyone walk? He called the weather line: rain all day. He showered and dressed and sat by the window, watching the raindrops splatter puddles like boiling water. He waited and waited, changing his mind every minute, finally deciding that he would just go to the registration point in Central Park, turn in his pledges and contributions, and then leave. When David got to the park, he was surprised at the number of people who were already there. Pausing atop a rock that provided a view of the Great Lawn, he was astonished by the sight of thousands of umbrellas, moving in and out of large random patterns like the kaleidoscopes he used to hold up to his eye as a boy. How could he leave now when everyone else was staying?

So David remained and walked.

That same morning, when Barry woke up he was curled around a guy with a goatee who snored through his mouth. He could not remember the guy's name, had no idea where he was in the city or if he even *was* still in the city; but he did remember they had met at a club near Avenue A last night when he had been waiting in the line for the restroom. When Barry slipped away from the guy and stood up beside the bed, he felt the chill in the air and heard the taps of raindrops against the window, just as the heaviness in his head shifted toward a headache. As he slipped on his jeans, the guy with the goatee rolled over, opened his eyes and looked at Barry, studying his face as if trying to memorize a criminal he would later have to identify, and then, without saying anything, closed his eyes and went back to sleep. On the street, Barry realized he was still in the East Village, and darted beneath awnings till he reached the corner of St. Mark's Place. Waiting for a cab on Lafayette, Barry noticed in a store window a poster for the AIDS Walk. He looked at his watch and then back at the poster. He knew he was too late. It had already started. And the rain made him feel really lousy. He hadn't planned on going anyway. Everyone at work had asked if he were participating. It was as if, because he was gay and positive and open about both, he was *expected* to participate. Barry hated that expectation, which is why, when he finally found a cab at the corner of 13th and Broadway, he decided only at the late, last minute, he would go to the park. When the cab dropped him off, umbrellas were streaming out of the park onto Central Park West like a long, black river.

David, practical and worried about his health—he was always catching cold—was dressed in layers. He wore a T-shirt underneath a long-sleeve T-shirt underneath a sweatshirt, a sweater, and a denim jacket. He wore his chino pants because he felt they would dry out quickly, two pairs of socks, and his heavy winter boots. Wes, David's friend who now lived in Los Angeles, would have wisecracked that David looked like a walking Gap ad. David carried the wide, oversized umbrella he normally hated using in the city because it meant dodging everyone else's umbrella. By the time he had walked to 96th Street David's pants were soaked, his shirts and sweatshirt and sweater were damp, and he knew it was only a matter of time before he would feel the water seeping through his boots, chilling his toes. But he let none of this bother him. Around him everyone else was soaking wet too; as people passed him, David noticed everyone was collectively laughing or moaning or singing or chanting—the ever-resourceful New Yorkers had turned towels and shopping bags and banners and plastic garbage bags into survival gear.

Barry had stopped into Woolworth's to buy a cap before joining the Walk. He was soaked after the first five minutes; the wind had started whipping the crowd, and not even the long windbreaker Barry always wore around the city could keep him dry. *I'm such a jerk,* Barry thought, and lifted his head up to the gray sky, thinking about a way out of this madness.

Barry first noticed David when the crowd reached Riverside Park and volunteers were distributing frozen yogurt in small plastic cups to give the walkers energy or optimism or both. David, who was trying to hold his umbrella, eat the yogurt with a plastic spoon, fight off the wind and rain, and walk—all at the same time—had gotten his legs tangled in a discarded plastic bag. It was this cartoonish lunacy that captured Barry's attention, the waiflike

Chaplinesque figure struggling with the weather and the attacks of urban garbage. But what pulled Barry even closer was David's scrubbed, boyish face—the fair complexion highlighted by the dark, doe-like eyes and the thick brown hair weighted down into curls from the pressure of the rain. Barry followed David to an overflowing garbage can where David lightly tossed his uneaten yogurt onto the top of the pile and untangled the garbage bag that was twisted around his foot.

David first noticed Barry when he turned and headed back into the crowd to continue walking. He noticed him again a little later when he switched the umbrella from his right to left hand. But it wasn't until David thought he noticed Barry shiver that he moved in closer. Barry's clothes stretched heavily against his body, his sneakers left wet footprints behind him, even in the rain, and he had turned his cap backwards and now walked with his hands clasped behind him, like a penitent priest, his head bowed to meet the onslaught of the weather. David noticed the jeans ripped just above the knees, the dark hair of Barry's arms matted against his skin where he had pushed up the sleeves of the windbreaker, the left ear triple pierced, the pendant—a cracked heart—that bounced atop his black T-shirt, the neatly trimmed black beard that covered Barry's face, even the raindrops suspended on the surface of the hair.

David held his umbrella higher, not shielding his face, worrying that if he were wet and cold, Barry, so lightly dressed, must be freezing. Finally, out of so much genuine concern, David walked over to Barry and asked, "Do you want to get under?" at the same time lightly shaking his hand that carried the umbrella. Barry turned and looked at David as if for the first time, moved underneath the umbrella and said, "Do you want me to hold it?" The voice is what caught David—the pitch so deep and heavy, so unexpected from such a slender man—almost magisterial, David thought, like that of an old, overweight English actor.

"No, I'm okay," David said, and then realized Barry's height and lifted his hand, as if holding a torch, so Barry would not have to stoop. Barry moved in closer and draped his arm around David's shoulder.

The physicality did not strike David as odd. Everyone was huddled and twisted together beneath umbrellas. But what happened as they walked and asked each other simple questions—"Are you from the city?" "Did you do the Walk last year?"—was that their eyes would lock as they looked down or up at each other and their touch would shift—David placed his arm around Barry's hip, Barry twisted his chilly fingers beneath David's T-shirts for warmth. They walked this way, smiling and embracing, till they reached the park again. By then the rain had almost stopped and what was left of it was a soupy drizzle. That was when Barry turned to David and kissed him. David, caught up in the moment—the Walk, the rain, the closeness of Barry—lifted up onto his toes and leaned into Barry, feeling the water trapped within Barry's beard ribbon down his chin.

When they broke apart they looked awkwardly away from each other, till Barry took David's hand and led him to a bench. Barry sat on the top frame, his feet resting on the seat, and pulled a pack of cigarettes from the pocket of his windbreaker. He offered one to David, who stood beside the bench and shook his head no, then lit it with a lighter he pulled from the pocket of his jeans.

"You should know I'm positive," Barry said, blowing a stream of smoke into the air.

David's back stiffened. In less than an hour he had imagined falling in love. Now, in two seconds, he was breaking up. "We should dry out," David said. He looked around, wondering what to do, knowing he was being tempted and tested. "Come on," he said, and this was when he took Barry's hand.

Fearless

"I'm not far from here."

They caught a cab at Columbus Circle, holding hands till the driver dropped them off at Ninth Avenue.

"Welcome to the slums," David said, unlocking the street door of his apartment building. "It's a straight climb to the top."

"Straight?" Barry said, grinning, and turned and kissed David. David, now, was slightly embarrassed, wondering if passersby on the street could see them in the building vestibule.

Inside David's apartment, Barry again kissed David, testing him once more, wanting to see if there was any fear in his kiss. David pressed his tongue into Barry's mouth and Barry gasped for a moment, pulled back and slipped his hand beneath David's shirts.

Now David leaned back and removed the denim jacket he wore; it landed on the floor in a wet *thlop*. He led Barry through a tour of the apartment till they stopped, standing, in front of the bed. Barry again kissed David, this time at the neck. David felt the bristles of Barry's beard, one moment prickly, then wet, then slick like an animal's fur. David slipped his hands along Barry's forearms, amazed at their leanness, the tendons and veins popping right up to the skin.

They continued to peel wet clothing from each other—jackets, sweaters, shirts—rubbing their hands along the dampness that remained on their bodies, warming and drying each other's skin with the friction of their touch. Barry stepped easily out of his sneakers. David sat on the edge of the bed and unlaced his boots, then Barry leaned down on top of him and lifted their bodies into the bed. As they removed the rest of their clothing—socks and briefs—Barry was amazed by the thick muscles of David's body—the heavy arms, the wide shoulders, the deep muscles of his back, like those of a wrestler or a high school coach; he had imagined David would have had a more lean, boyish physique. David

69

was mesmerized by the dark hair that covered Barry's entire body—coarse and bristly about the legs, flat and silken as it traveled up his stomach and splayed across his chest. He was surprised, too, by the narrowness of Barry's bones at his shoulders and hips—so slender and precise they appeared almost feline. He held on to Barry as they continued kissing; David was not really sure where his movements were going to carry him and he felt his body tensing instead of relaxing. It had been a long time since David had allowed himself to enjoy sex, a long time since he had even allowed himself the touch of another man.

Barry was not frightened at all. He held on to David and stroked him and kissed him. Sensing David's anxiety, Barry straddled David's thighs, his knees pressed against the mattress, next to David's hips. "It's okay," Barry said, and David felt the voice reverberate through his chest and he closed his eyes as Barry stroked him till he came. Barry then lay down beside David, and David turned his body toward him, their eyes locking as Barry then slowly jerked himself off.

David found a towel, dipped a washrag under the warm water, and returned to the bed, cleaning first himself and then Barry. Barry stayed and fell asleep and David held him from behind and watched TV in the darkened room. Through his mind ran the list of safe and unsafe guidelines. How safe was kissing? Jerking off? A shared washrag? David knew he was being silly; hadn't he done more dangerous things than kissing? Hadn't he cleaned PJ's catheter daily, washed shit off of Neal, wiped up Jeff's vomit? Just when David himself had nodded off, he realized Barry had gotten out of the bed, and he lifted his head away from the pillow and heard the shower running. David lay there until Barry came back into the room, a towel draped around his waist. "Everything's still wet," Barry said.

"There're some T-shirts in the top drawer," David replied, motioning to a bureau against the wall. "You can take one of those. And there's a pair of sweatpants in the bottom. They're probably too small, but they'll last till you get home."

"I'll give them back to you the next time I see you," Barry said.

There was a profound pause between them, as if neither wanted to say the next thing. "Will I see you again?" Barry asked.

"There's no reason why you shouldn't," David answered and watched Barry get dressed.

By the next morning David had made up his mind that he wouldn't see Barry again, that he had only been caught up in the moment and that he and Barry weren't really compatible. Barry smoked, after all. And, though David would never admit it to anyone else, he was scared of becoming infected himself; this was something that could potentially lead to his own death. But there were photographs of the Walk in the newspaper. At home, after work, there it was again on the news. All those people in the rain. Wouldn't David's fears about contracting the virus make him, in his own way, homophobic and bigoted? This was something he knew he had to confront. David called the number Barry had left, and when Barry answered, he asked how his day was, did he see the paper this morning, was he watching the news? Barry said he hadn't seen any of those things, but he had been thinking about David all day. They talked briefly about how wet they had been; wasn't it amazing, they laughed, David fully entranced by the sound of Barry's voice.

They made arrangements to see each other two days later.

They met for dinner at a crowded Mexican restaurant in Chelsea; Barry brought along the T-shirt and sweatpants he had borrowed from David. At a table in the back Barry ordered a margarita and lit a cigarette. This momentarily confused David; wouldn't someone who had tested positive give up smoking and drinking? "Is there a reason why your ear is pierced three times?" David asked instead.

The question surprised Barry. They knew, at this point, so little of each other that this seemed to him such an odd question to ask.

"The first time was for myself," Barry said. "The second time I don't remember. The third time was to really piss off my boss."

Barry explained he worked at a bank on Wall Street where everyone tiptoed around the conservative executives. He hated the job, hated the hours—he was a night person, really—hated wearing suits. His grandmother had found him the job when he had left home because he could no longer get along with his father. His first week at the job he grew his beard. The second week he was promoted. He didn't understand any of it, he said, lighting another cigarette.

David said he had moved to the city fifteen years ago, after graduating college, to become an actor. This made Barry turn pale, and he stared at David, stopped his talking by placing his hand on top of David's.

"How old are you?" Barry asked.

"Probably older than you," David answered.

"How old do you think I am?" Barry was stunned, caught off guard.

"Probably close to your thirties."

"I'm twenty-two."

"*Twenty-two?*" This stunned David. How old had Barry been when he had tested positive? David wondered. David sat there, shocked, wanting to cry.

"I thought we were the same age," Barry said.

David felt his face redden. "I'm flattered, I think," he said, hearing his own voice turn high and thin. "But I've been through a lot."

It was then that Barry realized how little he knew of David, and now, sensing this gap, this difference in age, he felt his caution returning, not wanting himself to know any more details about David. Every time he had gotten close to someone he ended up being pushed away. The virus, the damn virus. He wasn't even sick. It was particularly harder, he had discovered, with the older men. Those that remembered what it was like before the epidemic began.

"How old are you *exactly?*" Barry asked.

"Exactly? Thirty-seven," David answered, "and seven months."

What saved Barry that night was David staring straight back into his eyes. *What does one say to a twenty-two-year-old?* David had thought at that moment, and heard himself rambling into a monologue about how he had never been able to make it as an actor because he didn't have the self-confidence to make it through auditions. Then he began talking about the job he had lost, the friends who had become sick, and he realized he was dropping his cards and guts and baggage right there on the table. At times, he admitted, he just wished he were someone else. Barry ordered another margarita.

"Do I scare you?" Barry asked.

David knew exactly what he meant. "Yes," David answered.

It was then that Barry realized that he had been sitting there with an erection.

They spent the night together at David's apartment.

༄༅༄

When he was alone David could not sleep. He kept worrying. Why was he doing this? His gums bled easily when he flossed, his hands were full of paper cuts, he always nicked himself when he was shaving. There were a million ways he could become infected. He would work himself up into such a state of frenzy that the only way he could become calm was to remind himself that no one *really* knew what was going on, no one really knew what was causing this craziness. Then he would think of all the positive men he had kissed or had sex with in his lifetime. But that would lead to a roll call of the dead and David, now near tears, would sit in bed shaking his head, wondering, why was he here—negative, healthy, and depressed? What was going on? Finally, he would turn on the TV or the radio, hoping the sound would keep him from thinking too much, and he would lie down again, curling into a tight fetal position, waiting, waiting for sleep to return.

Barry, too, had trouble sleeping; he had come to believe things were now divided into "Us," the infected, and "Them," the healthy. He knew too many guys who had been dumped because they were positive. But what kept Barry up at night was the worry of who would be there for him if he got sick. He had never been able to ask others for help, but then he had never even tried to get close to anyone, not even the members of his support group—when he reached a point of connecting or caring for someone he usually asked to be placed into another session. At night Barry would imagine himself sweating from a high fever in a hospital bed, totally dependent, and he would be seized with panic. He did not trust his doctor. But Barry knew, too, he had progressed beyond his fear of being abandoned because of his serostatus. He had pushed everyone away himself. He would get out of bed and walk around his darkened apartment, reminding himself it was not too late to find someone; he still had time. But it was important, he knew, not to get hurt. He had to protect himself, too.

Fearless

They met again on Saturday to see a movie in the Village.

David was already at the corner of Bleecker Street when Barry arrived and greeted him with a kiss on the lips. David gave Barry a weak and embarrassed smile, and as they walked together toward the theater, Barry took hold of David's hand. David, surprised, looked down at their hands, joined at his side, as if they were a scar or a blemish he were not supposed to acknowledge but had to inspect. David had never been comfortable with such open public affection between men, and he wondered now if Barry had misread him from their rainy walk last week. He looked out at the people passing them on the sidewalk, hoping to spot another male couple holding hands, but all he saw were startled expressions, eyes focused in their direction, right at their hands. David moved their joined arms so that their hands fell behind his back as they walked, trying to rationalize his timidity and uneasiness. Wasn't Barry's public affection just another thing he had to overcome or adjust to, like his youth and smoking and serostatus? Weren't they, after all, walking in the *Village?* Wasn't this *their* part of town? Finally, however, worried by the stares they were still receiving, David just let go of Barry's hand, knowing it must *really* look queer to be *holding* hands and *hiding* them.

By now David had reached a foolish state of confusion. He had not dated anyone in over nine months, not since his blitz period—the period during which he had answered personal ads, joined a dating club, and started calling a phone line—with predictable results: too many dates with too many wrong guys. But even in his younger days, even when he had been Barry's age, David had never been able to master the protocols of dating. He had never known when to be aggressive, when to wait for a phone call, when to flirt with someone or how to catch a stare on the street. In those days he had felt awkward and unattractive, always standing on the outside of gay life; even the clues and codes mystified him—what were all those keys and colored handkerchiefs *really* about anyway? But sex had always been obtainable for him—he was always approached at the bars or the baths; in fact, he went to those places to find reassurance that he was *not* awkward and unattractive. In those days dating to him meant having sex. It's why he got together with a guy for a second time. No matter what incompatibilities there were, sex was a way of connecting that made them compatible, even if only briefly.

Now, everything about Barry bewildered David—the touching, the holding hands in public, the fuzzy feelings David felt inside while they were together. But David also thought that his relations with Barry so far showed he had not made any progress after all these years; what did they have in common with each other, really, besides their desire to have sex with each other? David had hoped that by now, at his age and having survived this far into the plague, he would have reached something *beyond* a sexual relationship. Was he merely using Barry as reassurance of his own attractiveness or was he instead simply smitten by the attentiveness? Was he afraid of falling in love or worse, falling in love and being abandoned, or worse still, falling in love and watching someone die? Was the real issue Barry's serostatus? Or had David accepted that through the act of sex? Was David simply *incapable* of a relationship? But David could justify even now that Barry wasn't physically his type. Wasn't he usually attracted to and more interested in guys his own height and age—those boyish, actor friends, conservative and nonthreatening, who knew the same subjects he did and could talk in the same shorthand about the theater or books or movies? But even this was discouraging; somehow everyone David knew or met these days was already attached to someone richer or better looking or taller or smarter. Perhaps what David needed was someone younger, someone uninhibited and dauntless.

Though Barry was drawn to David because of his boyish

looks, Barry knew he and David were really not compatible. And it had nothing to do with David's age, nothing to do with David's reticence or overeducated response to everything. Emotionally Barry typically found himself drawn to men who were adventurous and willing to take risks, the reason why he was captivated by the spontaneity of the club crowd, and those who were ready to just go out there and dance and sweat it out. But physically he was also wildly attracted to those macho-masculine men who were tall and unapproach-able-looking, rough around the edges, the straight construc-tion worker/cowboy types, the kind who presented as much danger as domination. "In other words, someone unavail-able," a woman in his support group had laughed the night Barry had explained this. That was the first group Barry had left. He had changed therapists for the same reason when, in a session, his doctor suggested that perhaps what he was searching for was a surrogate for the father he felt had aban-doned him.

When Barry had brought the subject of David up at his support group meeting that week, Ken, an older man—even older than David—who believed he specialized in being dumped, warned Barry to be prepared for the worst. "People don't change," Ken said. "If he hesitates now, he'll hesitate later." Dustin, a year younger than Barry, yelled at Barry and said he should just forget about David. "It's his fault anyway, man," Dustin said. "They fucked around for years. Those kind of guys gave us AIDS." That prompted an argument within the group, angry cross-examinations and challenges displacing Barry's appeal for advice.

Earlier that week, when David had phoned his friend Stuart and asked if he, Stuart, would ever date someone who was positive, there followed that notorious gap of silence. By the time Stuart spoke, David already knew his answer.

"You're putting your life at risk," Stuart said. "No one

else. *You* have to make that choice."

When David pressed him harder, what would Stuart do, Stuart again avoided the question. "I have a lover," Stuart said. "I'm lucky I don't have to be out there."

David called his friend Wes in Los Angeles and asked him the same question. This time there was no hesitation. "No," Wes said bluntly. David and Wes had slept together years ago. Now Wes worked for an organization that raised funds for AIDS research. When David pressed Wes to explain his decision, Wes answered succinctly, "I can't work with it *and* live with it." Later, toward the end of their conversation, Wes asked David, "Do you feel something for him?"

"Yes," David answered honestly, but then he remembered he had also felt something for John-Boy on *The Waltons* and Michael on *thirtysomething*.

David wished Barry was negative. Barry wished David was positive.

They held hands throughout the movie.

Afterwards, Barry took David home to his apartment on the Upper East Side.

david had not been aware of how much money Barry had; it was certainly not apparent in Barry's choice of clothing or restaurants, not even hinted at in his attitude. Barry's apartment was on the top floor of a Park Avenue building, decorated with dark, bulky wooden antiques and tapestries, large floor-to-ceiling windows providing a city skyline view. Barry explained that the apartment and furnishings belonged to his grandmother, though she had not used the place in several years, since Barry had asked to move in; she now stayed at her house in Westchester.

"Do you want a drink?" Barry asked, and David, disappearing into the cushions of an overstuffed couch, shook his head and said, "No, I'm fine," and noticed as Barry opened the bar, the crystal ice bucket and glasses, the bar stocked with an assortment of foreign liqueurs.

For the last few years David had lived on the brink of poverty. David had paid for Neal's funeral with his own money, bought medication for Jeff, loaned PJ money he knew he would never see again. David had lost jobs, quit others, moved in and out of apartments so many times that he had now become so poor, so behind on all his loan payments and credit cards, that his creditors had taken to calling him periodically to check on his financial status—was he working, why were the payments late, could he send something in now, just a little? Sometimes David believed if it weren't for his regular collectors—Mr. Shaw from American Express, Mrs. Watson from Chemical MasterCard, Andrea from Citibank—his phone might not even ring at all. These financial problems had produced in David such a lack of self-esteem that he could no longer listen to his friends' stories of European vacations or trips to the Caribbean, no longer hear about the cars they were considering buying, no longer care, even, what new plays or restaurants or movies they had discovered—everything seemed so unattainable to him. Sometimes David tried to shrug it off with a joke, saying that he half expected one day to walk into a bank or a store and hear alarms go off and have security guards rush at him, yelling, "You owe us money! You owe us money!" But the truth was, David was worried that now no one would take him seriously; could anyone ever find him attractive when he was living with such troubles? David had also come to believe, in that same lighthearted manner, that the only person who could fall in love with him now would have to be someone obscenely rich. Or would have to be either a doctor or a psychiatrist, someone who could talk David out of all of his neuroses.

He told none of this to Barry, of course. Rich, well-to-do Barry. Barry who drank and smoked too much. Barry who could march in the rain without even an umbrella for protection. Barry who was fifteen years younger than David but looked four years older. Barry with whom he had such a difficult time finding things to talk about, finding interests they shared besides that crazy, intense chemical attraction of sex. Barry who was positive and seemed to live, not more carefully, to protect his health, but precariously, teetering on a ledge.

Always at the back of David's mind, of course, was Barry's status. What if Barry got sick? Would David take care of him? As he had done with the others. Could he *really* go through that again? David had never had a lover—a string of boyfriends, yes, but never a lover—and his closest, most intimate moments were the ones he had spent washing PJ when he was sick, helping Neal walk from the bed to the bathroom, feeding Jeff when he was too weak to do it himself. There was always the possibility that Barry was stronger than the virus; wasn't the news full of reports of weaker strains and longer life expectancies? But for David, there was always the looming possibility that he, himself, could slip across that line and become infected.

Barry was acutely aware of the division between himself and David because of the virus. It was an issue with every man he had met and dated since he had heard his diagnosis. Barry refused to believe that sex was a moral or legal dilemma for him. The problem was unsafe sex. He knew the facts; he operated within the guidelines. But what upset Barry was the way gay men had become interested in safe men, not safe sex. Most negative men would not even consider dating a positive man; ironic, Barry thought, that in a community so passionate about civil rights, discrimination, and antibias legislation, there were still men who would walk away from him the moment he explained he was positive.

Even the personal ads reeked of codes: *healthy playmate seeks same, responsible man wanted,* or, more blatantly, *negatives only need reply.* And now even the positives had made the division wider: special bar nights for positives, dating clubs for positives, special newsletters and support groups and circle jerks for positives. All Barry really wanted was someone who would not be afraid of him. The concept of safe sex was that safe sex was for everybody, but HIV had now become more than an opponent for some men; it had become, in this disturbed and distorted fashion, the antagonist of love. For years Barry had never really wanted a lover; what he enjoyed about sex was the raw, physical anonymity of it. When Barry left home at sixteen he knew nothing about safe sex—his parents had created such a protected environment for him that the equation of sex with death was not even considered. Barry believed that what had happened to him—his seroconversion in the early period of exploring his sexuality— was no different than what had happened to other men in the early days of the epidemic. He could not blame himself any more than he could really blame his parents or his teachers for their lack of perception. He discussed none of this with David, of course. Now, he joined him on the couch, placed his drink on a glass-topped coffee table and lit a cigarette.

David had given up smoking, drinking, pot and other recreational drugs. Sometimes David felt he had gone through every modern gay phase possible—the theater phase, the bar phase; the opera, baths, gym phases; the disco phase; even the twelve-step and activist phases. Sometimes all this history just seemed to have worn him down. What was left, David felt, was a hollow shell, waiting to be refilled. As David watched Barry take a deep, long drag off of his cigarette, he realized that of course Barry should smoke—it made sense—what did Barry really have left to lose? David reached out and touched Barry on the arm and it was here that Barry recognized, for the first time, that this was not a touch of sympathy or concern but one of understanding. Barry leaned over and kissed David, and David, at that moment, tasted everything—the cigarette, the alcohol, the passion and struggle of another man's life.

It was David who suggested they move to the bedroom; Barry led the way.

ʌʌ̂ʍʌ̂ʌ̂ʌ

David spent the night tossing, unaccustomed to the bed and Barry beside him. David had never liked sleeping over with someone; it always seemed to shift a relationship into a more intimate and awkward level. Barry woke up intermittently throughout the night, lifting himself out of sleep to remember who lay beside him; Barry seldom had overnight guests, pre-ferring instead to let himself be absorbed into someone else's life. Before them was a large window with a view of the night sky. David, waking, noticing the deep violet clouds, was reminded of those nights years ago when he would stumble out of a disco or the baths, his mind tinted by alcohol and drugs, and he would suddenly notice, upon turning a corner, a huge, wide pocket of the Manhattan sky. It always made him feel vivid and indestructible; but now, looking at it through his sleepy haze, it made him feel old and defeated. How could he deny or fault Barry for wanting that same illusion, the invinci-bility of youth? As the morning light began to outline the clouds like veins of marble, David reached out and drew Barry toward him. They made love again, and afterwards, David held Barry in his arms, Barry's head pressed against David's chest, David stroking his fingers through Barry's hair. They stayed that way, watching the morning sun bleed into the horizon and Barry felt, for the first time since his diagnosis, that something was attainable for him, a future was possible with another

82

man. David felt he was capable of protecting Barry from every harm, of helping him navigate the muddy river of youth.

Barry was the first to get out of bed. He dressed and went to the deli on Lexington Avenue and brought back the Sunday *Times*, bagels, and coffee. David sat at the grand piano and sight-read a book of Jerome Kern songs.

It was a beautiful spring day and Barry opened the windows, causing the light to break through in rays and the sheer curtains to billow and curl as they would in a movie. They showered and decided, each to himself, that they were not tired of each other nor ready to part, and they agreed to take a walk to Central Park, amazed that only a week ago it had been so rainy when they met.

On the way to the park Barry noticed young men everywhere: young men dressed in tank tops and shorts, young men carrying backpacks and gym bags, young men wearing caps and sunglasses and Walkmans. At one point they passed a young man holding hands with his girlfriend, a man Barry found so handsome that he upset Barry's balance, weakened his knees, made him momentarily lose his logic. Of course David had noticed Barry's reaction; David had also noticed the girlfriend noticing Barry. Barry knew he had to find a way to handle this distraction, knew that if he were to make a relationship with David work he would have to channel his obsessions in other ways, or at least *discuss* them and acknowledge them to David. David, however, knew he had to accept Barry's preoccupations, weren't they, after all, a distinction of being both young and gay? Near Fifth Avenue a gaunt man with a ragged beard crossed in front of them and it was here that David recognized the man as someone he had seen years ago in his gym. David averted his eyes, embarrassed and upset, feeling guilty once again for surviving, guilty for being alive and healthy and negative when so many of his friends and lovers and boyfriends and tricks were either positive, ill, dying, or dead. Barry, now realizing something had passed between David and the man, took David's hand, and it was then that David gave it willingly, here realized that one had to have such an immense courage to date these days—to be fearless, really—to fall in love. At that point David became immune to everyone's stare, existing blissfully in a moment of affection.

It was a perfect day for the park. They lay on the ground at Sheep Meadow watching a boy and his father fly a kite, then walked to the pond and watched the miniature sailboats, then rented bikes and cycled around the horse-drawn carriages. They ate hot dogs and ice cream from vendors. David felt as young as Barry had imagined him to be. Barry moved everywhere with the lightness of hope in his step. They did not part until twilight, kissing unashamedly in front of everyone at Columbus Circle, beneath a sky fading as brilliantly as it had arrived.

That was the end of their first week together.

What happened next was David got sick. A cold. A bad one. He had a fever and deep pains in his chest, as if he had pulled a muscle. Bad enough to cancel a date with Barry. Barry offered to come over anyway and cook David something, though when Barry heard himself saying that he thought it sounded false. Cook what? he thought; he didn't know how to cook. "I'll bring you some medicine. Or something," Barry said.

"No," David replied, not wanting to seem vulnerable. "I need to just shake this myself."

Barry was pissed when he hung up; he felt David was using this as an excuse to push him away. David was not really *that* sick; the issue was once again that Barry was positive. Barry went out to a bar, then to a club, then home with a guy named Allen.

Barry was not home when David called later that night. David left a message on Barry's answering machine that some medicine would be nice, so would some company. Barry did not get the message till the following day when he got home from work. When Barry called David, David did not pick up the phone, thinking it was Mr. Shaw from American Express, calling to inquire about when another payment could be expected. Barry was so upset he could not leave a message on David's answering machine. Days passed. Barry went out to another club. David, over his cold, agonized over whether to call Barry again, then decided, impulsively, to visit a friend out of town.

Time passed between them.

Months later, sometime near Christmas, David spotted Barry through the window of a store on Christopher Street, his arm draped around another man. It was then that David crossed the street to the other side, not wanting to become upset, wanting only, instead, to survive.

A Date with Dracula,
a Trick with Tarzan

Will was not the worst date I ever had—the worst was with the Romanian midget with short, baby-sized arms, a nasal whine, and a black shoe-polish toupee. A supposedly reputable members-only gay dating service had set me up with that one and we met for brunch at an Upper West Side restaurant. Not only did I have to endure the embarrassment of this bad blind date, but I also had had a bad blind date with our overweight waiter the week before. That date had not gone very well, either (he was thirty years older than he had stated), and the waiter kept coming over and spilling things on my creepy-looking circus companion out of revenge for my not having liked him (or believed his age) and I watched with terror (and amusement) as my midget date's face became redder and redder the wetter and wetter his lap became.

In the fifteen years that I had been openly gay I'd averaged about thirty blind dates every hour (and that's not counting the tricks). I quickly learned not to expect any sort of sexual chemistry from someone I had had a thirty-minute awkward phone conversation with trying to discover nonsexual avenues of interest between us, ranging through a wide spectrum of details about a number of subjects that I could "pull out of my hat," from the side effects of the drug DHPG to the Great Vowel Shift to the plot breakdowns of episodes of *The Mary Tyler Moore Show*, *Rhoda*, and *Phyllis*.

The most awkward part of a blind date, of course, is seeing if the person who showed up is as you had imagined him to be. (And how accurately he has described himself—one man who described himself as having salt-and-pepper hair was actually referring to the freckles on his bald scalp; another guy who said he was six foot seven was actually referring to his girth, not his height.) Men are very visually responsive sexual animals and gay males, in particular, are drawn to sultry hothouse flower sex-pot looks, and those first five seconds of a blind date, when you meet each other for the first time and shake hands and exchange those up and down glances—when he looks at you and you look at him— can be either wildly exciting or horrifyingly dismal. You know instantly whether or not you're going to work together sexually. Emotionally, it's usually another story, and the rest of the date can be rather frustrating: you either have to be polite and stick out the date and listen to him ramble on and on about his new dog Maxie and wonder if you will ever *evolve* into a romance, or just be rude and leave and say you forgot and left your dance belt in the dryer and you can't possibly afford to have it shrink any more because you just gained twenty pounds because of an ex-boyfriend, or wait and hope that he's as interested in you as you are in him, which usually translates into, will we trick together once or twice and how soon will it happen?

In the months I had been steadily dating a guy who lived on the Upper East Side who didn't want to be in a committed relationship, I had gone out on at least fifteen-thousand blind dates, desperate to find someone better to obsess on. During a rocky period, when I was certain this guy was seeing someone else, I had answered several hundred personal ads. I went through an ad-mania, actually, answering ads in

A Date with Dracula, a Trick with Tarzan

magazines and newspapers both legitimate and gay, as well as a few obscure and under-the-counter ones, from *The Village Voice* to *The Advocate* to *New York Magazine* and *The New York Review of Books* to those freebie grocery store coupon circulars like *The East Side Shopper* or *The Clinton Chronicle*. I weeded out several guys on the phone, of course, and a few others I never even returned the messages they left on my answering machine, deciding I didn't care what they looked like—even if they were JFK, Jr. clones—I simply didn't like the way they *sounded*. I did call and end up meeting a guy named Sal with whom I went bowling (and who was a bit too self-absorbed in the bed department for my tastes), a nudist who seemed rather shy about removing his cap when we sat down at the coffee shop where we met, a guy named Franklin who was so spaced out on drugs that he fell asleep before the coffee he had ordered arrived, and several theater queens who lived in my neighborhood, all of whom I had some witty and campy conversations with but nothing else. Will was simply another coffee shop stop on a string of coffee shop stops as I looked for someone I felt I could like as much as I did Mr. Upper East Side—hoping, of course, that I could just up and *replace* the jerk like a used set of AA batteries.

The afternoon I met Will he wore black shorts and a black T-shirt, which flattered his pale complexion and curly black hair and highlighted the scab on his nose (the cause of which was not explained). His eyes, dark brown with dark brown circles in the folds of the skin underneath them, were also accented with red veiny streaks running through the whites like interstate highways on a roadmap, and I assumed that it must have been from insomnia, the cause of my own occasional bloodshot eyes. It made him look like a sleepy Dracula who had stumbled outside into the sunlight. *Count Dracula is awake and sleepy and looking to date men in New York,* I thought, trying to keep myself amused and, well, amusing, too, one of the better ways I thought I could catch a guy. I had expected, from our prior phone conversation, that Will and I would have a rather boring conversation about psychiatry and a few good "links" talking about biking in Central Park, a shared passion. What I hadn't discovered was that Will was a heavy thinker, and that the pause between two consecutive words in one of his sentences could last...longer than most of my other blind dates.

"You said you were some sort of...," Will said, his forehead lined with frowns, thinking, thinking, *thinking* of the next word and then it finally arriving. "Actor." The result of his thought process was as dry and dull a delivery as opening an empty paper bag.

Actor? I thought, trying to take it all in. *Some kind of actor? Yes, I guess so. Here I am acting—pretending I'm interested in another boring blind date.* "Not really. I used to work in the theater," I answered, realizing my delivery was as barren of personality as Will's own. Even my sarcasm was missing. I had had so many bad blind dates that I had finally left my sense of humor behind in some coffee shop like a forgotten briefcase. Why couldn't I at least let him know up front that I was, well, feeling a bit too cynical about this less-than-sparkling encounter?

"The theater has gotten so out of control," he said.

"Certainly," I answered, nodding my head up and down, like a bobbing dashboard toy. (Why was I always agreeing with jerks? Why couldn't I just tell them they were dull, dull, dull?)

"Commercial," he added. There were those lines in his forehead again—he was thinking, thinking, thinking. "...Out to make a buck."

"Yes," I replied. "You have to take out a loan to see a Broadway musical these days." There. There it was at last. Some sort of sarcasm. A touch of humor. It made me feel, well, so all-at-once gay. Then I became worried that I was being *too* sarcastic. I was always watching my words on blind dates, imagining that every choice was being rated and dissected as harboring some secret clue about myself that I didn't want to acknowledge.

"I find museums much more...," thought, frown-line, another thought, another frown-line "...*in-te-rest-ing.* I find it helps me with my work."

"Your *work*?" I responded too quickly. "How so?" *Oh god,* I thought. *Now I am acting too interested in him.*

"My...," pause, pause, pause "...*draw-ings.*"

A few minutes later I discovered that Will was also an artist; he described his work as collages of portraits and words. He was having trouble articulating his style and technique (which I wasn't surprised to note) and he suddenly invited me up to his apartment around the corner to show me the etchings he was having difficulty summarizing. *Such a ploy,* I thought, when we hit the sidewalk and I was following a few steps behind his long-legged gait, knowing, of course, that we were on our way to having sex. When I stepped into his apartment a few minutes later, however, I thought I had entered an episode of *The Twilight Zone.* It was decorated in black—black walls, black sofa, black carpeting, black, black, black with black on black, as if it were a layout for a cover story for *Dungeon Times.* Will's "art" turned out to be black line-tracings of police mug shots where the whites of the eyes were outlined in red streaks like his own, with tiny words snaking around the skin and bone lines, giving a horrific skeletal effect to the pictures—as if an X ray of the skull had been taken and filled in with doctors' diagnoses.

Dracula, I thought, again. *Will is Count Dracula.* Count Dracula was alive and drawing bad art in Manhattan. I looked at him, and his eyes looked even brighter, more devilish. Will was so proud of his pictures that he soon stood behind me with his hands on my shoulders as I looked at them with my jaw dropped open. I could feel the parental pride flowing through him and touching my body. The next thing I knew he had me clutched in a bear hug and was dry humping me with his hips. I struggled with him, momentarily thinking, *this could be sort of fun in a kinky way, maybe he'll tie me up and we can have some unnatural counterculture sex,* but when I had managed to turn my body around, he began licking me as if he were a dog, and, before I had even had a chance to respond, he had pulled his dick out of his pants and was chanting in a tribal primate fashion. A few seconds later he had jerked himself off, his come landing in a gray blob on the black carpet. I don't know what stunned me more—that he could ejaculate faster than he could speak, or that my dick had not even moved a millimeter during the entire time. I was quickly escorted out of his apartment, as if I were a trick he had picked up on the street. A *street* trick—not even a blind date.

On my walk back to my apartment, despair over yet another bad blind date overwhelmed me, and I tried to find someone other than myself to blame for letting it unfold so disastrously—finally settling on just blaming Will because he, in the end, turned out to be a bigger pig and jerk than me. *Don't let the fact that sex occurred snow you,* I reminded myself. *He had sex. You didn't.* Yet I still felt somehow defiled. A victim. Dracula's *victim.* But even as I made my way back downtown I realized it wasn't the *worst* sex I had ever not had. (The worst was the time with the guy who had had his pelvis removed a few days before I showed up at his apartment. I had been so turned off by him, but so sympathetic to his condition, that I had been humiliated into shoving a dildo the size of Texas into his ass. A mercy fuck, I remembered, and once again I was a bigger dick than the dildo.)

All of this led me right into the arms of Tarzan, or, rather, right between his legs, which, when I met him in a vegetarian restaurant downtown, was exactly where I was hoping I might end up. I had answered his personal ad weeks before his phone message arrived; by the time we actually spoke with each other (in the hazy aftermath of the curse of Dracula) I could not remember any of the qualities he had listed that could have possibly intrigued me enough to respond. Despite all my bad dates, I wasn't the kind of guy to turn down one more—and there was something admirable about his voice that sounded responsible or caring, or caringly responsible, so after a brief phone conversation, we agreed to meet for dinner the following evening.

Glenn—that's his real name—turned out to be a god in a flannel shirt and jeans, which made me want to know what he looked like without them. He was close to six feet tall, with dark eyes and thick, curly hair and the kind of luscious black stubble that can never be shaved entirely away day or night. I was rather appalled by the restaurant he'd chosen— a vegetarian place housed in the basement of a building on a side street that seemed certain to be infested with all sorts of crawling city vermin. I'm a meat eater, always have been, since the day my mother introduced me to solid foods, and I've never let what they do to baby calves deter me from ordering veal off a menu. Vegetarian restaurants unnerve me, something about the combination of plants that do not grow anywhere near one another geographically and the way in which they are always lumped together into a soggy, luke-warm stew. And then there was the strange odor that always seemed to hang about this sort of place, as if a pile of lawn trimmings had just been dumped inside the kitchen door and was now baking in an oven.

But I took my seat opposite Glenn in a booth in this foul-smelling place he had chosen because I knew, immediately on seeing him, that I wanted to know more—no, make that *everything* I could find out about him, especially what was beneath his clothes. I thought I could break the ice by asking what he recommended from the menu, but right away this seemed to cause him some concern. "You're not vegan, are you?" he asked, suspiciously.

I could be for the right guy, I thought, but felt my reddening face betray the truth. Before I had a chance to think my answer through, I said, instinctively, "Oh, I'll eat anything that tastes decent."

I know my face brightened even further, because I felt the need to backtrack when I saw the sour expression on Glenn's face. Vegetarians, I have learned through many bad blind dates, usually have a defensive haughtiness which takes a bit of chipping away at to get them relaxed. "I usually just get a veggie burger," I said. "But I thought you might have a favorite dish here—something you really liked."

He didn't answer me. Instead, he buried his head in the menu, then said, rather softly after an acceptable—and condescending—pause, "The okra is *very* good here."

"I love fried okra," I answered, again instinctively and rapidly, and knew, immediately as the words left my mouth, that I would be corrected.

"The *stew*," he said.

I could not have been more appalled by this suggestion. Okra. Slimy, slippery, smelly stewed okra. I tried not to roll my eyes and scrunch up my nose. But I was desperate to try to find a way to connect with this guy, so when the waitress arrived, I ordered the stew. The *okra* stew.

And so I sat there picking at my tepid okra stew and holding back the gagging motions in my throat. I wanted nothing more than to lean over and run my tongue along the black stubble of Glenn's jaw and felt defeated with every swallow. But the meeting wasn't a complete disaster, or at least I wouldn't let it veer in that direction for too long. And I wasn't really at a loss for words, even though I was so smitten with Glenn's looks I could feel my blood throbbing in the veins of my throat and neck. In fact, I actually knew a thing or two about holistic herbs and organic foods. During my years of moving from one thankless job to the next, I have often been so poor and without medical coverage that I've had to explore herbal treatments when I can't afford a doctor or am unable to raid a friend's antibiotic stash. And soon I had worked our conversation from his favorite vegetables to my detailing the subtle differences between kava kava, valerian, skullcap, and Saint-John's-wort for uses ranging from depression to anxiety. Thankfully, my display of knowledge was enough to make Mr. Body Beautiful in a Flannel Shirt want to do more than eat strange-tasting food with me in a smelly restaurant.

After we had finished dinner (and which hovered in a bitter aftertaste at the back of my throat), we split the bill and Glenn invited me back to his apartment to watch a movie. As with my other dates, I hoped the "movie" was merely a euphemism for some other kind of activity.

His apartment was a small third-floor studio and he had made it look more spacious by refusing to own any furniture except for the absolutely necessary items. This meant that everything was on the floor—books, kitchen pots and pans, pillows to be used as chairs, and his TV set. Apparently his one major furniture investment was the pair of bunk beds against a far wall and when I asked him why he had succumbed to this sort of sleeping arrangement, he explained that it was a concession to his sister, an actress who sometimes stayed over when she came to town to audition for a role.

The whole experience of sitting on the floor of his apartment, propping myself up on my elbows and watching a low-level TV had a sort of urban "roughing it" feel, as if I were a Boy Scout in front of a campfire with a friend, or, to be more exact about the fantasy, as if I were Jane at home with Tarzan in our tree fort, lying back and kicking off our sandals and listening to the sounds of the jungle around us. By now I was ready to find out every detail of Tarzan's body and had no interest in the movie, and I knew from our dinner and our conversations that Glenn was not the type of man who wore cologne, deodorant, or anything that would harm the ozone. He exuded a damp muskiness that periodically wafted its way tauntingly to me, and soon enough, I had angled my pillow so that we could cuddle and I could inhale his hypermasculine odors.

As I'd hoped, the cuddling turned into some heavier action and soon Tarzan and I were stripping to our underwear, my tongue was at the back of his throat and my hands were wherever he would allow. He wasn't the Johnny Weissmuller type of Tarzan, nor the tall, skinny Ron Ely sort of guy, or even the pretty-boy Miles O'Keefe/Christopher Lambert kind of jungle man. He reminded me more of Mike Henry, the Tarzan who starred in *Tarzan and the Valley of Gold* and *Tarzan and the Jungle Boy*, heavily built in the shoulders with a nice amount of fur trailing down his chest and over a six-pack stomach.

As we groped and tussled with each other I imagined myself as Boy being taught some wrestling holds; our twisting and grappling quickly turned into a sort of physical competition between the two of us—Tarzan wanted to best me by proving that I could not best him, and of course he could because he was a good deal taller and heavier and more muscular than I've ever been, even at my fittest. But he was also willing to concede when he wanted to concede, which was often enough, and soon my hands were slipping off his underwear and gripping two tight and very hairy ass cheeks.

When it was over, when we had both reached orgasms, we were sweating and gulping in deep breaths of air. I lay

A Date with Dracula, a Trick with Tarzan

there thinking that I could get used to this sort of thing—I could build up my stamina for this type of sweaty, heavy action—and deep in my gut I knew I could convince this man to invest in some real furniture.

Later that night, alone back at home, still dizzy from my dream date, I paced back and forth, wondering how soon I might reasonably call Tarzan and say I wanted to get together again. Too soon would make me look too eager to have another go at great sex; too late would make my interest seem too casual.

I waited till the end of the following day, dialed his number, and got his answering machine. By then I had rehearsed what I would say if I had reached him or if I got his machine; in fact, I had scribbled a script down on a piece of paper so that I wouldn't stumble through my message, though I did anyway.

"I really, *really* had a good time the other night," I said, and then, thinking my voice sounded too high, I cleared my throat and tried to say in a deeper pitch, "I hope we can get together soon." Then I left my phone number, even though I knew he had it, slowly repeating my digits just in case he had tossed them into the trash or they had mysteriously fallen into the jungle canopy after I left his tree hut.

He didn't call back that evening or the next, and another day and night passed by before I decided to break down and call him again. By then I knew he most likely wasn't interested in seeing me again and I was disheartened and deflated, but I held out hope that maybe for one reason or another he hadn't gotten my first message—maybe there was a garbled tape or Cheetah had ripped the machine out of the wall in a jealous rage, so I dialed his number and got his answering machine. Again, I left some silly high-pitched oh-please-please-like-me sort of message and when I had hung up I realized that he would never, ever, call me back under any circumstances and even if he were to do so, I doubted I would get together with him another time. We didn't really have anything in common, there was no connection that could grow into anything but a few more hot and sweaty sexual sessions—but for a few days afterwards I boiled and sautéd an assortment of vegetables and fantasized that he would call and I would transform myself into a meatless sort of guy. Luckily that obsession ended when a friend called and asked me if I wanted to be set up on a blind date and, feeling vulnerable and needy and bloated from all the fiber, I could not think of one decent reason why I should object to spending time with another stranger.

What You Learn

You are fifteen years old. It is summer; school is out. Your father is letting you drive to the pool. He mentions a stop sign you are approaching and you tap the brake pedal to begin stopping. The car has power brakes. It lurches with your tap, lurches again when you release the pedal. You let out a giggle. Your father tells you not to be so nervous and to turn on the left turn signal. You feel a bit of sweat beneath your arms and on your forehead. You think about turning down the radio and turning up the air conditioner but there is too much to think about already in front of you. You are glad when you finally reach the country club.

Your father tells you to park away from the other cars. He points to a spot that makes you turn your head. You turn the wheel at the same time. You almost cause a collision with a passing car but you right the wheel at the last possible moment. Blood has drained from your dad's face. He doesn't speak as you lurch the car to a stop. Then, when you have turned the ignition off, he says, "I'll meet you back here after your class."

Inside the club, you sign in and walk back outside to the pool area to join the other guys who are taking the class. Lifeguard Certification. Three hours every weekday for two weeks. Your father thinks it will help you get a summer job.

Desire, Lust, Passion, Sex

He thinks you can be a lifeguard at the country club. Your dad was an Eagle Scout when he was a teenager. Your older brother is a football player. Your dad thinks you need to stop reading so many books and get outside more often. The swimming class was his idea, not yours.

Outside it is bright and hot, but not as hot as it will be later in the day. You sit on the concrete shelf, tell your name to a man carrying a clipboard and wearing a whistle on a string around his neck. He has skinny legs, a big gut, and very hairy forearms. His face reminds you of a coach at school. His body makes you wonder if he would float. "Everyone in the pool," he yells and blows his whistle. The guy beside you dives in head first. You walk to the steps and edge your way into the freezing water, stopping when you reach your waist. You wait a few seconds until your teeth start chattering and then you dip into the water to your shoulders, take a breath, and swim underwater. This is your favorite way to cool off in the heat.

When you emerge, the man with the whistle is addressing the guys in the class. There are twelve of you. He says his name is Mr. Williams. He gives a spiel on the importance of safety in the water and being serious about looking out for others and how swimming is a serious matter than can mean the difference between life and death. The guy beside you treads water. You stand in shallower water, on your tip toes, balancing yourself with your outstretched arms. You like to rock in the water as if you are dancing. While the instructor is talking, you sing pop songs in your head while you rock.

The first part of the class is the qualification. You have to swim and swim and swim. You do one lap, then have to do another, and then another. Mr. Williams yells to change from sidestroke to breaststroke. Your heart is beating in your ears. You swim and swim. Your chest is full of air one minute and gasping for more the next. Your lungs begin to hurt. Your arms grow heavy. When you finally finish the guy next to you is coughing up water. Mr. Williams blows his whistle and everyone gets out of the pool.

Next you have to retrieve a brick from the bottom of the pool. You are number seven. The first two boys are like seals. They easily retrieve the brick. The third guy doesn't like to open his eyes underwater. He has to dive several times to get the brick. Mr. Williams turns red in the face but seems to forget it when the fourth boy is a seal, too. When it is your turn you hold your breath and dive. You swim easily to the brick but find it heavier than you expected. The weight is a shock to you and it takes you a couple of seconds to get a good grip on it before you surface.

Mr. Williams taps you on the back when you get out of the pool and says, "Good job." You sit and catch your breath and watch the other boys dive and retrieve the brick. Number nine and number twelve struggle with the brick, too. Only number ten, a skinny boy with scabs on his knees, can't bring the brick to the surface.

Next you have to swim with the brick without using your hands. Mr. Williams begins the numbers backward, with boy twelve. Number ten keeps dropping the brick. You sit in the sun squinting, getting nervous. When it is your turn you jump into the pool holding the brick. When you surface Mr. Williams yells for you to swim with the brick and not dog-paddle in place. You hold the brick in front of you, as if it would float on its own. It doesn't. It can't. Your arms grow tired. Your legs become more tired. Your lungs hurt. You keep looking over your shoulder hoping Mr. Williams will blow his whistle when your time is up. When the whistle finally goes off you drop the brick. Mr. Williams yells at you, tells you to dive and pick it up and bring it back to the surface.

In the car after the class, your father asks you if you

Desire, Lust, Passion, Sex

want to drive home. You shake your head no and turn on the radio.

The next day at the pool there are only ten boys in the class. You remember that number eight's name is Andy. Number five is Craig. Two is Steve, who was in your algebra class last year and never spoke to you because he is tall and on the basketball team and you are short and only in the marching band. You begin the class by swimming laps. Mr. Williams makes you tread water, surface dive for the brick, and swim laps with it before you get out of the pool. After class your mom picks you up and you drive the car home.

On Wednesday, you float. You spend minutes and minutes and minutes and minutes on your back with your stomach and eyes to the sky. The sun is very bright and you have to squint while you float. Water fills up your ears. Chlorine sinks into your skin.

After floating you practice tossing a rescue tube in the water. Water continues to stay in your ears. The chlorine makes you itch. While Mr. Williams is talking you keep shaking your head to dislodge the water and scratching your arm. Charlie, number six, keeps coughing so that you can't understand the instructions. Steve, the tall basketball player guy, picks dead skin from between his toes.

After class, your older brother picks you up. He does not let you drive home.

What You Learn

On Thursday, it is not so sunny. There are only nine boys in the class now. Number six, the guy who was always coughing up water, has decided to drop out. Mr. Williams gives a lecture about the importance of safety. As the sky grows cloudier, he says he will teach you how to resuscitate a victim. He makes you line up according to height. He breaks the class into pairs. Since you are now the shortest guy in the class, the odd one out, Mr. Williams tells the class that you have the honor of being his partner. And guinea pig. He makes you lie on your back on the cement. You feel silly, let out a giggle, then try to become serious. He kneels beside you, on his knees. He explains to the class how to open the victim's airway. (He tilts your head back so that your mouth opens.) He leans his face over you and tells the boys how to check a victim's breathing. (You feel a bit of sweat under your arms even though the air is cool.) He explains that if the breathing is not normal, pinch the nose and ventilate. (He presses his fingers against your nostrils and his lips cover your mouth. His mouth is moist and full of energy. The whistle around his neck thumps against your chest. You cannot understand anything else he is saying because all of this is a shock to your body.) When he pulls away from you, you hear someone snicker. Mr. Williams reminds the class that this is a serious matter.

When it comes time for the class to practice CPR, Mr. Williams lies down on the cement, tells you to practice with him. You lean over him. His face seems huge. The pores of his face are filled with stubbles of black hair. Hair grows up from the collar of his shirt. Behind you some boys giggle while they practice, others grunt and say to their partners, "Come on, just do it and get it over with."

Looking down at Mr. Williams, you don't think that you can stretch your mouth wide enough to cover his mouth. It is full of big teeth and a thick tongue. Stubbles of hair ring the border of his lips. You open your mouth wide, wider than a yawn, and press your mouth into his. You force two breaths of air into his mouth and realize, when you break away from him, that something of him remains with you. You cannot exactly place what it is. It is more than the taste of him. More than the moist, warm feeling of his mouth. Something, you think, has been left inside you.

When Mr. Williams tells the class to switch positions and continue practicing he stays on the ground. "Do it again," he says to you. "And don't be so nervous this time."

⋀⋀⋀⋀⋀

After CPR, Mr. Williams demonstrates how to handle a struggling victim. It is still too dark and gray and cold to swim. He continues to use you as the class guinea pig. "Don't sacrifice your life trying to save someone," he says. "If a victim lunges toward you, place an open hand against his chest."

Mr. Williams places the palm of his hand against your chest. His hand is moist and warm against your skin when he touches you. He turns you toward the class. "Lean backwards and submerge rapidly away from him. Keep your blocking arm extended."

Mr. Williams now takes his hand and presses it against your shoulder. His hand is so large you believe you can feel the weight of each of his fingers. He turns you away from the row of watching boys. He makes you clamp your tiny fingers around his thick, slippery, hairy wrist. "If a victim grabs your arm or wrist, quickly submerge the victim by reaching across with your free hand and pushing down on the victim's shoulder while kicking upward for better leverage," he says.

Mr. Williams presses against your shoulder so that you are forced to your knees. His strength is surprising, but his touch is still moist, warm. You look up at him as he says, "This leverage allows the rescuer to pull his hand free. You may also reach down with your free hand to grab your other hand, and jerk upward. Swim clear of the victim and reassess his condition."

Mr. Williams motions for you to stand up. He squats so that he is about your height. He takes both of your arms and places them around his shoulders. You can feel the power of his body. His eyes meet yours. "The front head hold escape technique allows you to escape from a victim who has thrown his arms around your head and neck," he says. "Take a quick breath and tuck your chin into a shoulder while shrugging your shoulders upwards. Then take a strong stroke and submerge instantly. This drags the victim below the water."

Mr. Williams shifts his squat so that he moves in closer to you. He moves his hands to rest below your elbows. His touch is surprisingly soft now. "Grasp the victim's elbows or the underside of the upper arms." You feel the energy building up in him. It seems to come from somewhere in his squat, somewhere in his legs. It moves up through his body until your hands are suddenly tossed up into the air. "You have to thrust the victim's arms upwards and away," he says while you are trying to reign in your thrashing arms. "Be sure to keep your chin tucked and shoulders shrugged to protect your throat."

The class ends with a demonstration of the wrist-tow and the cross-chest carry. Mr. Williams' hands surround you, warm you. His chest is against your back, your head is locked in his elbow. Then he is kneeling so that you can surround his chest with the hook of your arm. He looks up at you. You look down at him. You meet his stare. He meets yours. You feel his strength, the muscles in his arms, the strength in his legs, the dampness in the hair of his forearms—all within the clutch of the power of your elbow.

Desire, Lust, Passion, Sex

After class, the wind gives you a chill when you walk out to the car. Again, your brother does not let you drive home.

✺

On Friday, you are back in the water. Mr. Williams is again your partner and he joins the class in the pool. He takes his shirt off and dives into the water without a splash. His body is huge and covered with wet black hair. You practice escapes and holds and tows with him for three hours. He keeps your energy focused on him.

✺

Over the weekend, you tell your dad that you do not want to be a lifeguard because you want to work in the record store. He says no, that's no place for you to work. Your dad thinks Satan sends messages through certain kinds of music and books. Your mom does not dispute him. Your older brother, who smokes cigarettes sitting on the roof outside your bedroom window, tells you it's all a phony game so that adults can control the world.

Your mom lets you drive to the mall so that you don't spend all weekend inside reading a book. Your two younger sisters sing Bible camp songs in the backseat and make you nervous. You spend the whole time at the mall in the record store, forcing your littlest sister to find you and tell you when it's time to leave. Your mom is so annoyed at you for keeping her waiting that she does not let you drive home.

✺

On Monday, Craig is not at class and Mr. Williams pairs you up with his partner, Steve. Practicing rescues and holds and tows with Steve is not the same as it was with Mr. Williams. Steve has no coordination in the water. His grip is too tight. At one point you must knee him to prevent him from choking you. Since he is the largest boy in the class and you are the shortest, the rescues are awkward and you must fight off the urge to scream at him. By the end of the class you are so angry and upset that you decide you never want to come back to this pool again. You are glad to see your brother waiting for you in the parking lot. It means you don't even have to try to want to drive home.

᜵᜶ᜃᜎᜈᜃ

On Tuesday, Craig is again out of class, though Mr. Williams does not say if he has dropped out for good or not. After twenty minutes of laps, you are once again paired with Steve. Each team of partners must demonstrate the rescue of a victim for the rest of the class. Since Steve is the tallest in the class, your demonstration is the last of the pairs. You sit in the sun while the four other teams thrash through the water. Andy and his partner use a float, which seems to sink the moment it is needed. When it is your team's turn, Steve decides that he will be the victim and you must rescue him with a cross-chest carry. Mr. Williams nods and Steve dives into the pool, swims to the deep end, and pretends to need help.

You dive into the pool, slice easily through water. You swim toward Steve. Steve grabs you by your left wrist when you are close to him. He is strong enough to push you underwater before you have a chance to react. You are smart enough to remember how to break the grip underwater, but when you surface Steve is behind you and grasping his long thin arms around your neck. You go back underwater to release his grip, like you have practiced, but his legs are so long and awkward you misjudge his thrashing. He kicks you first in the arm. Then in the stomach.

The air goes out of you while you are underwater. You feel water rushing into your mouth. At first, everything goes blurry. Then, everything goes black. When you blink your eyes open, you are lying on the tiles at the edge of the pool. Mr. Williams is leaning over you. His face is close to yours. You can taste him inside of you. He has saved you from Steve. He has saved you from drowning.

After class, you wait in the car while Mr. Williams talks with your father. You see the disappointment register on your dad's face as he walks to the car. He asks you if you want to drive home. You shake your head no. You don't want to talk to him. He doesn't understand what happened. He doesn't understand that Steve kicked the wind out of you. You feel like crying. You don't want to be a lifeguard but you don't want to be a failure, either. About a block from home, your dad says that Mr. Williams wants you to take the class again next year. "You just need to be stronger and older," your dad says. "It'll help you keep up with the bigger boys."

You decide your older brother is actually right about something. The world is a conspiracy of adults. And bigger boys.

Thirteen years later you are two inches taller and thirty-three pounds heavier than you were the summer you drowned and were saved by Mr. Williams. You remember the swimming class while you are at the gym. The memory doesn't happen right away. It floats to the surface when a guy steps on a treadmill next to the one you are using. You see his face in the mirror in front of you. It is not the same face, but it is similar enough to dislodge the whole set of memories of what happened the summer you were fifteen. It is not the same body either, but the stocky, hairy build is enough to make you remember Mr. Williams.

You walk on the treadmill until it is comfortable enough to jog. You run at a slow pace, keeping your steps even. You glance in the mirror. Yes, the face is similar. Too similar. It is the same nose, the same wide stubble of blue-black hairs. The same jaw. Your throat tightens. For the next twenty-two minutes you remember everything you can of Mr. Williams and then you want to forget him.

After the treadmill, you move to the other exercise equipment. You are ready to repack the memories now that you have examined them. You move from the leg machine to the back machine to the bicep machine. You don't look back at the guy on the treadmill. Your life moves forward. Your workout continues. You lie on the mat and do sit-ups. When you finish and walk across the room to the free weights, you notice he is no longer on the treadmill. A quick glance through the room shows you that he is no longer on this floor. You relax and continue exercising. By the time you make it to the locker room you have forgotten him. The memories have been repacked.

You change into your swimsuit and take a quick shower. You walk out of the changing room into the small corridor that leads to the Jacuzzi. This part of the gym is coed, used by both male and female members. It is a large, glass-enclosed space in the area between the entrances to the men and women's locker rooms. Since there is so much walking back and forth in front of the glass wall, most members don't use the wet sauna because it is like sitting inside a television set. Everyone looks to see what you are doing. You hate this part of the gym, too, though you love sitting in the hot tub for a few minutes before you change back into your everyday clothes and walk across town to your apartment.

Desire, Lust, Passion, Sex

Today, the water is hotter than usual but you adjust to it easily. You are the only person in the Jacuzzi. You lie back with your head against the ledge of tiles, going through a list of things you want to do before going to work tomorrow morning, the faint smell of chlorine haunting your memory. You close your eyes to concentrate and relax, even though the gym is emptier than usual today because it is a summer weekend. Most of the members are out of town or out at a private beach somewhere. (Your soon-to-expire membership was a generous gift from a boyfriend who has already expired beyond his usefulness. You could never afford this kind of place on the kind of money you make and the larger amount you owe, so you journey across town as often as you can to use this gym.)

When you open your eyes, only a few seconds later, you are surprised to see him entering the hot tub. It is like you have entered a dream. Or a dreamworld. You cannot believe this is happening but you cannot decide if it is pleasure or torture.

He takes the steps slowly into the water. His body is covered with dark hair that becomes darker when wet. He is wearing a small black swimsuit. He stretches his arms out on top of the water, dips his body in and out. He does not look at you as he settles into the water beside you. At this point you have decided it is torture. You think about leaving but you are too embarrassed to step out of the Jacuzzi. You are already aroused. You would have to reveal all that you have. You cannot leave the Jacuzzi until you can find a way to hide your interest in him.

You try not to stare at him. You look at the empty hallway, the empty walkway, the streaks of humidity on the glass wall. He stretches out his legs in front of him and flutter kicks. His leg grazes against yours. He pretends not to notice it has happened. You pretend it has not happened, either.

What You Learn

He shifts in closer to you. You shift in closer to him. He changes position, dips his body up and down, his hands now underwater. His touch grazes you. He pretends it has not happened. His face is a warm, stubbly stare. He is a torture-machine and you will not let him know it. You pretend he has not touched you either. Your heart is beating in your ears.

He shifts closer to you. Underwater, his hand presses against your swimsuit. You glance over his shoulder. You look again at the empty hallway, the empty walkway. Your face does not reveal your pleasure though your body reveals every inch of it. You are flushed with blood. When you move your hand to his swimsuit, you feel he is erect, too. He is ready for you. He is a torture-machine of pleasure, you decide. His face remains motionless as you shift your hand inside his swimsuit. When he touches you, he easily finds what he wants.

The encounter continues without conversation or interruption. Your facial expression does not change to accommodate his stroking hand. His black-stubbly jaw does not shift to recognize yours. All of this continues out of sight, underwater. He has easily aroused you because he is so familiar. At one moment you close your eyes and imagine he is Mr. Williams. Seconds later this is all over. The water has revealed nothing that has happened. The man has been satisfied and he is leaving the wet sauna. You watch his black swimsuit and furry black legs disappear into the locker room. After all these years, this fantasy is over as quickly as you can come.

When you are alone again in the water, you shake your head, trying to dislodge water that has somehow become trapped in your left ear. Your father told you the day that Mr. Williams saved your life that your instructor was willing to make an exception and keep you in the class if you wanted to remain, though he didn't think that you would pass the final examinations and get your lifesaving certificate. Your father had decided it was not the right path for you, that one close encounter with death was enough to chance in a summer.

"He's a fast learner," Mr. Williams had said to your dad. "A few more years and he'll be a strong swimmer, too."

You realize it has taken thirteen years to understand how smart you were that summer. You never forgot the taste of that something Mr. Williams left in your mouth when his lips pressed his breath into yours. It was not something that you could easily explain at age fifteen. But it was also something you knew you could not let drown.

Impromptu

They met in the most casual way, outside the AVA office in the Venice terminal. There was a long wait by the time Jesse took his place at the end of the line for available hotel rooms. The man with the mustache began the conversation the moment he took the spot behind Jesse.

"They told me it would be impossible to find a room here," the man said. Jesse had his back to him and hadn't realized that he was being spoken to until somewhere in the middle of the man's next sentence. "But I've heard that everywhere I've been."

Jesse turned his neck and gave the man with the mustache a weak smile. His backpack was cutting into the flesh of his shoulders, the weight pressed down against his spine in an uncomfortable way. He thought it would be at least an hour before he made it to the reservations counter, but he wasn't willing to let go of the notion that it wouldn't be too long a wait and admit that he should remove the backpack and put it on the ground. He certainly wasn't in the mood for a conversation; the flight had tired him and he'd lost track of time zones.

"I heard they can book you in Mestre, the next town over, but I would rather stay in Venice if I could find a room," the man was saying now.

It seemed impolite to Jesse to continue keeping his back

to the man, so he turned sideways in order to acknowledge that he heard the man speaking. The man was a big man, but not out of shape. The mustache was black and gave the man a fatherly look. He was neatly dressed in khakis and a button-down shirt, which made him seem out of place in the line of lean, hungry tourists and students on a budget. Jesse had lines and wrinkles around his eyes, but he had been able to keep looking boyishly slender even into his mid-thirties, and his T-shirt and faded jeans, shredded at the left knee, made him look like he belonged in the line.

"Is this your first stop?" the man asked Jesse.

"Yes," Jesse said. "I came from the airport. I should have booked a room there. The line wasn't this bad. I thought they might have better rooms here, closer in."

The train terminal was crowded with passengers coming and going, and there was enough to look at without maintaining a conversation with a stranger. But it had already started and both the wait and the conversation were sure to continue. Outside the terminal, a few steps away, Jesse could see the edges of the Grand Canal. Ahead in line, three girls exited the door of the AVA office and told another group of girls that there were "No more rooms in all of Venezia!" The young couple behind them tensed up and began directing questions at the girls. The remark made its way down the line where the man overheard it and began to talk to Jesse again.

"I mean if I have to I can find a room somewhere else," he said. "It's still early enough to do that and I really don't mind. I could spend a few hours here and be off somewhere else. The trains run late. But I really wanted to stay in Venice."

Jesse had wanted to stay here, too. He had looked forward to this summer vacation for months and when things ended with Wade, he had made up his mind he would not give up this trip. His only regret now was canceling the hotel room he had reserved—Wade had wanted to stay in a four-star hotel and had made a reservation at a place near the Piazza San Marco. But that was a luxury Jesse could not afford now, he reminded himself; alone, he needed to travel more cheaply.

The man with the mustache continued to talk to Jesse. He talked about the convention he had been to in Milan, the week afterwards he had spent at Lake Como and then the next week in Florence with friends. Somewhere in the conversation he introduced himself. His name was Burt and he was from Columbus, Ohio, and had a wife and two sons. He was due back in Geneva in three days to make his flight back to the States and he had decided impulsively, at the last moment, that he wanted to see Venice before he returned home.

Jesse did not mention the abrupt change in his travel plans, only that he had arrived in Italy for a week's vacation and was planning to stay at whatever places he could find.

"I love being impulsive," Burt said. "I don't get many chances to behave like this."

⋀⋁⋀⋁⋀⋀

At the counter, Jesse waited for a long-nosed woman with thin black hair to process his request for a "single room, cheapest possible." While she was looking through the list another woman with blonde hair and dark, raccoon-like eyes answered the phone and heard of a list of cancellations at a hotel in the Dorsoduro. Jesse waited while the woman helping him phoned the hotel and found out the types of available rooms. Four singles for two nights each. Two rooms had showers, two had baths. Jesse took a room with a shower even though the price was slightly higher than he had budgeted.

On his way out of the AVA office, Jesse nodded good-bye

to Burt and whispered that he might be in luck, there were a few cancellations for single rooms that just came in and one might be left when he went to the counter. The woman behind Burt overheard the comment and Jesse, even walking away, was aware of the good news making its way down the still-long line.

Outside, beyond the steps in front of the terminal, Jesse fumbled his way through buying waterbus tickets and deciding where to board the boat. It was a warm, August morning, the air full of humidity, and any other place in the world he might have set out on foot instead of relying on public transportation. But he balanced himself on the deck of the waterbus when it arrived, the noise and energy of the engine rumbling beneath his sneakers, and he giddily studied the architecture of balconies and gables and turrets and minarets as the boat made its slow course down the Grand Canal.

At his stop, Jesse tightened the straps on his backpack and set out on the path the AVA clerk had drawn for him in red ink on a map of Venice. It seemed like an easy route to take, but once Jesse proceeded in the direction of the hotel, he realized he was looking too much at where other alleyways and overpasses were headed and was lost, though he happily backtracked—twice—until he finally found the hotel.

His hotel room was small but generous because of the shower. The shutters of a tiny window beside the bed opened to reveal the red tile shingled rooftop of an adjacent building and a small square patch of the green water of the canal. It was a relief to finally take the backpack off his shoulders—he had never removed it during his long wait for a room—and he took the opportunity to shower off the dust and dampness of his journey. After cleaning up and unpacking, he decided a nap would give him more energy so he lay down on the bed and closed his eyes. No need in rushing out right away and becoming lost again, he thought. A nap would make everything easier.

Up from his nap and back out exploring, Jesse discovered that Venice was nothing like he had expected. It was a dizzying, confusing jumble of archways and alleys and bridges and courtyards and *campi* and canals. He spoke not a word of Italian, had not even bothered to bring along a phrasebook or a guidebook. All he wanted to do was walk and forget everything about his life back in Boston. He wanted to forget the paralegal job he had worked at for years now at a Boston law firm, where he had never gotten more than a tiny raise and a few words of thanks during the end-of-the-year holidays. He wanted to forget about the tiny closet of an apartment that kept flooding or leaking or breaking or falling apart. But more than that he wanted to forget about the disastrous year he had spent waiting for Wade to make up his mind about whether to leave his lover, Kevin.

Wade and Kevin had been together for close to twenty years, since they had met in college, but they had become more and more incompatible during the last five years, which was why and how Jesse had met Wade one night last summer at a bar in Cambridge. Two weeks before their trip to Italy was to take place—their first together—Wade had accused Jesse of becoming too demanding and needy and broken things off, just as Jesse felt that he was becoming more seriously involved. It was an unexpected blow even though Jesse had known the long-term affair with Wade would never amount to more than just that. But walking from one courtyard to another and making his way around groups of laughing tourists and guides holding small flags above their heads, he was aware he hadn't been able to leave the longing and loneliness behind. His eyes continued to roam to windows and balconies and across canals for any distraction his mind would allow. Soon he found his way into a museum and then into a church, where he listened to a small ensemble perform a concert of music by Vivaldi, and his mind was able to settle into the music and away from other things. When the concert was over it was dark outside and the city had transformed into shadows and reflections and a different color of longing and loneliness. Jesse wandered that evening over bridges and beneath archways until he was too tired to continue. By the time he found his hotel again it was late and he had to buzz the night clerk to open the door. Inside, he stopped at the bar for a drink before going upstairs to his room. The small glass of wine he had made him instantly exhausted and he slept easily through the night, even though he had fallen onto the bed without undressing and with the shutters still wide open.

They met again at breakfast the next morning. Jesse was seated at a table in the small dining room on the ground floor of the hotel when Burt came up to the table. "You're here, too?" he asked. "Mind if I join you?"

Jesse nodded and Burt took a seat and began talking about how difficult it had been to find the hotel the day before, his confusion over how to stamp the waterbus tickets, his wrong turn down an alley before he discovered the path to the hotel. He'd spent his day at the *Accademia* and the Guggenheim and had sat at an outdoor concert at a *campo* not far from the hotel. Jesse mentioned the concert he had gone to the night before but didn't say much more as he sipped at his small cup of thick black coffee; still, he was rested and didn't at all mind dining with Burt—in fact, he thought him surprisingly more handsome than when they had

Impromptu

met in the AVA line.

Before breakfast was over, Burt asked, "Any interest in going together out to the Lido today? I saw it's the last stop on one of the boat lines. You can't come to Venice without seeing the Lido. Not after they make you read that book in college."

Jesse accepted the invitation, though he was torn with spending too much time with a stranger and a busy talker at that; he wasn't sure how much conversation he could maintain without revealing a side of his life that might not be acceptable to a man with two boys and a wife somewhere back in Columbus, Ohio, USA. Talking on the waterbus, however, was nearly impossible. The motor rumbled loudly enough to prevent anything being heard except what was shouted when necessary, and for Jesse that was close to nothing. The ride was not as long and oddly not as scenic as he had thought it might be; once on shore they stopped at a store to buy bottled water before proceeding toward the beaches. Above, the sky was a pale blue with a promise of more heat, the humidity as thick as the day before.

They walked and talked. Burt talked about how surprisingly urban life in Venice must have been centuries ago with neighbors so close by and relying on boats for transportation; he had grown up in a landlocked county dry of both liquor and lakes and never understood city life until he went to college in Chicago. Burt tried to recall books and movies he knew of that were set in Venice. He could not remember the plot of the famous book he had read in college, though he remembered a movie with Julie Christie where everything was dark and ghostly and there was something about a dwarf that kept confusing him. Jesse mentioned a few British authors who had set scenes here in their novels—he had been an English major in college and remembered how even small passages in books could cast an enchantment over the area. But it wasn't until Jesse stretched out the map and tried to decide their route to the beach that he had a hint that there might be more to Burt than what the fast talking revealed. While looking at the map, Burt leaned in close to Jesse's face. His hand pressed against Jesse's shoulder and the fingers clutched deeply through his flesh toward the bone as if trying to make a statement. His breath was sweet as he breathed in and out against Jesse's neck and the mustache came so close that at one moment it grazed against Jesse's skin. Then, Jesse traced his fingernail along the map and folded it up and they were walking again; soon, the beach was spotted and Burt was trying to remember things he had learned about the Adriatic.

⋀⋏⋀⋀⋏⋀

The beach was crowded and Jesse had the impression that they had wandered to a place where they shouldn't be or didn't really understand or belong. Cabanas and umbrellas and colored towels atop the sand seemed to indicate that this section was reserved for this set of people or this area was reserved for that group and this color indicated this guest at that hotel or that one over there. They took off their shoes and socks and walked in the water to keep cool; the sand was surprisingly pebbly. They had both been smart enough to wear shorts and T-shirts that morning because of the heat. Burt talked now about genealogy and reincarnation; he didn't know his family history beyond where his grandfather was born, and he said he felt drawn to Italy for some strange reason that wasn't because of heredity. He laughed and said maybe he might have been born here in another life, even though he confessed that this was the most absurd thing he had ever thought and said to someone he didn't really know that well.

Jesse mentioned vaguely that he had left behind a relationship before arriving in Venice. They stopped to eat a snack at a café before taking the waterbus back to San Marco; they had gone all day without eating lunch. By the time they stepped off the waterbus it was twilight and the Piazza was full of tourists and vendors. Jesse took photos of the sunset against the bell tower; Burt took photos of Jesse against the water.

While the sun disappeared behind the horizon, they watched a young girl feed pigeons and then walked toward the water and watched the gondoliers luring tourists toward their boats. The sky darkened and lights became shadows and stretched and deepened. When they followed the crowds along the waterfront, they stopped on an overpass where they could look down the canal at the Bridge of Sighs. Burt said he had no idea why the bridge had been given that name. Jesse, in a moment of weakness, watching a couple kiss as their gondola passed underneath, said, "But it's awfully romantic no matter why it's called that."

For dinner, Burt chose a small trattoria, a place that could only be found by going through an alley and underneath an archway and behind a building and down a few steps. During the meal, Jesse had a glass of wine and it loosened him up a bit; he confided that he had been through a string of bad relationships even before the last one had ended and he had thought about just canceling the trip to Venice and staying home, in the dark, watching TV. "I was in Paris a few years ago," he told Burt. "It was so wonderful and beautiful and just like everything I had always imagined it to be. I was miserable the whole trip because I was alone. I was there by myself so I didn't see my happiness reflected through someone else. I know it sounds awful but I decided I would never go back there alone again. I felt that Venice would be like that, too—too romantic to handle—because even though I've never been here before I had all these romantic images of Venice, and I was just frightened about dealing with them alone. But I needed to get out of town, as they say. I needed to just get away to forget about a few things, so I didn't cancel this trip. I came here anyway."

After dinner they decided to walk back to the hotel because they both felt they had eaten too many courses and drunk too many wines and the walk would help them digest and sober up. "Last night I followed the signs that say 'Accademia,'" Burt said. He was pointing to a building at the corner of an alley. "They're stuck on the second floor of the buildings and it's like following a trail of bread crumbs— sometimes they are there and sometimes they aren't, but it worked last night. I made it back to the hotel that way."

That night it didn't work so easily, however; one alley led to another, which led to a side street with led to a passage which led to a *campo*. One sign was there but not another one ahead. Somewhere on their route they both stopped and began laughing. Burt drew close to Jesse and pressed his hand again against Jesse's shoulder. That was when they began kissing—in a spot in a doorway where they could not be seen by anyone passing by. By then, Jesse had expected it to happen. In fact, he had even encouraged it; since dinner he had walked as close as he could to Burt, brushing his hand up against Burt's body. He hoped it might signal to Burt that this diversion was what he needed and why he had made the trip after all; he wanted it to be spontaneous and impromptu— the way it was, indeed, happening. He wanted to be caught up in the romantic moment. He wanted Burt to kiss him. And that is exactly what happened.

⚡︎⚡︎⚡︎

Back at the hotel Burt continued talking. They were in Jesse's room, undressed, lying together in the single bed. Burt said, as he broke away from kissing Jesse, "I don't do this a lot. It just struck me as something that could happen here." His body seemed larger in the small room, so large it amazed and overwhelmed Jesse. He ran his lips against the coarse black hairs of Burt chest and twirled his tongue around a nipple. Burt's large hand cupped Jesse's balls, warmed and kneaded them, then his fingers were around Jesse's cock. "It's not like I was searching for this. Or expecting it to happen," Burt said, his mustache grazing against Jesse's neck now. Jesse's hand held Burt's cock, which was large, as if it belonged with this broad body. "I thought about it when I saw you in line. I thought that this was something that could happen here. This was something I could do that I might not do anywhere else."

Jesse had not expected any of this to happen, either, though he hadn't arrived unprepared for it, if an opportunity like this were to come along. He pressed his hand against Burt's chest, pushed him flat against the bed, and rolled a condom over Burt's cock. The attention, the sensation, seemed to make Burt speechless. His large brown eyes followed Jesse's movement as he lubed the cock and positioned his hips above it, slowly consuming it while he said, "I didn't expect this either. But it is a nice surprise. I'm glad you decided to strike up a conversation."

In the room they were as close and deep as two men could become with each other. Burt twisted himself up off the bed so that his face was buried in Jesse's chest. Whatever he said then, whatever words came out of his mouth, was lost in Jesse's body, deep inside the guts of him.

※※※

They did not say good-bye. There were no phone numbers exchanged, no hints or hopes of this happening again, of their finding each other back in the States or even back in Venice, years later, on a planned rendezvous. Burt disappeared while

Desire, Lust, Passion, Sex

Jesse showered; he was booked on a train a few hours later to Geneva. Before he left the room he stuck his head in the bathroom and his voice bounced off the white tiles. "I'll remember this," he said. "You gave me something I won't forget. I'll remember this about Venice."

Jesse leaned his head out of the water. "Yes," he answered. "So will I."

The next morning Jesse slept late, so late that he almost missed the hotel's checkout time. Outside, he adjusted his backpack so that it was not uncomfortable for walking. He set out for the train station, trying to decide where to go next. His head was full of impromptu destinations: Pisa, Vernona, Milano, Firenze.

Elvis is Alive
and Working on
Eighth Avenue

I have no doubt that I could have been elected the National
Cover Boy for Obsession (and I'm not talking about the
Calvin Klein cologne, either). For the truth was, the sad hon-
est-to-goodness-no-bare-bones-about-it truth, I couldn't get
my troublesome boyfriend Peter out of my mind. He was
locked inside my body, infecting every cell as if he were some
kind of yeast-growing herbal-resistant bacteria. He had
burned my skin and contaminated my body fluids. He was in
my blood, my sweat, my piss, my spit, my hair color. My obsession with him had made him a part of me. When someone
says he doesn't want you, you only want him more, something
that my friend Evan failed to understand when, in response to
all my moaning and groaning, he suggested that I have an affair.
But I didn't want *another* boyfriend to obsess about. One was
enough, thank you very much. How could Evan have suggested that? An affair wasn't going to make me happy. It was
going to make me ballistic, bonkers, ready-to-be-committed-
in-a-straitjacket-at-Bellevue. What I needed, I believed, was to
find a way to make what I already had with Peter work.

I will just live with my pain, I decided one afternoon at a
temp job where my primary responsibility was to maintain a
full pot of decaf coffee for a pair of shoulder-padded,
pantsuited, officious Amazons. I had had a full day to just sit

and obsess about Peter and watch a coffee machine irregularly drip. *I will just make the pain Peter inflicts part of my day-to-day consciousness,* I decided. *I will make it a part of me.*

But once I had hit the hot pavement on my way home, my mood became as foul as sour milk. *Fuck him,* I reconsidered. *I will just move on. It's over. O-V-E-R. Over!* It was mid-June, I remember, and I was walking up Eighth Avenue along that troublesome stretch of the low 40s that resembles what 42nd Street between Seventh and Eighth Avenues used to look like before Disney arrived and changed the neighborhood— discount stores; honky-tonk, open-door dark bars; and neon-signed, mirrored-window porn shops. It had turned into another unbearably blistering, humid day and I had taken my white dress shirt and tie off and put them in my knapsack and was wearing just a T-shirt with my chinos as I headed uptown. Fuck Peter. Fuck this job and fuck this city and fuck this starving no-money no-air-conditioner life I had chosen that kept pulling me down, down, down into the stinking, smelling sewer.

The heat and misery had put me in a scurrilous mood. That aging, bitter, dragon lady persona was overtaking my formerly happy-go-lucky-chorus-boy personality and it was not a pretty sight. I had nothing to do that night. My apartment was sure to be overheated. I was too broke to see a movie, too broke to even rent a movie if I had been able to watch one in the dusty, sweltering jungle of my apartment. It was too hot to rollerblade or bike. So I decided to slip into one of the air-conditioned porn shops to cool off for a moment before I faced returning to the Sahara.

Peter, of course, was my real motive for entering the store. Sure, sure, you might be thinking—wasn't I just another aging guy looking to get his rocks off easily and cheaply? Had I come to *that?*

No, no, no, I told the other side of my brain. I was

considering buying Peter one of those bootlegged versions of those too-too-buffed West Hollywood gay boy porn tapes when I cashed my next paycheck; I felt it might smooth over that nasty-edged memory of our jealous confrontation over his infatuation with the strippers on *The Robin Byrd Show.* This particular porn store—with aisles so narrow you had to shift sideways every time another customer wanted to pass you— was notorious for their cheap, bootlegged videotapes, or at least that's what Evan had led me to believe a few months back when he had confessed to having been there.

So I was standing there looking at a shelf full of titles, conscious of the big-eyed attendant looking over my shoulder from some omnisciently high counter and suspicious of my every move—trying to read the badly reproduced color photocopies of the original covers that had been slipped behind the plastic sleeve of the black video cases, thinking I might splurge and get Peter one of those Bel Ami or Kristen Bjorn movies—when a tall, slender-framed boy passed behind me. He was wearing bell-bottom jeans, sandals, and a blue T-shirt that read *Cheers,* and had a mop of thick, curly, sandy-blond hair and long sideburns styled as if he were stuck in the '70s. When I noticed him I thought I had entered a time warp, or, rather, I thought he might have stepped out of one of those ancient high-priced video classics that were shelved behind a locked glass counter. Unfortunately, the boy disappeared as soon as I'd turned sideways to let him pass.

I soon gave up on the idea of buying Peter a video, however, when I realized I couldn't even afford to buy one of the bootlegged versions of the bad homemade video-cam-and-available-light porn tapes. Then I grew angry at him for making me feel as if I owed him a gift because of his inappropriate behavior. He had *caused* my jealousy, hadn't he? I had every right to be upset. By the time I had made it to the end of the aisle I had decided that I didn't even want to have a boyfriend anymore, that I would just up and end it with Peter, and as I turned the corner I faced a wall where dildos were displayed. Maybe I should just get a dildo, give it a name, and make *it* my new boyfriend, I thought. At least he would be there when I needed him, wouldn't he? And when I got tired of him I could just change his name, put a condom on him and call him someone else, or better yet, just go out and buy another one.

I stood there looking at the wall. And this wall had it all: there were huge double-headed jelly dongs, super stretch penis sheaths, deluxe super stretch masturbators, latex massage mitts, "feelistic" flesh-colored plastic supremo dongs with balls, anal balls on a stick, triple ripple butt plugs, inflatable dildos, natural penis extensions, and realistic dildos with a suction cup base—all with names like Plumber's Delight, The Emperor's Joystick or The Anal Invader.

The tall, thin boy approached the wall and I looked over at him and moved to let him pass. Instead of sliding behind me he stopped and looked down at me. When I tried to look at him, I noticed he was so tall my eyes were level with his belt buckle.

"You came to meet Elvis, didn't you?" he asked me, his brown eyes wildly searching out my own, his face leaning down so close to mine I could see his acne scars as though they were craters on the moon.

I gave him one of my silly flat-lipped expressions, the kind that just invites anyone to come up and begin a conversation with me, even though I seldom deliver. "Elvis is *here?*" I asked him.

He motioned for me to follow him, and as I did so I thought, *boy, am I dumb, dumb, dumb for doing this?* Still, what Southern, almost-trailer-park-white-trash boy living in Manhattan could refuse an offer to meet Elvis? *Elvis! Elvis is here on Eighth Avenue!* It was an experience I couldn't pass up.

As I followed the boy's swishing bell-bottoms, we moved

through the last aisle and entered a small corridor lined with cubicles sectioned off with curtains. The boy turned to make sure I was still behind him, then went down a set of dimly lit stairs. I continued to follow him, thinking, *Well, the joke's on him. I have no money in my wallet if he mugs me. Won't Elvis be surprised?* I am poor, poor, poor. Poorer than Elvis *ever* was. I don't even have a working credit card.

At the bottom of the stairs was a small, shadowy room with a toilet and a sink lit by a dangling low-watt lightbulb. The boy peered up and over his shoulder then leaned down and gave me a mischievous smile.

Here it goes, I thought. *Here comes the first punch.* Just as I was squinting my eyes and tensing my body to lessen the impact of his blow, he unbuttoned the fly of his jeans and slipped his pants below his hips, revealing a pair of white briefs that soaked up all the light the weak bulb above him could emit. Next he slipped his briefs down over his hips enough to reveal a thick clump of sandy brown hair at his crotch but not enough to reveal his cock. I thought, *Well, he must be going to show me a tattoo of Elvis or something.* Instead, he slipped his briefs down lower and took out his dick with his fist.

Flaccid, his dick was about as wide as a beer can and about ten inches long. It was an enormous cock that looked shockingly huge against the boy's slender hips and undefined waist, like an industrial strength vacuum cleaner hose attached to a portable dust buster. When the boy pulled his cock out I had to take my eyes away from it and look at his face, to make sure he was old enough to own that type of equipment. He met my eyes right away. That look was exactly what he wanted.

"The King," he said, waving his hand down the length of his shaft.

The next thing I knew he was groping my crotch with one hand and stroking his dick with his other. I am not sure where my hands were at first, perhaps I had clasped them against my cheeks, ready to howl like McCauley Culkin in *Home Alone*. Because as the boy groped my crotch his dick got bigger and bigger. I know my hands must have ended up there, because at one point I was comparing the length of it against my forearm and trying to decide which one was wider and longer. I was smart enough to know that my own cock should not be revealed. Even with my ample regulation equipment, I wouldn't have dreamed of putting it alongside this—*this huge one*. Instead, I felt like a kid who had wandered into the freak tent at the circus.

Before I knew it I was on my knees, adrift in the joyous surprise of watching him play with his stunning cock, now erect and at least fourteen inches long, so huge it crowded the room and seemed to pin me captive against the wall. And I could no longer touch it myself; I wasn't interested in suck-ing on it, wasn't interested in playing with it, had no desire to even consider putting it *near* my backside. All I wanted was to watch it. I had moved into the combined role of admirer and voyeur—so much so, that the boy reached a point of self-consciousness.

"Take your shirt off," I whispered urgently.

He grabbed the hem of his shirt and made as if to yank it over his head.

"No, slower," I said. "Make it sexier."

The boy looked at me, then realized what I had asked him to do. He pulled his shirt up to reveal his stomach and its light fuzzy line of hair that drifted down from his navel, then lifted it further to reveal his flat, hairless chest, gathering the shirt beneath his armpits while he continued to stroke his huge, beautiful, fleshy hose.

Slowly he inched the shirt suggestively off, then looked back down at me for his next cue.

"Stroke your chest," I said.

And he did so.

"Grab your pec and pinch your nipple."

He tilted his head back and smiled, one hand exploring his chest, the other still working his cock.

"Move both hands down to your dick," I said.

He did as I said, swinging his cock as though he were a batter warming up to hit a home run.

"Keep your hips moving."

He tilted his head back again, sagged at the knees and did a stationery pelvic dance.

"That's it," I said. There was something miraculous in watching him dance so freely, swaying a cock of that size back and forth. I ran a hand up to the side of his rib cage to make sure he was a real person and not some fever hallucination. He shuddered at my touch, as if my fingers were cubes of ice. I could feel his orgasm quivering this high inside him and I watched him come, pumping several short, quick drops into the darkness of the floor.

"Want to see me again?" he asked me as he was buckling himself up. I had watched his dick disappear back into his jeans and was trying to study the impression that it left against the fabric, but the shadows were creating their own optical illusions.

"Sure," I said, flattered that he would be interested in seeing *me* again. What had I done except provide an audience? I hoped he didn't expect me to pay him. Wouldn't he be surprised to discover that he had just stripped for free? And I hadn't even *tried* to blow him. "You could drive people crazy with that thing."

"I really get off on seeing people's reactions."

"I would think so," I answered. "You must be very... *proud* to own something like that."

He smiled back at me and then followed with a torrent of questions as I walked upstairs. Where do I live? (Around the corner.) Is this my first time here? (Is this *your* first time here?)

Desire, Lust, Passion, Sex

What do I do for a living? (My occupation is to struggle.)

This last one made him laugh, and as he did so I studied him harder in the brighter upstairs lights of the store. He was remarkably handsome in a Jimmy Stewart, stoop-shouldered sort of way, or at least maybe knowing what he had to offer made him seem more attractive than he really was. Perhaps it was his youth that contributed to his attractiveness, for he had showed a boyish enthusiasm during our entire encounter. I was full of questions for him myself, but I couldn't have asked them without seeming like a dizzy old sex-mad queen. (How many times a day can you get it up? How many times a day can you get off? Where did you get a dick like that?) Upstairs at the counter by the door, he borrowed a pen from the attendant and wrote his name and number on a scrap of paper. When he handed it to me he said nothing about any amount due for services rendered.

"Elvis," I said, reading his name. Then I introduced myself. "Are you from the South?"

"Memphis," he said. "My mother knew Elvis Presley."

"Really? Did she date him?" I asked, harboring twenty million more unasked questions. (Was it the young Elvis or the old Elvis she met? Did she sleep with him? Did she see *his* dick? Are your dick sizes related?)

"I think so. She doesn't talk much about it."

He followed me out onto the sidewalk, walking so close beside me that his thigh brushed against mine, or, rather, his thigh brushed against my *shoulder*. I had to take huge steps to keep up with him, or change my pattern to shorter, quicker ones. "How long have you been in the city?" I asked, feeling as if I had just stepped on a treadmill at a gym.

"A year," he answered.

"Have you done any movies?"

"A few solo scenes," he answered. "My boyfriend doesn't like me doing them."

"Your *boyfriend?*" I looked up at him and his face was unreadable, really, though I imagined that he was moving an unseen muscle somewhere forlornly. "How long have you been together?"

"Since I was in college," he answered. "About four years."

"You moved up to the city together?"

He nodded and I stopped walking. We had reached the block I was going to turn down to reach Ninth Avenue and I was once again breathing heavily from the heat and humidity and the exhaustion of the day.

"I can't give it up, though, you know?" he said. He looked at me as if he knew, just knew, I would understand his dilemma, or, rather, that I wouldn't see his dilemma as, well, a dilemma at all. "As long as he doesn't know about it, it's okay."

"It's amazing how much you don't know about someone no matter how intimate you are together."

He narrowed his eyes as he took in my words, then exploded them wide. "Yeah," he said, nodding and smiling. "Yeah. But it's not just all about him or me. It's about us. The thing we are when we're together. I love coming home to someone, you know?"

"Yeah," I answered, realizing nothing inside me had exploded in recognition. I stood there wondering how did someone so young get to be so lucky and wise, and then mischievously thinking that, well, maybe he *thinks* with his dick. If that were the case, then he must be a genius.

"It's hard to keep it from being so static," he said.

"*Static?*" I asked.

"Sex," he answered, giving me a perturbed look as if my thoughts had wandered away from him, which they had. "Our sex life is nothing like it was years ago."

"And him?" I asked Elvis. "Does it still work for him?"

His smile moved into a frown as he pondered my question. "He doesn't need it as much," he answered. "He's older."

Desire, Lust, Passion, Sex

"*Aaaaaahhhh*," I smiled back at him. "That's when you really need it *more*. Take my word on it."

He gave me a *sure-sure* roll of his eyes, as if he really didn't believe my statement. "You're much younger than he is," he said and I was once again flattered, the hideous dragon lady complimented back into being just an aging chorus boy by someone who could truthfully describe his genitalia as titanic. And then he stretched his hand out for me to shake.

"Let's get together again," he said.

"Sure," I said, grasping the flesh of him, bonding with him for a final, real moment. "Long live the King," I added. And then he was gone. As I walked away I was smart enough not to look back to see if he bequeathed me a lingering look. Back in my own mind and my own stride, I realized I had forgotten all about Peter. Maybe Evan was right. Maybe I did need to have an affair to balance my relationship with Peter, or, rather, to offset my obsession with a man not interested in obsessing over me.

Expatriates

Dru watches Mikey exclaim over the stripper's breasts. It is an amazing bachelor's party. Mikey is thirty-seven and has never been married. Dru admires that. Mikey outlasted lots of girl-friends. He even refused to marry Melissa, a cheerleader from Walton High, fifteen years ago when she announced she was pregnant. It turned out to be a false alarm and they broke up a few days later. Mikey doesn't even know where Melissa is now. Dru doesn't either. Probably Allentown. Or Harrisburg.

Mikey smiles at the round table cluttered with empty beer glasses, smeared cake plates, and ashtrays with cigar stubs, a few still smoldering. A large cake with the message, *Lost for Good* now reads *Lo—od.*

A whoop rises up as the stripper undoes her bikini top and flashes her breasts at the guys in the room. "I'm glad I know it's nothing final," Mikey jokes with his brother JT. JT has been married twice; the last divorce has lasted six years, longer than any of his marriages. "This is kinda fun so far," Mikey says to Dru. "Sorta like Christmas."

"You should have done this with a few others," says Dru breezily.

"No way," Mikey laughs. "They'd all want me to support them. Let's just hope you wise up before you make the same mistake."

Desire, Lust, Passion, Sex

Dru is as much a guest of honor here as Mikey is. Betty Sue, the stripper, dances in front of Dru's chair. Ever since Dru asked Annette to get married, JT and the other guys have been telling him horror stories about marriage. "She's going to make you clock in and out," JT said. "They want to know where you are every minute. Always, always, always, have a shopping bag with a new pair of socks in it in your trunk. You'll be surprised how handy it comes in. 'Just stopped at the mall for a pair of socks, baby.'"

Dru looks around at the guys in the back room of Lenny's Restaurant. JT is standing, his thumbs looped behind his belt buckle. Mikey looks happy because Betty Sue has taken her bikini off. Tassels taped to her nipples swing back and forth as she dances. Betty Sue danced at Sam's bachelor party three years ago. Now Sam is having an affair with a cashier at the pharmacy in Stroudsburg. His marriage is not expected to last, even though he has a two-year-old boy and his wife is due to have another in three months.

After Dru decided to ask Annette to get married, he started a full-time job at the lumber yard and now only does construction work part-time on the weekends for JT, helping to build decks or fences for the new condos being built along the Delaware. When Dru told this to Annette one morning when they were lying in bed together, he knew she was pleased. She had suggested the idea, telling him he needed to think about things like health insurance and benefits. His arms were behind his head, folded beneath the pillow. Her chin was against his chest. He felt in command. Authoritative. He thought he was moving ahead of things.

At the bachelor party Mikey is drunk and watching Betty Sue twirl her tassels. He throws a look at Dru and yells, "Dru, what are we doing? Marriage is a death sentence. Look at all we're giving away!"

Expatriates

Dru has only been engaged for a week, and there is one person he still wants to tell. He wonders if Rusty will be disgusted when he finds out. Rusty is not usually that kind of guy—he's as easygoing as Mikey and JT are rowdy. On Saturday, before going to the flea market to find Rusty and tell him, Dru decides to wash his car. Even while soaping up the black Mustang he has had for three years, Dru knows it's going to be one of those sticky, uncomfortable days. He feels the sun hitting his forehead and arms and the black paint of the car soaking up the heat. He rinses the car and lets it dry in the sun instead of wiping it off. He decides not to wax it today and goes inside his apartment and sits in front of the television and the air conditioner. He decides to eat something before heading out to the flea market. He makes a turkey sandwich and watches cartoons while he eats. When he is finished he decides to wear jeans instead of shorts. He takes another shower to rinse off and feel cooler.

It is afternoon before Dru leaves for the flea market. It is hotter and more humid than before and in the car he wears the dark shades Annette brought back from Atlantic City. He looks at himself in the side view mirror, waves his hand across his short hair. He has been thinking about Rusty all morning. Dru tries to shake away his concern over Rusty's reaction by reminding himself that he knows very little about Rusty. Rusty lives about ninety miles away, in Sterling, and he travels to the flea market every weekend with his sister. Dru met him at the flea market last spring. Dru had gone there with Annette to look for sweatshirts. Annette likes to wear giant sweatshirts and colored stockings around the apartment when she cleans or works out to a videotape her sister gave her. Dru doesn't think it's a great look for her—sort of like a tomato with pipe-cleaner legs, but she usually changes to jeans and a nice blouse when they go out to the mall or to a movie.

The day Dru first met Rusty, Annette had wandered ahead and stopped at a booth where a chubby, blonde-haired woman with pink eyeglasses made floral arrangements out of dried flowers. "I can preserve your wedding bouquet under a glass dome like this one," she said to Annette, pushing her eyeglasses further up the long bridge of her nose. "Or dry them and press them flat and make a wall portrait out of them."

"They're gorgeous," Annette said, smiling and flipping her hair behind her neck. She turned to look for Dru's reaction but Dru had walked over to a silver van behind the booth and lit a cigarette. He was aware of a man standing beside him, chewing on a toothpick and watching him watch Annette at the booth. The man had a thinning stubble of black hair that matched his shortly clipped goatee. He was a tall, lean fellow and wore a yellow down-filled vest and a plaid shirt tucked tightly into his jeans. He was handsome in an unexpected way—like a bulldog or a horse—and he slouched his shoulders and cocked his leg as if he were posing for a camera. He shifted his weight and said to Dru, "You planning on getting married?"

"Someday," Dru laughed. "My girl's more eager than I am."

"She does good work," the man said, indicating the booth where Annette was browsing.

Dru sensed there was some connection between the man and the blonde woman behind the booth. "That your wife?" Dru asked.

"Nope," the man answered flatly. "My sister. We're both hitting midlife crises. She wanted to get away from her husband. I wanted to get away from the city. So here we are. Together."

He introduced himself as Rusty and told Dru he helped

make the frames his sister used for her floral portraits. "Our parents were really into this stuff," he said. "They used to come to this thing years ago. When my mom died this spring—my dad died a few years back and then my mom married another fellow she met doing this—Faith and I thought we'd spend some time at the house she had. After a few weeks of it neither of us wanted to go back and we couldn't bring ourselves to sell the place." He stopped talking for a moment to check some papers in the pocket of his yellow vest. He studied a piece of paper and then put it back in the pocket. "We're originally from Mississippi but our mom sold everything when she left there," he said. "So this was all we had. You grow up in this neck of the woods?"

"Yep," Dru answered. His apartment was in the basement of his parents' house, but he felt embarrassed to tell the man that information.

"Faith's really into all this stuff now," he said. "My mom left behind baskets of flowers and frames and stuff. Faith says it makes her feel artistic and special. Something that her husband never did. I told her he just wasn't a good man. Some men are good. Some aren't. You just have to learn from experience how to tell the difference." He let out a laugh that sounded like the beginning of a sneeze. "Still don't know which kind I am. But Faith never dated much when she was in high school. She jumped for the first guy and has been miserable since."

Dru shifted uncomfortably and threw his cigarette to the ground, stubbing it out with the toe of his boot. "I don't know," Dru said. "Annette and I've been dating since high school. I saw a couple of girls but none I liked as much as her." He hesitated next, not sure of confiding in a stranger. He looked out at the booth, then felt a need to continue talking. "She keeps nagging me to settle down with her and get myself a better job. She wants a baby so bad you can just see her toting it against her hip."

Desire, Lust, Passion, Sex

"Baby'll tie you down real good and quick," Rusty said. He stretched his shoulder and Dru became aware he was staring at the guy. Their eyes connected for a second till Rusty nervously broke away and looked back over at the booth. "When I was your age I couldn't keep it in my pants," Rusty said. "I'd do whoever wanted it. And I mean anyone. I got a lot of jobs that way. Used to do some acting."

"What did you do?" Dru asked. His voice was wobbly and tentative. "Movies?"

"I did some extra work on a few," Rusty said. "Most of it was commercials or print work. Got to go to a lot of places. Some guy was always flying me off to some beach so that he could photograph me in the surf and then spend the night in the sack."

Dru let the words sink in. *Guy. Sack.* He jerked his gaze around, unwilling to let it settle anywhere for fear it would reveal something about himself. He didn't move. And he didn't say anything else, either. His head and eyes tried to contain his brain's instant panic reflex. After a few seconds Rusty continued, as though he were unaware of Dru's edginess. "Like I said. Your age I'd do anything. Fun is fun, you know, as long as you ain't hurtin' anyone."

〰〰〰

That first day Dru and Annette had left Rusty and his sister and wandered through the rest of the outdoor booths, a maze of hardware merchants, clothing vendors, and hobbyists hoping to sell their crafts. Annette bought a Christmas ornament in the shape of a carousel, even though it was just March. As they stopped at tables to examine an embroidered vest or hand-carved mailbox sign, Dru tried to sort out Rusty's remarks about sex. He had been surprised at the casual way the man had tossed out the fact that it happened whenever it happened. And with guys. Dru considered himself someone who had always toed the straight line; he didn't have the kind of stories that JT or Mikey had about meeting chicks at the Laundromat or at the gas station, or, Mikey's most recent conquest, hooking up with a married woman he met while chatting on the Internet.

But he had experienced a few confusing times. None that he had talked about with anyone before, though. When he was eleven a neighbor, Steve Finnerty—two years older than Dru—had convinced him to "show his equipment" in the basement of one of the new buildings being constructed in Shawnee. He and Steve had undressed and rubbed their dicks against each other. Dru believed it had happened more out of curiosity than anything else. Two young kids playing at being bad. Which meant it was fun. Even before he knew anything about having an orgasm, Dru felt what he was doing with Steve wasn't necessarily the "right thing to do." But they still continued to do it over the next few months, finding new ways to "beat their meat." When Steve moved away the following year, the temptation to continue "practicing" didn't leave. Dru found himself looking for another partner among his friends at school, but never got close enough to another guy to get up the nerve to initiate anything. Instead, he mimicked the other schoolboys' obsessions with girls and fell into teasing and chasing them. A few years after that he met Annette and they began dating.

⋀⋀⋀⋀⋀

Dru had not been able to shake Rusty from his mind that first day. After Dru and Annette had browsed the indoor booths of antiques and furniture, Annette fumbled through her purse and announced that she needed to use the ladies' room. At first, Dru waited for Annette outside the building where the

Desire, Lust, Passion, Sex

restrooms were located, then hoping a good piss might shake off his uneasiness, he decided to use the facilities himself. The men's room was crowded; a steady stream of big-bellied men in jeans and boots with long hair or sideburns or mustaches wandered toward the row of urinals against the side wall. At the sink were a group of young boys in oversized jerseys and baggy pants punching at each other and splashing water from the sink. An old man in a dark shirt and work pants was working as an attendant, handing out paper towels for a quarter. While Dru was standing at the urinal, he noticed out of the corner of his eye a familiar color move in beside him. It was Rusty's yellow vest. Rusty was standing beside Dru at the next urinal, looking directly at the wall. As Dru tilted his head up he thought he detected Rusty's nod. His eyes drifted back to the urinal and Dru shook his cock so that the remaining drops of urine fell into the latrine. He shifted his gaze momentarily to his side, catching the flannel sleeve and Rusty's wrist. Rusty was slowly stroking his cock, a long and slender shaft with a dark, mushroom-like head.

Dru lingered at the urinal. He slowly stroked his own dick until a wave of panic flooded over him. Instead of remaining, he quickly zipped up and headed out of the restroom to find Annette. Twenty minutes later, while Annette was sorting through piles of sweatshirts, Dru said he wanted to get a snack and check out the booth where they sold automotive supplies. Annette nodded and said she would meet him later—at their usual spot—somewhere between a half hour or more.

Dru maneuvered around the shoppers, their aimless, slow-moving gaits aggravating him. When he reached the aisle where Faith's floral booth was located, he waited behind a man and a woman wearing matching flannel jackets, peering around them to see if he could spot Rusty. Faith was showing a couple a bouquet of white flowers preserved beneath a glass dome. Rusty was not at the booth, nor was he beside the silver van where Dru had met him. He was about to give up when he noticed a pair of boots jutting out from the tailgate of a red truck. Dru walked to the side and saw Rusty leaning against the truck, smoking a cigarette.

"Got a great tape you can listen to if you want," Rusty said, when he saw Dru. He flicked the cigarette to the ground.

Dru felt uneasy; he shoved a hand into the pocket of his jeans and felt for his keys. As he approached the side of the truck he felt as though his feet were moving faster than the rest of his body, the "Sure" he responded with coming from someone else.

Rusty stepped up into the driver's seat of the truck and Dru opened the passenger door and slid into the seat beside him. Rusty leaned over the dashboard and inserted a cassette into the tape deck, turning the key in the ignition to battery power. Rusty's hand lingered by the tape deck until a woman's thin, slippery voice began to sing a country song about unrequited love. "My mom used to play Kitty Wells all the time when we lived in Mississippi," Rusty said, and let his hand fall against Dru's leg. When Dru made no motion for him to remove it, Rusty moved his hand closer to Dru's crotch.

Rusty rubbed his hand up and down the inside of Dru's thigh, then squeezed the fabric of the jeans at Dru's crotch, catching Dru's dick in his grasp. Dru had been hard since he had approached Rusty at the truck. Now, a thin line of perspiration broke out on his upper lip. His heart was beating loudly; he couldn't understand any of the words coming out of the speakers. He felt the sweating increasing—on his brow, then at his armpits.

There was no talk between them, only the sound of the guitars and the wobbly voice of Kitty Wells. Dru looked out the dashboard at the back of the white tarps which tented the booth where Faith was handing a business card to a couple. Beyond her, the slow, confused march of shoppers continued up the aisle. Rusty unbuckled Dru's jeans, first the belt, then the buttons at the crotch. With the flap open, Rusty slipped his hand beneath the white briefs Dru wore and clutched his fist around Dru's dick. Dru felt the pressure of Rusty's grip and the heat and smell of his own body drifted up to his nose. Rusty looked straight ahead, his other hand tapping against the steering wheel as if all they were doing were listening to a country song. Dru shifted himself so that his dick was exposed. He looked down, watching Rusty's wrist, thick and covered with dark hairs, pump against the end of his reddened cock.

He came easily. Rusty popped open his glove compartment and reached for a wad of napkins, wiped off the back of his hand, and offered the napkins to Dru. Dru dried himself and buttoned himself back up. He mumbled, "Thanks," and hopped out of the truck. He wanted to look back for Rusty's reaction but he didn't. He made his way back to the crowd.

For the rest of the day Dru could not erase the presence of Rusty's hand on his cock. It came to him while he was watching TV, while he was eating dinner, while he was in bed, later, with Annette. "You're sure wired up, today," Annette said, when he had left the bed to shower. The next morning, when he woke up, Rusty's presence was still there in his mind. When Annette left for her mother's house, Dru went back to the flea market.

"Thought you might like to have lunch," Dru said, when he found Rusty shifting boxes in the back of his sister's booth. "Your sister let you go for a while?" Faith was polishing the glass of one of her picture frames and she lifted her eyes up at Dru and said, "Hey."

"I could use a good lunch," Rusty said. "I need to pack these into her van first." Rusty lifted a stack of small plastic boxes which looked like they contained sand, and Dru followed him to the van which was still parked behind the booth and next to Rusty's truck. Rusty slid the side door of the van open and stepped inside, settling the boxes into the back. Dru lingered outside the van as Rusty, on his haunches and his neck bent, shifted boxes about. After a few seconds that seemed like forever, Dru bent his head and looked inside the van. "This was my stepfather's van," Rusty said. "It's more than ten years old now but it still runs like new. He took good care of this. When the weather's not too chilly, Faith and I just roll our sleeping bags out instead of checking into the motel."

Dru was inside the van watching Rusty's back. He felt uncomfortable resting his weight in this haunched position so he sat on the metal floor, the coolness seeping through the seat of his jeans.

Rusty twisted himself so that his hand fell against Dru's leg. Once again, Dru was hard. He looked worriedly out through the open door of the van then leaned forward, breaking away from Rusty's touch, and slid the van door closed. Dru slipped further inside, unbuckling his jeans before Rusty's hand arrived at his crotch. Rusty's hand played with Dru's hard cock and Dru tentatively touched Rusty's shirt, pressing against it to find the stretch of his stomach. Before he had a chance to explore Rusty's body, Rusty leaned over and took Dru's cock in his mouth. Dru let out a moan of surprise and he tried to hold his orgasm back for as long as possible, watching Rusty's head and lips move over him. This had never happened to him before. The pleasure confused him, but he made no motion for Rusty to stop.

Rusty pulled away just as Dru was coming, as if he knew when it would happen. He smiled and offered Dru an old shirt to dry himself, leaning back and waiting for Dru to button up and leave the van. Instead, Dru positioned himself over Rusty and unbuckled Rusty's jeans. Rusty wore nothing underneath and Dru leaned down tentatively to taste the semi-hard head of Rusty's cock. He licked it and smelled it, then slowly worked it into his mouth, conscious of the wiry

Desire, Lust, Passion, Sex

hairs of Rusty's groin touching his lips. "Careful of the teeth," Rusty said, and placed his hands against Dru's shoulders. "You done this before?" Dru pulled away and shook his head *no*. Rusty guided Dru's mouth slowly back down to his cock. Dru felt Rusty's cock grow harder in his mouth until, a few moments later, Rusty gently lifted his mouth away and jerked himself off.

Dru's first instinct was to run away, but he stayed and waited for Rusty to buckle up his jeans. They left the van as if nothing out of the ordinary had occurred. They walked to a food stand and ate lunch together at one of the indoor stalls. Dru had a chili hot dog and a beer; Rusty had a sandwich and a soda. There was no talk of anything that had happened between them in the van, no plans made to get together again. Rusty talked about his job at a printer's in Sterling, saying that he was thinking about investing in a good camera. He wanted to try and sell photographs of covered bridges. "Everybody loves a covered bridge," Rusty said. "It makes them think of an easier way of life."

Dru said that he would start a job next week enlarging a deck at a house in Montgomery County for his friend JT's company, grateful for the work but unhappy about the lengthy drive from his house. They stood away from the aisle and watched the shoppers roam back and forth, finishing their drinks and laughing about a woman haggling a vendor over a framed poster of Elvis. They parted a few minutes later with a handshake.

〰〰〰

Dru had never thought he could be queer. It wasn't like his friends were queer or he sought out the company of gay guys. He had never been to the bars in Easton or New Hope that attracted gays, nor had he felt the urge to see what they

154

were like. He liked being in the company of men—liked talking about football rankings and vintage cars and baseball stats.
But Rusty had aroused in him something he had assumed
he'd grown out of. Soon he found himself noticing the
glances of fathers shopping at the grocery store, the way men
leaned and shifted and tilted their bodies as they pumped gas
into their cars, the way guys never talked about being close
to or romantic with their wives. Then he found himself
appraising other men physically: were they good-looking or
heavyset, young or tired-looking? He began wondering why
JT had an earring in his left ear, what possessed Mikey to
grow his sideburns into points like the spiked toe of a boot,
why Sam wore his shirts with the top three buttons open.
Everything became more sexual to him. And the more he
noticed and thought about all this, the more he found himself
seeking out Annette's company, as if her companionship could
dam up his fantasizing about Rusty.

When Dru began meeting Rusty regularly on weekends
at the flea market, Rusty always seemed to have a plan for
where they could go. All Dru had to do was appear and they
were suddenly headed somewhere else. One morning they
drove out to the rest stop that overlooked the Delaware
Water Gap, another time they ended up in the parking lot
behind the bus terminal in Stroudsburg. Though the anticipation of it happening haunted Dru throughout the week, the
actual event was always accomplished quickly—pants
unbuckled and buckled up again in nothing more than fifteen
minutes. Rusty and Dru never kissed each other, never held
hands, though they'd share a beer or a cigarette or a meal
afterwards. Their conversations never contained a hint of
intimacy. Dru liked the distance and the familiarity. He didn't
act possessive, didn't expect Rusty to call him during the
week. When it was Dru's birthday, Rusty made nothing of it
since he had no way of knowing, but on another day at the

flea market—two and a half months into their friendship—he bought Dru a baseball jersey from a well-built young guy who called everybody "buddy." His name was Coy and he worked at a booth that was run by his parents, who were away for the day visiting his grandmother at a nursing home. At first Dru enjoyed the way Rusty got along with Coy, teasing him about working out to impress his girlfriend, till he realized that there was some kind of chemistry going on between the two of them that had nothing to do with a conversation about women. Coy appeared to be about the same age as Dru and he found himself jealous, wondering if Rusty had the same kind of thing going on with Coy that he did with Dru. When Dru asked Rusty how he knew Coy, he said, "He's out here every now and then. He wants to get out of the country and move to the city. I recommended him to an agent I know who's trying to help him out."

Later, the notion of something going on between Rusty and Coy continued to bother Dru. He tried to rationalize that there was no reason to be jealous. He was with Annette, after all, not Rusty. Annette was his future. Rusty was not. But the next few times Dru and Rusty got together he found himself wondering if Rusty had any kind of feelings for him. So Dru began bringing Rusty casual gifts—items that appeared to have been picked up in a moment of inspiration—a photo magazine, for instance, or another time, a guide book for the Poconos. Rusty accepted these things with a "Hey, thanks," and a pat on Dru's back, but nothing that confirmed any sort of emotional attachment. Even when Dru began wearing the jersey Rusty had bought him— a large, gray one with a Yankees logo on it—Rusty made no mention of it. On one hand Dru was relieved that there was nothing more serious going on; on the other, he wondered if he wasn't a little let down. If what he really wanted was something more from Rusty.

Expatriates

Later that summer Annette went on a trip with two girl-friends to the Jersey shore and Dru stayed behind to finish a fence for one of JT's clients. That Saturday evening, Dru asked Rusty to stay over at his apartment. He wasn't worried what anyone might think if Rusty's red truck was spotted in his driveway—by then Rusty was friendly enough with Dru's family and friends. He'd been to the house several times to have a beer with Dru and watch a ballgame, and once to help Dru and his younger brother move an old upright piano Dru's mother wanted to donate to a church in Stroudsburg. But the other times Rusty had been over, Annette had been around. That Saturday, on his own with Rusty, he hadn't known what to expect, or how to act, or even more, what he should be feeling, and Dru was nervous from the moment Rusty arrived. But it wasn't like Rusty wanted more out of this, Dru convinced himself. This was just something different, not something deeper. They were just two guys who enjoyed each other's company.

For dinner they grilled steaks and corn on the cob. Afterwards, they settled on the couch in front of the television with beers to watch the baseball game—Dru at one end, Rusty at the other. They'd done this before when Annette was around. There wasn't much of a conversation going on between them and gradually Dru felt a disappointment overwhelming him, as if he expected something else should have been happening.

Things changed after the game when they made it to the bedroom. Rusty suggested they shower together. Dru, immediately aroused by the suggestion, was fully erect before he had undressed. In the bathroom he realized that he had never seen Rusty completely nude. Before he'd had a chance to study Rusty's body more closely, they were kissing each other beneath the warm jets of water. Dru had never kissed another man. Rusty's stubble burned his lips and Dru found himself struggling for short gasps of air. Then Rusty's hands moved over Dru's body, soaping him up, and brought him to an orgasm. Dru, catching his breath, reciprocated. While he was toweling off Dru decided that this was what he liked best about Rusty—being taken out of his life and into someplace new.

In bed, Dru realized all his thinking and the sex had made him exhausted. As he turned on his side to fall asleep, Rusty mirrored his position, roping his arm around Dru's waist.

"This is what I miss," Rusty said.

"What?" Dru answered.

"This," Rusty said. "The cuddling. Even after things had stopped with Nick we still used to sleep like this together."

Dru tried to imagine sleeping with a guy like this night after night. He had always assumed he was the kind of guy who didn't enjoy the closeness of someone else while he was sleeping—he had always found it difficult to get a sound sleep when Annette was staying over—but now he realized he didn't mind Rusty's embrace at all. In fact, he moved himself a bit closer.

"How long were you together?" Dru asked.

"'Bout five years," Rusty said. "He looked a bit like you. Except his body was firmer. He was obsessive about working out. He didn't have an ounce of body fat on him."

Dru wondered if Rusty liked him less because his body was not as perfect as Nick's. "How come you left him?" Dru asked.

"Didn't leave him, he left me," Rusty answered. "I had an acting teacher once who said never date an actor. I never thought he'd be right. Nick left to take a job in LA. Mom was sick and I went to Sterling."

"You ever thought about getting back with him?"

"Nope," Rusty laughed and Dru felt the sound of Rusty's voice again. "He got a part on a TV sitcom that ended after half a season, but before he did he married this model we knew for a cover. He decided he liked it and they've got a kid now."

"That's why I want to get married," Dru said. "I want a family."

"They're good to have," Rusty said. "Nothing wrong with that."

In the morning they had sex again; Rusty had brought condoms and a bottle of lubricant. He lowered himself over Dru, taking Dru's cock slowly up his ass. Dru lay in bed disbelieving that this was happening to him—watching his cock move in and out of Rusty as if it were disembodied.

When Rusty left for the flea market after another shower, Dru tried not to let what had happened overwhelm him. Instead, the image came back to him over and over. He found himself wandering through his apartment, clutching and stroking his cock until he could bring himself to another orgasm. He did this for two more days while Annette was away—thinking about Rusty but trying to stay away from the flea market.

When Annette returned a few days later, Dru surprised her by telling her he had joined a gym. "Just trying to get in better shape for you," he said, offering her a smile. He gave her a gift he had found at the flea market, a Christmas ornament—a papier mâché angel. "It made me think of you."

"That's so sweet," she said. "It's beautiful. I got something for you, too."

She reached into the large bag she carried and pulled out a pair of sunglasses. Dru put them on and checked himself out in the mirror over his dresser. "Neat," he said, waving his hand through his hair. He liked the way he looked in them.

Later, after dinner, when they were in the bedroom, he asked her if she wanted to live together. Sex had been awkward, Dru self-conscious every time he touched Annette. At the back of his mind he knew he was complicating things—

he was lighthearted over his growing feelings toward Rusty, giddy over the adventure of it, but aware he was headed into more uncertainty. A stronger, more committed relationship with Annette—once a logical direction, the path he'd always imagined taking someday—now seemed equally confusing. He had hoped this decision would help anchor him, make him feel more responsible. Instead he drew Annette closer, placing her head against his chest, and felt crowded and crushed, unable to breathe.

⋀⋁⋀⋁⋀⋁

In the six weeks Dru had been going to the gym he had dropped two inches from his waist. He had also taken to cutting his hair shorter, tucking his shirts into his pants, and wearing aftershave. Even though Rusty had said nothing about these changes, they made Dru feel more confident about his appearance. Dru now spoke with a deeper and calmer voice; his eyes were less skittish. The last time he had seen Rusty they had met at the flea market and driven to a shopping center in Shawnee. They parked the van and went into a camera store where Rusty picked up a roll of film he had dropped off to be developed.

Next door in the ice cream shop, Rusty ordered a milk shake and Dru got a low-fat frozen yogurt. When they had taken seats at a table, Rusty showed Dru the photos. Inside the envelope were three pages of contact sheets which held more than fifty small black-and-white photos, all of them of Rusty in a series of different poses for the camera. Rusty leaned over the table and scrutinized each of the poses carefully, drawing back from time to time and pointing one out to Dru to study as well.

"These are great," Dru said. "Where did you have them done?"

"I had them taken with the new camera I bought," Rusty answered.

There were a series of poses where Rusty wore a jacket, then just a shirt, then a pair of boxers. Studying those poses, Dru saw how familiar Rusty had become to him, the tanned, muscular arms, the ridges of his waist, the goatee like a vacuum cleaner brush. "Where did you find this photographer?" Dru asked.

"Coy did them," Rusty said. "He's gotten pretty good. Says he likes doing this better than modeling himself."

Toward the bottom of one of the pages was a pose of Rusty nude, his body angled so that his genitals were not exposed. Dru was bent over the page examining the shot when he realized he was wondering again about Rusty's relationship with Coy.

"My old agent contacted me about a month ago," Rusty said. "He's gotten Coy a couple of jobs. He's been bugging me to get some new shots done so that he can send me out again."

"Are you going to go back to it?" Dru asked.

"Depends on whether Faith feels okay on her own," Rusty said. "Coy's been talking about getting a place in the city and I could stay with him for a while."

Back in the van they drove to a rest stop at the base of the Delaware Water Gap, parked, and climbed into the back. Unbuttoning Rusty's jeans, Dru was shaken by a painful and tender rush of emotion. Did suddenly being so afraid of losing Rusty mean he was "in love" with him? He felt like a stranger arriving at a foreign city he has studied for years in photographs, only to realize the camera has distorted the view and he is somewhere else.

Back at the flea market they shook hands as usual, but Dru felt a growing knot in his stomach. At precisely that moment, the idea of asking Annette to marry him came to him. He thought about asking Rusty's opinion, but thought better of it, not wanting to look like he was giving Rusty a reason to break away if he still had any doubts. As Rusty left to help his sister at her booth, he looked back over his shoulder at Dru. "See ya next week," he said.

"See ya," Dru answered, grateful nothing was coming to an end.

The humidity is heavy when Dru reaches the flea market. He parks the Mustang and walks across the black tar lot toward the booths. Already he is sweating. He should have worn shorts, he thinks, not jeans. Everyone else is wearing shorts today because of the heat. He buys a soda from a man who pulls a can out of a bucket of melting ice. Dru holds the can to his cheek and then pops the top open. The familiar aimlessness of the crowd at the flea market makes him anxious today. Again, he wonders if Rusty will be disgusted when he tells him he is engaged. Out in the sun, Dru browses through a box of record albums even though he doesn't have a turntable. He looks through the rock collection, but there is nothing he wants. He skirts around bins of cassette tapes and overhears someone saying, "I wouldn't pay a nickel for Cher." Dru smiles, remembering how Rusty claimed to have met her at a theater. He stops and looks at a bin of sweatshirts to see if there is a color Annette doesn't already own. He buys a pair of white, athletic socks from a woman with a toothless grin who stops fanning herself long enough to make change from the bill Dru hands her.

As he continues through the aisles he notices the familiar canvas tent of Faith's booth but he doesn't see Rusty's truck. Faith is sitting in an aluminum folding chair, working a piece of ice around her neck that drips and stains the T-shirt she is wearing. She seems to be a trusty fixture to Dru, something stable and permanent, like a boulder fallen into a mountain stream.

"That girlfriend of yours pin you down yet, hon?" Faith asks when she recognizes Dru.

"Sure did," Dru says. "She's gonna come lookin' for you to do her flowers."

"I'll do a real special job for her," she says. "Since you're always a friendly face here." In front of her is a rectangular bucket of sand. "Lookit here," she says and picks up a flower out of the sand. "Someone gave me magnolias to do. Aren't they beautiful? These here are my roots."

Dru leans forward to look at the flowers and nods and smiles. He says, "Have you seen Rusty today? Where's your brother?"

"Rusty's gone for a while," she answers. "Got a modeling job in Long Island this weekend. The Hamptons. That lucky boy is at the beach splashing in the waves and gettin' paid for it."

"So he's going back to it," Dru says.

"Yeah," she answers, with a smile. "Beats sittin' here watching flowers dry out."

Months later, at his own bachelor party at Lenny's, Dru sips a beer and watches JT try to shimmy with the stripper. Betty Sue was booked so another girl, Cherie, has taken her place. She has a long, leggy look to her, like a chorus girl or a Rockette except that her breasts are too big for her body, or so Dru thinks. Dru believes she has implants but Cherie hasn't taken off enough of her top for anyone to see if there are scars. Cherie holds JT's head between her hands as she dances, not so much to display affection as to keep JT slightly at bay. JT has already had plenty to drink. The table is littered with beer bottles and empty glasses. Dru pulls JT away and hands him another drink. Cherie smiles and mouths, "Thank you, honey," to Dru. She twirls in a circle and dances now with him.

Dru feels strange dancing with the stripper, as if he is impersonating a drunken, rowdier version of himself. His head is swimming. From behind him Mikey yells, "Come on, baby," to Cherie. "Give us a peek." The stripper unhooks her bra and waves it in the air over Dru's head. Underneath is another bra—thinner and briefer than the one she had been wearing before.

"You still have till morning to wise up," Mikey yells at Dru as he dances with Cherie.

"I'm wise enough," Dru yells back. "Look who's making a fool of himself now."

What You Find

He kisses you on the lips and says good-bye in a whisper. As
you hear the door click shut behind him you are suddenly
wide awake, aware of the morning stillness in his apartment.
This is the first time you have been left alone in his apartment
after seven months of dating him, sleeping over occasionally
at his apartment on the weekends, and you stretch your legs
out in the bed, tensing the sleep out of your muscles. You feel
the space where he slept last night next to you, still warm,
you think, then run the palm of your hand over the flat empty
space of the sheet and draw his pillow up to your face,
breathing in the remaining scent of him. You think a moment
about last night's sex, feeling yourself getting hard. You play
with yourself for a moment, slipping your hand beneath your
underwear, stroking yourself, then cupping your balls. You
sigh loudly and get out of bed.

In the kitchen you make coffee, fiddle with yourself in
your underwear some more, wanting to keep yourself semierect and edgy as long as you can. You sit at the table and eat
a cranberry muffin he bought for you at the grocery store
yesterday. You look at the digital clock on the VCR. It reads
9:17. You calculate he won't be back for another four
hours—gone to his daughter's graduation in Connecticut.
You don't know what amazes you more—the fact that he is

Desire, Lust, Passion, Sex

forty-nine years old and has a daughter old enough to graduate high school, or the fact that he is still married and filing for a divorce. You glance outside the window as you chew on your muffin, happy as you taste the burst of a cranberry in your mouth. You stare at the trees in the park across the street, the tops of which are puddles of deep green leaves. He says he's gay, though he won't admit it to anyone except you and the tricks he meets at his favorite bar on the East Side. He's not told his soon-to-be-ex-wife the reason why their marriage is ending, hasn't told his daughter why he no longer lives at home. He has no plans to come out on the job, no plans, either, for you, except to have sex when his schedule permits. He doesn't want a relationship, after all, you remind yourself—only someone to have a good time with. That's all you want out of this too, you tell yourself, but you know that's not true. You've spent the last two decades of your adult life looking for a lover, and just when you found someone you want to fall in love with—just when you are ready—he tells you he wants to date other people and doesn't want to settle down.

The story of my life, you think with a big sigh. You get up from the table. You wash your coffee mug in the kitchen sink and place it in the dish rack. You wonder why he has left you alone in his apartment—after months and months of insinuating that he was dating other men, that you weren't the *only* distraction in his life, that he knew you were the possessive and jealous type, did he think that you had changed after all this time? Or has he changed, you wonder? Is he ready for a relationship now? No, you remind yourself again. It's sex, not a relationship. You're just fuck buddies who go to the movies together.

At least it's good, you think. The sex. At least you find him sexy. At least he appreciates you appreciating him. At least it makes you feel good to make him feel good. Well, most of the time. You walk out of the kitchen and again are drawn to the view from his window. The light is bright this morning and you cast your eyes downward, following the tiny figure of a jogger in an orange sweatshirt as he enters the park from the street. Before he left you alone you had made up your mind you wouldn't snoop through his things—you knew enough about him already, and what you suspected of him you didn't need confirmed. You're thirty-nine years old. You're a mature, open, honest gay man. You don't need to snoop through a married boyfriend's stuff. You don't need your jealousy piqued, your possessiveness inflamed. You already have enough problems with this pseudo-relation-ship—his age, his marriage, his money, his ego.

You suddenly smack yourself in the head with the palm of your hand, listening to the sound it makes. *Why, why, why are you here?* you ask yourself. Are you that desperate for attention? That needy for *any* kind of relationship? *Yes*, you answer. You're such a fool. And Kevin's dead. So are Dean and Tony and Greg and a lot of those other boys you used to play with. Peter thinks he is in a relationship now. And then there is Jack. Emotionally unavailable Jack.

You turn on the television and check the weather on NY1—the box in the corner reads sixty-nine degrees. You turn up the sound so that you can hear it above the stereo and wait for the newscaster to read the forecast, running your finger across the head of your cock. The newscaster predicts that it may reach the high eighties today. You stand in front of the TV playing with yourself, looking out again at the view, this time looking at the rows of buildings that frame the other end of the park. You think about him sucking your cock, then think about sucking his cock, then imagine him on the couch with his legs apart, and you feel yourself grow harder, frustrated. You fight off the urge to masturbate—he's coming back, you know, and he'll want to have sex—and so will you. You surf through the channels with the remote control, lingering for a moment on a wrestling program, admiring the body of one of the wrestlers—thick and muscled about the arms and shoulders. You wish for a moment he had a better body. Wish he were younger and better looking. You wish he were the wrestler. You're still hard and you squeeze your cock now, stroke it back and forth really good a few times, then click the TV off with the remote just when you're ready to want more. You switch on the stereo and begin stretching your neck, twist your waist back and forth and side to side until you feel loose, supple, and awake.

You turn the stereo up louder and wander into the bedroom. You slip on his sneakers, hoping you'll stretch them out of shape. You laugh. Your feet are bigger than his. But he has the bigger waist. You look at yourself in the mirror over his dresser. You look better than you have in the last ten years. You've lost fifteen pounds since you've started dating him—anxiety over trying to make it work for you, too, you know. But it has made you look younger, more attractive, you think. You certainly notice you get more looks now on the street. And you never walk out of a bar alone these days. You stare at your waist. Twenty-nine inches. You can even see the muscles in your stomach. You couldn't when you were twenty-nine years old.

You turn on the treadmill in the corner of the room, start walking at a slow pace. You turn up the speed, punch the reset button. Your erection drops off fast as the pace of your feet gets faster and faster. Even if he doesn't want you someone else will. Even if this ends there will be someone else. He's not the only person you're seeing. Your little joke on him. *As if he even cared*, you think. You walk and walk, noticing the furniture in his bedroom. You remember when they delivered the dresser. You suggested he get the mission-style headboard because it would work well with handcuffs.

What You Find

You were with him when he bid on the Hockney at Christie's. You notice an unfamiliar envelope on the top of the dresser and it disturbs you. You don't know what it is. You think about stopping the treadmill to snoop, but you don't. You keep walking, turning the speed up even faster.

He'll never lose the weight, you remind yourself. He eats too much junk—snacks and cookies throughout the day, every night potato chips, chocolate ice cream, and a carafe of wine before going to bed. How does he do it— consume so much food? You don't even have an appetite anymore. All you want is to feel good about something. All you ask from him is some kind of affection, which is the last thing he is willing to give.

You stop after thirty-one minutes and two-and-a-half miles. You are drenched in sweat. Your cock is small, wet. You get off the treadmill and check the envelope on top of the dresser. It is the invitation to his daughter's graduation ceremony. You look at the clock. Two hours and forty minutes left. He could get back early, though. You lie on the floor and look at the ceiling, then force yourself through one hundred crunches. You roll over and lie on your stomach, lift yourself up into a position for push-ups. Your feet slide against his polished wooden floor. You inch your way down till the heels of your feet are against the bottom drawer of his night stand. You do fifty push-ups and then rest. You make a note in your head to remind him to invest in a chin-up bar. He will never do it, you know. It would ruin the aesthetics of his apartment. You do fifty more push-ups, purposely banging your heels against his dresser drawer. That's where he keeps the dildos and lube. Where the condoms come from. Where he stashes the magazines he picks up at the bar.

You roll over and open the drawer and look inside. *Oh hell*, you think, *you've started snooping. Just find it all out and get it over with.* You've seen all the toys in this drawer before.

Desire, Lust, Passion, Sex

Three sizes of dildos—thin, regular, and extra big with a double head. Nothing is new that you can tell except the recent issue of *Next* which is dated this weekend. That means he went to the bar this week.

You close the drawer and sit on the bed. You untie his sneakers and throw them on top of the treadmill. You open the top drawer of the night stand. You've never seen him open this drawer. On top are his pay stubs. You read the year-to-date earnings column. You estimate he makes close to $400,000 a year. You are stunned. You had no idea he made *that* much. He did say once that he made more money than a doctor. Then you get angry. You pay for half of everything you do together—the movies, the theater tickets, the occasional restaurant, the trip last month to Boston for the weekend. You barely make $25,000 a year. You try to shrug it off, but you can't. He once told you he would like you more if you made more money. *Jerk*, you think. *Pig*. All he's after is sex. All he wants is a good time. He's just using you. Using you for the sex. And you're not even getting paid for it.

You look through the rest of the drawer. There are scraps of paper with numbers and addresses written on them. You read each one. John at a Chelsea phone number, Paul on East 80th Street. There is another pile of business cards he must have gotten from tricks at the bar. You become perturbed because there are so many of them. You even find one of your old boyfriends in his pile. Small world, you try to console yourself, then laugh because you think they both deserve each other. *They're both jerks*, you tell yourself. *Both nothing but pigs.*

In the back of the drawer you notice a membership card to the East Side baths. You look at the expiration date and are relieved that it expired one month before you started dating him. *What a pig I've found*, you tell yourself again. Why would you want to be in a relationship with a sex junkie?

What You Find

Why has this affair lasted this long?

You shake your head. That's not what you want. You wonder if he will ever want to settle down. He was up-front when you confronted him with it after you had been dating each other for six weeks. He said he just got out of a twenty-two-year marriage, why would he want to settle down with someone right away? You remind yourself that it was your choice to continue this. Then you remind yourself that since he cheated on his wife when he was married—of course he's going to cheat around on a *boyfriend*. Then you tell yourself that "cheat" is the wrong word. There's nothing going on between the two of you, after all. At least not from his direction. It's just sex. Just dating. You close the drawer. You don't want to know any more. You try not to get upset. Don't make him into someone he's not going to be.

Pigs, you think. *They're all pigs.* Rich men, fat men, gay men. They're all jerks. Even yourself. When did you ever have a decent boyfriend? When were you ever a decent one yourself? You never told him about your ongoing thing with Jack, never mentioned the ad you placed in *HX* two months ago, never mentioned the string of blind dates you had, never mentioned whom you met on the phone lines. *But he provoked it,* you tell yourself. Didn't he *make* you look by reminding you of your every imperfection over and over? That you are far from the perfect boyfriend for him? That you weren't rich enough or young enough or cute enough or hot enough? And weren't you just hoping to find someone better than *him*?

You go into the kitchen and get a drink of water. You look at your watch. Ninety more minutes. You could read the book you brought, look through the notes of your novel that you think will never be finished. Suddenly you are aware that you will never have any money. You're a gay writer, you write gay stories, you write about gay life. You will never have this kind of money. You look back at the view of Central Park. If you give him up you will never see this view again. But you would never feel this lousy again, either.

When you first started dating him all you did was have sex. Sex in his new bed, sex in the kitchen, sex on the ottoman, sex on the floor. He was so cheap, he didn't even take you out for dinner. You wonder for a moment if you had his kind of money would you be dating someone like him? No, you think. You would be out of here quick. But you don't like him for just his money. And you want him for something more than just the sex.

You remember how much you have in your wallet. Two dollars. You just paid the rent on your fifth-floor walk-up in Hell's Kitchen. You're broke. You don't even have enough to go out for a sandwich. Instead you walk into the bathroom and rinse your face. You open the medicine chest and count the number of new toothbrushes on the shelf. Four. None gone. None of the packages have been opened since you were last here. You know he keeps them for tricks. Just like he does the stack of disposable razors. You pull down a razor he has saved for you and lather your face with his shaving cream. You smile at yourself in the mirror. *Fool*, you think. You're such a clown. At least you can pretend to be happy. Maybe you should have been an actor after all and not a writer.

You shave and then brush your teeth. You look at yourself in the mirror, admire your waist, flex your biceps, then think: *Treat me nice when I'm poor and I'll love you when I'm rich.*

You walk out of the bathroom and into his closet. You smell his shirts—freshly laundered and ironed cotton button-down. You touch his jackets, wave your fingers through the rack of ties, then thumb through them for the one he bought when you went together to Barney's. You play with yourself again and realize that you are already hard.

What You Find

You try on one of his shirts. It fits nicely, but you don't even contemplate trying on his pants; there's a five inch difference between your waists. You take the shirt off and look at yourself in the mirror nailed to the back of the closet door. You strike a pose. You run your hand up and down your stomach. You cup your balls, twirling the ends of your pubic hair. You would never shave your balls. You like it natural. You think about the times you've shaved his balls, the erection he gets as he's handled by you. You smile and then shake your head. *Where is all this going?* you wonder. *Right into therapy?*

You decide to explore some more. He once told you he kept cash hidden in the apartment, out of sight of his wife's lawyer. You wonder if you can find it. Suddenly, the prospect of this new game seizes you. You open his dresser drawers, looking beneath his underwear, between his T-shirts, inside his socks, through his shorts and under his slacks. You're obsessed with finding some money, any money, even if it's just a dollar bill or some coins he uses for laundry. You're not going to steal it, you just want to discover it, count it, touch it, know where it is because he makes such a big issue of how much he has and how little you have. Instead, you find a book of erotic stories under his jeans. You thumb through it. Nothing inside so you put it back. Maybe he's cash poor, you think as you close the drawer. Maybe he's just a portfolio— all stocks and assets.

The bottom drawer surprises you, however, when you open it—there is a row of neatly stacked videos. You pick one up. It is *The Best of Joey Stefano.* You look at the photo of the guy on the cover. Dark hair, dark eyes, unshaven pouty looks. You've seen him on the reruns on Robin Byrd's cable show a couple of times. *Didn't he die?* you think. *Didn't he have a drug problem?*

You put the video back in the drawer. You lift up another one. Same guy on the cover, full body shot, tattoo on his bicep. Joey Stefano in *Tattoo You*. You look at Joey. You look at yourself in the mirror. No contest, you think. He's younger. Hotter. Better arms. Better ass. You feel defeated. You put that video back and lift up one more. *Prince Charming*, with Joey Stefano's name in the cast list. As you turn it over an envelope falls to the ground. You pick it up and notice there is a phone number written on the front, 213 area code. California. You look inside the envelope, opening it carefully where it has been taped shut. It is full of small black hairs. Pubic hair, you think. An envelope full of pubic hair. It can't be *his*—his is gray. It must be Joey Stefano's pubic hair. *You have discovered an envelope full of Joey Stefano's pubic hair.*

What a pig you've found out you're dating. You had a big fight once over the porn. He wanted to watch it during sex. You wanted a little more attention from him. You sigh, aware that you will never be his ideal type—he's told you that, in fact. But you've never insulted him, however, never told him that you think he could lose a little weight, go to the gym a little more, that the bald spot at the back of his head really *does* reflect light. But then you're easier than he is. You're not so specific when it comes to men and body types and hair. All you want is someone to care—he doesn't have to look like a bodybuilder or a wrestler or the bouncer you once saw in front of a club. Okay, so you're jealous, you think. Deal with it. Get over it. Accept it and move on.

You go into the bathroom and flush Joey Stefano's pubic hair down the toilet. Then you open the medicine cabinet and find his nail scissors. You take off your underwear. You snip off some of your pubic hair. It is the same color as Joey's. You put it in the envelope and return it to the drawer with the videos. You kick the drawer closed with your foot, hoping you've made a dent in the wood.

You lie back on the bed again and stare at the ceiling,

playing with your cock. How do you make things work, you wonder. You don't want to give up. You're not a quitter. Something is going on with this man if he trusts you enough to leave you behind in his apartment. You look at the photo of his daughter on his dresser. You could always blackmail him, you think. You could earn your fortune by threatening to expose him to his wife and his boss.

Grow up, you tell yourself. He is his own boss. And you're too old to be a double-crossing boy toy. You would never do that. You're too gay yourself, too out, too proud to even think about doing something like that. What you want is to make something work, make this relationship work. But what if this is the wrong one? What if you've picked the wrong guy again?

You squeeze your cock, rub your fist over the head. You feel yourself getting hard. You close your eyes, feel the muscles of your chest tense. You think about the guy you saw in the men's department at Bloomingdale's yesterday. Black hair, great arms. Better looking than Joey Stefano, you laugh to yourself. You imagine him going down on you. The guy at Bloomingdale's. Not Joey. You lift your legs up in the air, wet a finger in your mouth, then begin to play with your asshole. You're hot, bothered, frustrated, and worked up. You pump your cock. Harder and harder. You push two fingers into your ass. Move them in and out as you work your fist up and down your cock. When you shoot you almost hit your nipple. You open your eyes and calm your breathing. You feel mean and nasty. You take some of your come and rub it onto his comforter. You're such a pig, you think. Why are all gay men such pigs? You're no better than he is. You get up off the bed and go to the bathroom.

You piss and then step into the shower. You use his soap and shampoo. You find a clean towel and dry yourself off with it, just to make another one dirty for him to have to wash.

Desire, Lust, Passion, Sex

You use his cologne and deodorant. You dry your hair with his hair dryer. You smell like him, you think, as you admire yourself in his mirror. He's all over you.

You look at the clock. He'll be back in about five minutes. Your heart begins to beat faster. You take a deep breath and hurriedly put on your jeans and sweatshirt, sitting on the couch and lacing up your boots. You get your jacket out of the closet. You take a last look at his view.

Then you leave. You open the door and just walk out, listening to it slam behind you. He will never find your jealousy, anger, and obsession again, you decide. And he will not find you in his apartment when he returns.

Flash Gordon at the Exclusive Dating Service for Men

The best way to get a guy out of your head, I knew from past experience, is to fuck him out of your head. And I wasn't thinking of my sometime-boyfriend Peter Gold and his million-dollar lifestyle when I remembered this either. I was feeling guilty over the way I had treated Alfie—poor, beautiful, young, exotic-looking Alfie. I had just up and dumped him, acting like every other horrible pig of a gay man I had ever dated and been dumped by myself. I was disgusted with myself over just walking out on Alfie at the bar that night, even though my friend Evan had obviously picked up the ball and run with it and Alfie hadn't shown much remorse over the abrupt change. Still, all I wanted—no, all I *needed* to do was to knock this onerous guilt out of my head by moving on to the next guy, looking for a quickie transition, really, before I could move on to looking for—no, *hunting* for—the *next* one—the next *good* one—the next guy, the one I *wouldn't* *want* to dump. In other words, the best way to get over being a jerk was to be a pig with someone else—to have a hot, sweaty, nameless, sexual session with Mr. Anyone-I-Could-Pick-Up-on-the-Street in order to forget The-One-I-Had-Just-Dumped-in-a-Not-Too-Polite-Way.

But the truth was that I needed to grow up. Here I was on the brink of forty, and I knew I couldn't always escape my guilt through anonymous sexual encounters—could I? I certainly wasn't getting any younger; exactly how many more hot quick-trick encounters did I have left in me? But the fact was I needed to *discipline* my sexuality better—I wanted to be worthy of a real relationship. Hadn't I dumped Alfie, after all, because he was getting in the way of my emotions for Peter Gold? Wasn't I trying to make things work out for me and Peter, or, at least, work them out in my mind so that they worked for me when we *were* together? So instead of going out to a bar or hooking up with someone via the sex lines, as I normally would have done when I wanted to forget a guy, I decided it was time to hunt for a serious replacement for my obsession for Peter Gold *and* get rid of my remorse over dumping Alfie. So I decided to cash in my coupon for three free dates from The Exclusive, a gay dating service, which Evan had given to me as a Christmas present over five years before.

The Exclusive Dating Service for Men, the only gay dating service in Manhattan that I hadn't tried before, was located in the basement of a townhouse on the Upper West Side between Columbus and Amsterdam. The day I impulsively showed up to cash in my gift certificate I was dressed in a sweaty T-shirt and knee-length chino shorts because I had been rollerblading in Central Park. The "Counselor on Duty" at The Exclusive that day (or so the nameplate on the front desk read) was a hunky Hispanic guy named Gordon who, I was surprised to find, was more skimpily attired than myself. Dressed in a gray tank top and sky-blue running shorts, he had the kind of body that belonged on physique magazine covers and a face suitable for a Calvin Klein ad. He was both intimidating and desirable, with his statuesque size, three-day stubble on his face and skull, and an unblemished caramel complexion. His wide, brown nipples disconcertingly peeked from his tank top like two inquiring eyes, the left one, in fact, pierced with what appeared to be a golden dumbbell (and

Flash Gordon at the Exclusive
Dating Service for Men

which made it look as though it were winking at me). Great, I thought, as he handed me a dating questionnaire to fill out, a Chelsea-cum-Bronx-Homeboy-Clone-Out-of-Water-on-the-Upper-West-Side—he'll never be able to match me up with what I want. Nor did he really want to, judging by the perturbed look he gave me when I unfolded the years-old coupon from my wallet, the edges frayed and the printing illegible in places where it had simply worn away with age.

Just like me, I thought, *worn at the edges,* as I took a seat in the chair opposite the Counselor-on-Duty's desk and began filling in the questionnaire, which required me to describe my idea of an ideal partner, as well as rating my own qualities and characteristics. I'm a firm believer that dating services are for losers, but a real loser in my book was also a guy who wanted a lover and did nothing about it. Nonetheless, I stumbled at the first question: *What do you do?* Do I respond "Wanna-Be Writer" or "Too-Tired Temp?" I felt lost before I had even started this process, so I looked up from where I sat, right at the eye-of-the-nipple of Mr. Very-Large-and-Too-Pretty-Dating-Counselor and asked in my most cynical, dried-up old faggot dragon lady voice, "Can I be put directly into the file of guys who are not concerned with what kind of income I make?"

The question seemed to take Mr. Big-Muscles-with-Pierced-Nipple by surprise. "Our matches are determined by all of your responses. Are you *done* yet?" The attitude he used on *done* seemed to indicate I should just *shut up and finish the form,* so I smirked at him in my own best haughty manner and looked back down at the questionnaire, still conscious of those thick nipples of his just pointing out of his tank top, itching to be licked and sucked.

I wrote "Writer," down on the occupation line and then began to fill in the details of my physical appearance: height, weight, age, hair color, eye color, any distinctive tattoos. The second part of the questionnaire was more difficult; the questions focused on what I desired in a lover. The truth was, I didn't care so much what the would-be date would look like physically. (Okay, he had to be *presentable*—I wasn't going to settle for a troll, after all—but I'm not *soooo* shallow that I would only settle for just one specific kind of guy.) I didn't care if he was clean shaven, had a mustache or a beard, was hairy-chested or smooth, short or bald. What I wanted was for someone to want me as much as I wanted him. Was that asking too much? All I wanted was the right guy for me and here I was at the mercy of Mr. Hot-and-Exotic-Homeboy-Clone-with-Heavenly-Nipples-Counselor-on-Duty.

The further along I got with the questions, the more I realized I wanted a clone of Peter Gold, except I wanted that clone to be more interested in pursuing and maintaining a relationship with me, me, me—not someone else. Certainly not with a rich, out-of-town, younger-than-he-was, socialite boyfriend on the side. The questions veered wildly between requesting specific details to offering absurd choices. *Do you wear cologne, aftershave or use talcum powder?* was one of the questions. *Do you prefer to take a date home on the first night?* was another. *How many times a week do you go to a gym?* (Not enough, I responded.) *How many mirrors do you have in your bedroom?* (Too many, I answered.) And then there were the questions that I refused to answer, like: *What is the longest committed relationship you've ever been in?* (Excuse me, but define *committed* for me—what *exactly* does that mean, and does a four-day, very passionate out-of-town affair count?) And then the questions turned philosophical, or a combination of philosophical and silly. What kind of question was this: *Do you prefer a man who acts more from his thoughts or one who acts from his feelings?* Or this one: *Do you want someone imaginative or realistic?* I just couldn't sit there with my mouth shut and not react to these absurdities, so I lifted my head and

Flash Gordon at the Exclusive
Dating Service for Men

asked the Nipples-That-Belonged-to-Man-Who-Must-Have-Changed-His-Name-in-Order-to-Be-Called-Gordon, "Must I answer *every* question?"

"It will help us make a better match for you," he answered, squirming in his chair so that the left side of the dumbbell of the pierced nipple got snagged on the gray tank top. It was so momentarily disconcerting to watch that nipple peek out again that I felt my dick fatten and I began to grow uncomfortably hot over Mr. Too-Beautiful-But-Not-Mr.-Right-Counselor-on-Duty.

A better *match,* I thought, taking in a deep breath. *But not a perfect one.* "But I don't have to answer *all* of them," I said firmly back to him, or, rather, to the *nipple.*

"No, we don't *require* you to in order to make a match."

"Then, I'm done," I answered and slipped the form across the desk and into the direct sightline of Gordon's nipples. He puffed up his chest as if he were babysitting me and exasperated with my behavior. I leaned back from the desk and simply gave him my heaviest cruise.

"Do you want to wait for your matches, or should I phone you?" he asked, running his fingertips along the edges of my filled in questionnaire. He looked up and smiled at me, locking his stare into mine, and I swear I detected sparks then, tiny little bursts of fireworks suggesting that I should stick around because this could be fun.

"I'll wait," I answered, arching my eyebrows.

He nodded, took a pencil, and began making notes in the margins of my answer sheet. I glanced around the office as he busied himself with my form, noting that this basement office looked about as dusty, worn-out, and dumpy as my Hell's Kitchen apartment. On the bookshelf beside the desk was a stack of magazines and I picked the first one on the pile, the current issue of *Advocate Men.* As Gordon sorted through index cards, referencing them against my questionnaire, I flipped through the magazine, once again unable to hold my thoughts inside. "*Him*," I said and turned the magazine so that Mr.Very-Big-and-Juicy-Nipples could see the full-frontal nude male model I had found in the magazine—an all-American football type with a neck as thick as his thighs. "Can you fix me up with *him?*"

Gordon's only response was a sneer, but a rather bemused, campy one, I thought, and when I found another *in flagrante* model (a much younger, thinner, and blonder one with a bigger dick), I repeated my routine, asking Gordon this time, "Do you think he acts with his feelings or with his thoughts?"

He laughed briefly, and then said that he was almost done with my application. He got up from the desk and went to a file cabinet and began pulling photographs from the back of a drawer. He returned to the desk a moment later, but instead of sitting in his chair, he stood over me and leaned forward, arranging photographs in front of me with his very meaty caramel forearm flexing right under my nose. I felt the electricity jumping right out of his skin and into my forehead like alien brainwaves, but I was even more conscious of his flapping tank top and the likelihood of those big, brown chewy nipples brushing up against my earlobe. I knew he was a little too close for comfort, or a little too close not to *get* more comfortable. And with all my years and years of training, I knew those sparks weren't just happening on one side of the table, either.

"What do you think of him?" Gordon asked, pointing to a photograph on the far end of the desk of an older man with an obvious Ralph Lauren obsession—wind-tossed hair, rugged-looking skin, a craggy face like worn leather luggage. The Exclusive was one of those dating services that at least gave you a look at someone before you went out to meet him. "I think I might like someone a little more codependent," I answered.

Flash Gordon at the Exclusive
Dating Service for Men

Since Gordon's face was slightly behind me, I couldn't tell his reaction unless I turned around to look at him, and, just as I tried, he stopped me by asking, "What about him?" I looked to where his overly-muscled arm stretched over my head and his finger pointed to a photograph of a much younger-looking man than the first one, this one with floppy black hair and very thick, pouty lips.

"I'd love to sit on *his* face," I said.

"He's even hotter in person," Gordon answered, chuckling close to my earlobe now—so close, in fact, that I could smell the sweat on him.

Did I mention that it had been an exceptionally muggy afternoon and that the basement offices of The Exclusive Dating Service for Men had neither a window nor an air conditioner, the air trapped and stale and warm all around us, hence Gordon's skimpy attire and sweat, and the reason the place had the smell of a locker room or a jerk-off club?

"Sorry it's so warm in here," Gordon said next, and then he took his hand and wiped the sweat which had collected at the back of *my* neck, and wiped it against the sleeve of *my* T-shirt. I wouldn't have thought anything about his action—it could have been construed as a friendly gesture—except for the fact that he returned his hand to my neck and began massaging it, causing me to sweat even more. *Sorry?* I thought, as his fingers kneaded my flesh, *who's sorry about this heat?*

The next thing I knew I had turned around in the chair and slipped Gordon's shorts off and he was sitting on my face, his balls slapping against my chin as I licked and blew his cock. I reached up to squeeze his nipples, slightly worried as to how hard I should be twisting the pierced one and wondering if what I did to him was going to influence who he would match me up with. I soon stopped with the nipples, but continued sucking and licking my way from the head of his cock to its base, fingering his balls occasionally and then slapping his ass cheeks, testing to see how hard and how loud he wanted me to go with this before I used both of my hands to reverse his position, giving me a full view of his backside as I moved my face toward the crack of his ass. As I did so, I noticed that he had a lightning bolt tattoo outlined in red and yellow streaks on his left butt cheek. *Flash Gordon,* I thought. *I'm having sex with Flash Gordon. I'm having sex with a comic book hero.* Flash me, *Flash. Flash me* hard. The thought of it really amused me and I leaned over and lightly bit and sucked on his tattoo.

The next thing I knew we were on the floor, my shorts and shirt were off, and I was sitting astride Gordon's chest, *my* balls bouncing against *his* chin as I moved *my* cock in and out of *his* mouth. Flash Gordon's left arm was wrapped around my thigh and his other hand was jerking his own cock as he pulled and slapped it against my ass. Almost immediately he began breathing hard through his mouth and I felt the muscles of his body tense underneath me as his come splashed against the left cheek of *my* ass, just about the spot, it occurred to me, where his tattoo was on *his* left cheek. I came not long after he did, right on that beautiful, wide brown pierced nipple.

A fantasy fuck, I thought when I was back out on the street, snaking my way through the crowds as I walked downtown, the harshness of the summer afternoon pleasingly liquid-like against my skin. That's what had just happened with Gordon. Nothing but a fantasy fuck. A comic book fantasy fuck that would never be repeated. At least not with Gordon. By the time I reached 57th Street I knew that I wouldn't call any of the numbers Gordon had given me before I left the office. For one thing, none of these guys were as good as Peter Gold, and, for that matter, I didn't *want* any of them to be as good as Peter, didn't want to *see* if they *could* be. And what I wanted to have happen had already happened.

Flash Gordon at the Exclusive Dating Service for Men

Alfie was history. He was out of my mind. I hadn't wanted any thoughts of Alfie potentially jeopardizing my feelings for Peter. Pity, I thought, as I climbed the five flights of stairs to my apartment. I'm just another gay gratuitous-sex-pig-devil myself. No wonder Peter Gold wanted nothing to do with me. But the joke was still on him. I knew his other boyfriend was no good either. Hadn't Brad been out and about with Scott behind Peter Gold's back? I reminded myself. Didn't I have proof that Brad, too, was just another big gay sex-pig-devil? Weren't we all just rutting in this heat and mess together? I realized that I had probably had enough sex in my lifetime to last *three* lifetimes and what I wanted, really wanted, was a relationship—a true, honest-to-goodness, down-to-earth committed relationship—something, well, more meaningful than a very passionate out-of-town four-day affair. The next thing I felt was guilt over looking around for another boyfriend behind Peter's back. But then I remembered I didn't know where Peter was or what he was doing at the very moment I had been sitting on Flash Gordon's face. *Hell*, I thought, when I opened the door of my apartment and was blasted with a wall of hot air. *Welcome back to Hell.*

A Kiss

In the afternoon the wind changed; the breeze that had drifted across the sound was pushed back to the sea. By evening, the air was hot and stagnant and humidity coated everything like a thick, dense fog. Clarke stood outside by the country club pool. He was fifteen and dressed in a navy blue tuxedo that had been rented for his cousin Melissa's wedding. He wiped his face with his sleeve and as he moved he felt the jacket stick to his wet shirt where the sweat had rolled down his back. The lights at the bottom of the pool bounced up and kicked the deck chairs and umbrella-topped tables. The water gurgled. It never fails, he thought, relief is always an irrational jump away. Still, he wanted to be anywhere besides the noisy ballroom where his mother or his aunts were constantly trying to pull him toward the dance floor.

Clarke hated weddings; this one had ruined a whole day. He had wanted to go with his friends Andy and Mack to Edisto Beach. Instead, this morning his parents made him mow the yard and pull the weeds from the flower beds in case anyone dropped by before the wedding. This afternoon the church was sweltering hot. Clarke had been an usher at the wedding. Escorting the women down the aisle was like trying to walk underwater. His mother sat in a pew and waved a fan she had made from a piece of paper she found in the back of a hymnal. His father coughed and shifted continuously in his seat, flapping the ends of his jacket away from his thighs. Reverend Bensen kept the vows as short as possible; when he stopped to apologize for the broken air conditioner, Clarke noticed that Ronnie, the groom, was sweating so much the collar of his white shirt had become translucent.

After the wedding everyone headed to the country club for the reception and dinner, racing as fast as they could to the air-conditioned ballroom and the bartender. Last year, Clarke's cousin Lexanne's wedding had been at the same church and in the same room of the country club, though he remembered the weather was not as oppressive. This year, Uncle Howard's face turned bright red before he even had a drink and Aunt Alice kept patting the bones of her neck with a lace handkerchief she kept crumpled in her hand. In the last year Clarke had grown four inches and was now taller than his father. Today, his three aunts overwhelmed him with attention, reaching up and cupping his cheeks with their hands even though they saw him almost every day of the year.

At dinner Clarke sat between Aunt Colleen and Aunt Joyce. Uncle Howard and Uncle Stan and his parents were also at the table. Clarke was uncomfortable every time he became the focus of their conversation. What was he going to do about a summer job? Where did he want to go to college? Did he have his eye on any particular girl? Across the room Jennifer Hammond, who was in Clarke's geometry class at school, sat between Ted Lambert and Steve Riley, two friends of Melissa's sister Robin. Clarke had once considered asking Jennifer out for a date. She was short and pretty and had large brown eyes and a cute, upturned nose. But it wasn't the lack of courage that had stopped him from asking her out; it irritated him that she always seemed to be looking at him, studying him, and then flipping her long brown hair off her shoulder and turning away. At her table, Wes Taylor, one of Melissa's friends, smoked a cigarette with one hand while the other was draped around Nancy Jo Crockett's shoulder. Clarke's mother must have sensed he was unhappy seated at a table full of adults, and allowed him to have a glass of champagne after dinner to toast the newly-married couple.

It wasn't hard to tell who was having a good time. Aunt Alice made Uncle Howard waltz with her, Aunt Joyce and Aunt Colleen did a jitterbug together like two little girls. A group of Melissa's friends started a line dance. Clarke was surprised his mother or his aunt didn't object to the way Wes held Nancy Jo's buttocks with both hands when they danced to a slow song, but then he saw Aunt Alice nudge Uncle Stan and whisper, "They'll be next." Clarke tried to imagine himself holding Jennifer that way, but couldn't, and grew annoyed when he noticed she was hanging around his table. So he walked outside into the hot night and stood by the edge of the pool.

The sound of a trumpet and laughter filtered through the large windows of the ballroom. Clarke turned away from the country club and followed the flagstone path down the bluff to the piers and the boats harbored in the cove. Before him the view was as motionless as a painting, the moon lost behind a haze of clouds. The tide was soundless and the sail boats stood inanimate in the water as though docked on dry land. He followed the path to the boardwalk but stopped when he reached the boathouse. He tried to peer in a window, couldn't see through the grimy glass, but felt as he pressed his hands against the sill a cool breeze seeping through the seams. He went to the door and twisted the knob. It was unlocked so he walked inside.

Inside the cool air chilled his damp clothing. He closed

the door and was relieved by the quiet and darkness of the boathouse. Suddenly he heard footsteps and the rustle of a jacket and he was seized by the embrace of two arms about his shoulders. "Finally," Clarke heard the deep whisper of a man's voice. The hands slipped up to Clarke's neck and he felt a rough, tingling brush against his cheek. His lips parted in surprise and were met by the warm, liquid taste of a kiss on his mouth. The stranger pulled away quickly and gasped, and then fled through the door.

Clarke was startled. Fear and excitement were trapped together in his lungs. His heart was wildly thumping, so rapidly he thought it might explode. He approached the door of the boathouse and stepped outside, but no one was there. There wasn't a sound, not even the footsteps of the retreating stranger. He shoved his hands into the pockets of his coat to steady himself, perplexed and embarrassed as though he had stumbled upon someone else being passionately kissed. But then he realized this had happened to him. The heat was now so unbearable he jogged up the bluff to the country club.

When he walked into the ballroom he almost instantly turned around to go back outside, worried that someone could tell by the way he looked or walked or breathed that he had just been kissed by a man. Instead he took his seat at the table and wiped the sweat from his face with a napkin. His parents were dancing. Uncle Howard and Aunt Alice were busy talking with Melissa. He realized no one had noticed his absence, so he relaxed and tried to sort through what had happened in the boathouse. He rubbed his neck, pressing it as it had been touched by two strange hands. His left cheek, where he first felt the tingle of another man's skin, trembled with a slight, burning sensation. He tightened his shoulders, as though they were being pushed together, and felt an unusual surge of exhilaration. For a moment he felt restless, tickled by an urge to laugh or jump or shout. Trying to keep his motions as calm as possible, he stood up from his seat and headed around the dance floor toward the bar. But when he passed Jennifer Hammond he gave her such a silly smile, she approached him with a puzzled look.

"Nice dress," Clarke said, but walked away from her before she could reply. At the bar, he turned around and noticed his parents were still dancing, and Aunt Joyce and Aunt Colleen were circulating through the room with cameras in their hands. He turned to the bartender and asked for a beer. He returned to the table and sipped the beer from the bottle, his mind trying to solve his mysterious encounter. Why had it happened? The man must have arranged to meet someone at the boathouse, Clarke thought, but what about the word he had whispered as he approached. "Finally," Clarke heard the man's voice echoing again, breathlessly, close to his ear. He must have been waiting for a while and, in anticipation, thought Clarke was someone else. It was an easy mistake. The boathouse was dark and when Clarke entered he had paused expectantly, as though arriving to meet someone. But was the stranger waiting for another man, or had he in his frustration mistaken Clarke for a woman? No, Clarke decided. He must have been waiting for a man. There was the way his thumbs brushed lightly against Clarke's skin and his hands clasped together at the back of his neck and fingered his short hair. He must have known Clarke wasn't a woman. There was the way, a second after the kiss, the man ran his hands down the collar of Clarke's jacket.

But who was it, he wanted to know, and glanced around the room. Could it have been someone here? It must have been one of the wedding guests. Wasn't there the rustle of the jacket? Wasn't there a taste of alcohol left in his mouth? And he must be as tall as he was, Clarke decided. There was the way the hands pressed squarely against Clarke's shoulders, not angled as though leaning up or down to kiss a person of a different height.

But who? Across the room Clarke noticed Wes removing his jacket and draping it over the back of his chair. Wes was as tall as Clarke and had a firmly built body and a deep, hoarse voice. Was it him? Wes laughed and Clarke thought the way his upper lip disappeared above his teeth made him look too much like a monkey. It couldn't have been him, he decided. And besides, he was constantly groping Nancy Jo Crockett.

Then who? Ted? Steve? Ted had deep brown eyes, a cleft in his chin and thick black hair which clustered over his brow and cascaded down the back of his neck. Steve had a more mischievous, boyish look. Straight blond hair and a smooth oval face, but the most breathtaking blue eyes of anyone in the room. But what about the mustache? The stranger, as Clarke remembered, had a mustache. Wes, Ted, and Steve did not. He looked again about the room. Uncle Howard and Uncle Stan had mustaches. So did Melissa's father and her new husband Ronnie. It couldn't have been Uncle Howard; he was much too short, and Melissa's father had a stomach wider than his shoulders. If it had been Uncle Howard, wouldn't Clarke have remembered the bitter taste of a cigar left in his mouth? And Ronnie? The mustache was just as Clarke remembered, thick, dark, and coarse. But could Ronnie have been unfaithful and untruthful to his new wife?

This is ridiculous, Clarke thought. *It's impossible, hopeless.* Yet he still searched for an answer. If he took Wes's body and added Ted's hair, Steve's eyes, and Ronnie's mustache, then perhaps he might have an idea, an image of what this man looked like. He assembled the pieces quickly together and when he had a clear picture in his mind he looked again around the room, but there was no one who resembled this man.

The band stopped playing. The bride and groom were now waving from the entrance of the ballroom. Clarke felt himself becoming depressed, distressed at not having solved his mystery. He finished his beer and placed the bottle where his Uncle Stan had been sitting, just before his mother tapped him on the shoulder and said it was time to leave.

Clarke followed his parents across the parking lot, removing his jacket and bow tie as he walked. At the car, his father handed him the keys and Clarke unlocked the doors, his father slipping into the backseat next to his mother. On the ride home, as the car crossed the Waterway Bridge, Clarke looked at the lights of the barges and boats harbored at the piers. As they passed out of view he adjusted the rearview mirror hoping to get one last look, and he noticed his mother and father in the backseat kissing.

At home, in his bedroom, Clarke locked his door and pulled down the shades. In the darkness he undressed and lay upon his bed, nude, fingering the strands of his hair at the base of his neck. Who was the stranger? Where did he come from? Where did he go, Clarke wondered, and felt the warmth return to his neck, cheek, and shoulders. Through his mind raced pictures of Wes and Ted and Steve and Ronnie and his uncles and his father. They twirled and blinked against each other and as they faded beneath his eyes into one, unknown man, he felt excited. And just as he became mesmerized by his combination of fantasy and fact, his mother knocked at the door and reminded him he had promised to sweep and clean out the garage tomorrow.

When she left, he rolled over on his side and slipped his hand below his waist and felt himself grow hard. He saw the stranger before him, leaning down to kiss him and then lowering his body to the bed to lie beside him, wrapping his arms around his body and drawing them close together. The night was silent, the house was quiet, and his bedroom was dark, but Clarke could hear the sound of his heart beating and, finally again, the rustle of the jacket. He curled his body tighter to maintain the sensation and felt spasms erupt within his groin. He felt embarrassed and possessed. Something strange and wonderful had finally happened in his life.

∿∿∿∿

Clarke fluttered his eyes dreamily. His body felt light, almost weightless. This morning he was awake before his mother had knocked at his bedroom door. Before she had made breakfast, he had arranged the garden tools on hooks and shelves and swept and washed the concrete floor of the garage. Now, he lay flat on his stomach, flat on a towel which lay flat on the white cement surrounding the pool, the morning sun burning into afternoon heat, his friends Andy and Mack on towels beside him. Around them shards of quartz embedded in the concrete shimmered in the sunlight.

This morning, before he got out of bed, Clarke had decided to tell Andy and Mack about his encounter with the stranger last night. After all, they were his closest friends; they all lived on the same block and had been in school together since kindergarten. As kids, they had roamed through the houses being constructed in the new subdivision across the street; sitting on the wood beams of unfinished homes, they told each other their problems, dreams, and secrets. Since junior high they had taken the same classes and played together on the basketball team. In the summers, they had always gone to the beach or the cove or the pool together, swimming, sailing, and sharing stories whenever something new or exciting happened. Hadn't Mack, when they were all nine years old, gathered them in a huddle by the mailbox on Andy's lawn and told them what his brother had

A Kiss

just told him that a guy could do with a girl?

Clarke relaxed by closing his eyes, tensing and releasing the muscles of his body. Fragments of the stranger jumped between the purple, red, and black spots beneath his eyelids and he felt the excitement and pleasure of last night still floating inside him. He wanted to share these feelings or at least explain them. He opened his eyes and turned on his side, propping himself up on one elbow. Mack was also turned on his side, away from Clarke, talking with his girlfriend Shelly, who sat cross-legged on another towel. Mack was already sixteen, had his driver's license and had been dating Shelly for over a year now, and the once hushed conversation he had shared with Clarke and Andy by the mailbox had turned for him into a firsthand, first-rate event. Clarke watched the hard knotted muscles above Mack's shoulder blades shift as he lifted a plastic cup to his lips. Mack was short and stocky but quick on his feet, and had a thick neck and long arms and skin which reddened instead of tanned. He was the oldest of the three of them, and it occurred to Clarke now that lately Mack never let the other two forget it, as though trying to counterbalance his extra weight and lack of height. Now, Clarke decided by the way Mack suddenly placed his large hand against the inside of Shelly's thigh, he wouldn't understand or comprehend what had happened to Clarke last night. He would consider it silly or ridiculous, perhaps even unimportant or perverted.

Clarke flipped over on his other side, again propped up by an elbow. Andy lay flat on his back listening to a cassette tape with earphones, his eyes closed as though sleeping. Andy's body was similar to Clarke's, tall and lean and tightened by the endless repetitions of exercise they did at basketball practice. For years, Andy had been the tallest of the three until suddenly this year when Clarke had leapt ahead. Clarke noticed the way Andy's body jerked as he kept time to the music and the way his skin, smooth and tanned on his chest and arms like a boy's, suddenly became dark and hairy like a man's at his thighs. Andy might understand, but he was so distant lately, lost in a book, a magazine or music. And there was the possibility he might tell Mack. Weren't they always telling him things they had already told each other?

A shrill yell—half scream, half giggle—pierced through the noise of a radio and the children scrambling around the poolside after a beach ball. Clarke sat up and saw Shelly, now standing, kick Mack in the leg and run her fingers quickly beneath the top of her bikini where Mack had slipped a piece of ice. Mack laughed loudly and turned to see if Clarke had noticed and Clarke gave a little chuckle to show he had. "That's not funny," Shelly said to Clarke though she kicked Mack again, and Clarke watched her stomp her bare feet against the cement to the other side of the pool and sit abruptly on a towel beside his cousin Robin and Jennifer Hammond. Robin was lying on her stomach, the straps of her bikini dangling off her shoulders, and she whispered something to Shelly and they both shook their heads. Jennifer ran a large blue comb through the dark wet strands of her long hair. Shelly looked across the pool, frowned, and stuck out her tongue at Mack, an expression Clarke knew meant she was mad right now but wouldn't be later. Now, even Andy was sitting up and laughing with Mack.

So who could he tell, Clarke wondered, if not Andy or Mack? Certainly not his parents or his aunts and uncles. None of them, he knew, would understand. They might turn hysterical, feel shamed, become angry or alarmed. They might even try to send him to a psychiatrist, the way they had all threatened to send his older cousin Bruce to a military school if they caught him smoking pot again.

Looking across the pool, he knew even his cousin Robin, who sat beside him every day during the school year when they rode the bus, wouldn't understand. She would gasp and fidget and warn him it was risky, maybe adding something like it was dirty or disgusting or he could get a disease from it and die. It was hopeless, he decided, and felt the heat pounding on his bare back. But it wasn't a dream. It was something that happened. And he knew how he felt. It wasn't a mistake, was it?

The sun turned intolerably hot. The noise of the voices and radios grew louder and louder. Clarke grew more restless and confused and stood up from his towel. He took a few steps and dove into the pool, his body and thoughts instantly chilled and silenced as he slipped into the water. He swam the width of the pool and when he reached the wall he stayed underwater until he felt his lungs would burst. He crouched and shoved off from the bottom. Hitting the air, he splashed and grabbed the tiles at the side of the pool. Jennifer looked up at him from her towel, her eyes widening.

"Want to see a movie tonight?" Clarke asked, catching his breath.

"Sure," she answered and flipped her wet hair over her shoulder.

∧∧∧∧∧

He picked her up at seven. She was dressed in a pink and white striped cotton sundress. Her hair was pulled back from her face, making its roundness look longer but softer. She smelled like a combination of flowers and baby powder. A thin strand of gold hung around her neck. He opened the car door for her and she took tiny little steps before she slipped inside. His father drove the car; they sat together in the backseat. On the ride to the movie he held her hand. It felt warm, moist, and small against his own.

"You got a lot of sun today," she said. "Look," she added and pressed a finger against the skin of his forearm. He watched it turn white then red and then back to a dark tan. "I can't stay out in the sun real long," she continued. "Unless I use a good sunblock. Otherwise I'll end up looking like Mack."

"He was such a jerk today," he said.

"But Shelly wasn't mad," she answered. "I think she likes him more when he does dumb stuff like that."

Waiting in line to buy tickets he was aware how delicate she was. Her legs were willowy, her neck slender. Though she only wore a light touch of makeup, her eyelashes were long and curved. She barely came up to the middle of his chest, but he kept his posture straight and erect, afraid if he leaned or stooped he might seem gawky, nervous or awkward.

"Are you going to be at the pool tomorrow?" she asked.

"Probably," he answered. "But my dad wants me to work at the shop next week when Bruce goes on vacation."

"We're going to Daytona in August," she said. "I hate it there, but my dad won't let me stay home alone. But in the fall, when we're seniors, he said he'll let me stay out after midnight. Are you going to play basketball again next year?" she asked.

"Probably," he answered. "If I can keep my grades up."

"I always thought you were a snob, you know, hardly talking to anyone except Mack and Andy," she said. "But Robin said you weren't. You could be real popular if you wanted to."

He bought her popcorn and a diet soda. During the movie they held hands at the edge of her chair. When it was over he let her walk slightly ahead of him up the aisle, his hand placed lightly on her shoulder.

"Melissa's dress was so pretty," she said when they were back in the car. "I loved the way the pearl buttons hooked together in the back."

"Yeah," he answered. "I liked your dress too," he added and clutched her hand tighter.

"I want to be married on the Waterway Bridge," she said.

"The bridge?" he asked. "Why there?"

A Kiss

"It's so romantic," she answered. "You know, the way it's so symbolic, the way it connects two pieces of land permanently together. But my mother doesn't like the idea. She says it's too dangerous, the way the wind can blow so hard there sometimes. And the water is so noisy because it goes real fast. She says it's because it's the closest place the Gulf Stream comes up to land."

"It's nice there," he said and noticed his father adjusting the rearview mirror.

"But of course I won't do it if the guy I marry doesn't want to," she added.

The car stopped at the curb in front of her house. He got out and walked her to the door, a yellow porch light guiding his steps.

At the door, she lightly touched the doorknob and said, "Thank you. I had a nice time."

He grasped her firmly by the shoulders and kissed her, his hands traveling slowly up to her neck, his fingers twisting around the soft wisps of her hair. She did not resist him; her mouth slipped easily into his. He pulled back from her, and let his hands fall down again to her shoulders. He said, "Good night," smiled, and left.

On the way back to the car he realized in two more weeks he would be sixteen. In another year he would leave home for college. He knew his life ahead held many questions. But for now he had found one answer. He was certain. It was real and true. His knowledge filled him with an intense and groundless joy, like a gust of air or a current of water. He imagined himself traveling along with the flow, as fast and as far into the future as it could carry him. His destination would have to be kept a secret for now and would be as difficult to pinpoint as a bottle tossed into the ocean. But he knew the direction he was headed; that was what he understood.

Grown-ups

Adam was five-eleven and thirty pounds overweight, even though his shoulders and thighs were still thick with muscle from his years in the Infantry; he'd survived Vietnam through discipline and patience, and he used the same approach when he returned home and joined the firm and climbed the corporate ladder to senior management. In the last round of lay-offs his cost-cutting plan had postponed a second round of buyouts. When his daughter married, he separated from his wife, Emily, after thirty-four years of marriage, and moved into a condo near Logan Circle. He was fifty-three years old and his bad eating habits had finally changed the width of his waist.

Josh was five-eight with a narrow waist, even at age forty-one, a product of his Franco-Italian genetics and a healthy obsession with working out. He kept up his gym trips even while working toward his MBA at night school. Most men were drawn to Josh because of his slender pretty-boy-on-the-circuit look. Josh had sworn off dating when his last boyfriend, Scott, walked out of a year-long relationship when Josh's mother died. Josh kept himself together without falling back on his former crutches: pot, booze, or the latest designer drug. In fact, Josh was glad he had finally reached an age at which he no longer felt compelled to party so hard. He was ready to be responsible and committed, which is why he worked such long hours at his job.

Josh was the token "gay boy" in his department, a moniker given to him behind his back because of his "slightly too casual" attire of polo shirts and khakis once the corporate dress code was relaxed to create a less rigorous office environment. Four years ago, Josh had been hired as an Employment Specialist in the Human Relations Department when he finished his MBA at night school and joined the firm, but after several layoffs and buyouts found himself doing the work of the department head without the benefit of the proper title or the salary. Because of these gaps in the corporate flow chart, Josh now reported directly to the Senior Vice President of Human Relations and Corporate Planning, but his new boss was too busy and too high up on the food chain to be a micromanager and their communication was limited to important e-mails, voice mails, and brief interoffice correspondence; they rarely both attended the same meetings. Things changed when Josh's boss retired and Adam, Senior Vice President of Advertising and Marketing, was given these new departments to oversee and felt it necessary to have weekly briefings in his office with Josh face-to-face, in order to make sure nothing slid by his attention.

Adam's military background kept his marketing and planning meetings perfunctory and impersonal, though he felt that this was not the right approach to use with Josh. In Adam's twenty-six years with the firm the company had made great strides in recognizing gay employees, adding sexual orientation and domestic partners to a variety of policies and plans. Adam admired Josh's openness and tried to find ways to commend that behavior, by complimenting Josh on the color of a shirt or his looking so fit.

Josh felt he was getting weird vibes from Adam. When their eyes locked at a meeting, Adam's face would redden.

Grown-ups

Josh lived in a gay neighborhood, worked out at a gay gym, and shopped at gay-owned stores, but at work he yearned for the company of anyone but other gay men. He found his gay coworkers too high-strung and needy, always wanting to confess their newest style dilemma or latest sexual conquest. Josh preferred having lunches with married women such as Lisa or Gwen, young professionals who could talk about their toddlers and preschool programs and take Josh momentarily out of the confined world he had created for himself. The death of Josh's mother had left him an orphan—he had no siblings, his father had died many years before of a sudden heart attack. At times Josh fantasized about moving to the suburbs and adopting a child, though the truth of it was he knew he could not go about it alone—he barely remembered to feed the fish he kept in an aquarium in his bedroom. Though Josh's sexual enthusiasm for random encounters with other gay men had diminished in the last couple of years, he had not stopped fantasizing about finding a good gay man who would want to settle down. In fact, in his mind, he carried on many affairs with a variety of men he would not have embarked on one with in reality.

Adam's affairs had always been discrete. In the army he had accepted an occasional blow job from another man, though he had not reciprocated the act until his service ended and he was married and living in Virginia. On out-of-town business trips, he had been able to go to a gay bar and find a guy to take back to his hotel room, though he never wanted or expected anything further from another man as far as a relationship or a commitment were concerned. Once, though, he flew to Orlando to meet a guy he had met in Atlanta, thinking a second time together might lead to other occasional trips of the same sort. Adam had never imagined leaving his wife, but as they both grew older their interests and outlooks differed—his wife had become devoutly religious and narrow-minded, whereas Adam fought off gaining

Desire, Lust, Passion, Sex

weight and tried to find more ways to seem enlightened, and he found his attraction to women waning and his desire to be in the company of men growing bolder. Adam never admitted it could be a distinctly gay change-of-life thing that was happening to him; rather, he felt he was an aging man attracted to the beauty of youth, and nothing was more hypnotic or alluring than being in the presence of a younger, gay man.

AIDS had taken a hard toll on Josh's generation. Josh had lost over a dozen close friends; his rolodex was filled with one-night, one-named men he was certain were no longer around. In the early years of the epidemic—before his mother's death but after his father's stroke—Josh had nursed Tom, his lover of three years, through his final months. Adam had not escaped the swath of the epidemic, either—a former army buddy had died early on in the epidemic and Adam had tested frequently to make sure he remained negative. Josh considered himself lucky to have remained negative throughout his party years. But this fact also came at a hard-earned price: Josh could not shed his guilt for surviving when others had not.

When Adam first imagined approaching Josh, he read Josh's employee file first. He found nothing to discourage him from continuing, though he knew he was incapable of making the first move. He was not about to "come out" at the office; for one thing, he was not exactly sure he wanted to give up sleeping with women, if, for example, he met someone he was attracted to or who could offer the right kind of distraction. Second, and more important, Adam would not risk jeopardizing his career. At stake were his seniority, his pension, his health benefits and all the money he owed his ex-wife; a potential sexual harassment suit could topple that, send his carefully constructed house of business cards tumbling to the ground. All he wanted was to find something to ease the loneliness his personal life had settled into; someone to hang out with, have sex with occasionally; someone without any demands or needs or complications. He put the idea of Josh out of his mind, even though he found his employee attractive and desirable. It was simply not the right thing to do. D.C. was full of other gay men. He didn't need to court this kind of trouble.

✣✣✣

It began with a recommendation. At a departmental lunch—another innovation of Adam's—he asked Josh for restaurant recommendations in his neighborhood. Josh thought nothing of Adam knowing the whereabouts of his apartment—employee home addresses were not a secret and were distributed freely amongst members of the department. Josh rattled off the names of some restaurants, mentioning a few that were more popular with gay men, but naming some other places where a mixed crowd was also comfortable. Josh assumed that Adam wanted the second kind of restaurant, someplace where he could take someone who was not gay. Adam mentioned that he had an army buddy coming in from California who was look-ing for possible apartments in that area, and they would proba-bly want to eat dinner in Josh's neighborhood.

On Saturday, after apartment hunting, Adam took Mark, his army buddy, to one of the restaurants Josh had suggested, one of the "gayer" places. As it happened, Josh was also dining there that night with Ricky, his workout buddy from the gym. Ricky was barely thirty years old, style conscious and flamboyant to an extreme that Josh was not. As Josh and Ricky were leaving the restaurant—they were on their way to see a movie—Josh spot-ted Adam and Mark. It was impossible not to say hello—their path to the door passed directly by Adam's table. There was a brief exchange between Adam and Josh, handshake introduc-tions between all the men, and then Josh and Ricky were quickly on their way out, worried about making the movie in time. Josh did not think it was strange to have found Adam eating at the restaurant; he had recommended it to Adam, after all. Adam thought Ricky might be Josh's current boyfriend or an ex-lover. Ricky articulated exactly what was on Josh's mind. "That guy is hot!" Ricky said. He was talking about Mark.

Mark was six-two, muscular, square-jawed, and blue-eyed. He was thirty-eight and hid the thinning of his blond hair by wearing it in a buzz cut; his pale complexion and low body fat made everything about him look exaggerated, from the small character lines at the sides of his eyes to the pulpy veins and muscles of his forearms and biceps. In the army, Mark had trained in surveillance. During his station in Germany, he had gotten a tattoo on his left chest; last year he added a chain design around his bicep, which always seemed to peek its way out from underneath whatever short-sleeved shirt he was wearing. After the army Mark stayed in California, his last station, and worked as a bartender before taking a job with a photo imaging lab where he could use the skills he had developed while in the military. Mark had dismissed the suggestion he got from many guys that he should become an actor or a stuntman—he was smart enough to know that he'd be no good at either one, but he did want to have a good lifestyle, so when a better-paying position opened up at another company—one where he could travel inspecting and developing new equipment, he jumped at the opportunity for bigger bucks and more responsibility. Mark's sexuality had always traveled on the edges of his actual proclamation of it; he hung out in adult bookshops or hooked up with an army buddy in the back room of a bar. The anonymity of the Internet had helped him progress to one-on-one hookups and private sex parties. What he had grown to like as an aspect of his sexual adventuring was the volcanic necessity of it—the spontaneous eruption of desire when he was with a guy for the first time. Mark seldom found a second time with a guy as exciting or fulfilling, and the truth of it was, he wasn't searching for a partner, a soul mate, a lover or a boyfriend. He got along just fine on his own.

Ricky was boyish-looking—dark-haired and wide-eyed, barely five-eight when he was wearing sneakers. He had a drop-dead gorgeous body, though many guys avoided him because he had a tendency to be too loud and too curious; Ricky was known for his sharp tongue and sharper eyes. He had grown up in the Maryland suburbs, though he had always considered himself more a Southern belle than a Yankee. At fifteen, he was hitchhiking his way downtown to meet guys. By the time Ricky moved into his Dupont Circle apartment after four stoned-out years at the University of Maryland, he had accumulated a small covey of friends with whom he'd either slept or shared drugs. Most of his little clique were now concerned with money or living well or the shape of their careers. Ricky's boast was that he was best the fuck in town, and Josh thought he probably was. Josh had had a terrific time when he slept with Ricky a few years ago, but neither one of them had wanted it to happen another time. Ricky was a party boy; he went through guys the way he took drugs, whatever was offered to him or available for the night. Ricky had cobbled together a variety of jobs for spending money—sometimes working as a personal trainer or a cater-waiter, or tricking for bucks with a closeted Congressman or lobbyist or someone who was "just in town" for something or other and needed some company. Ricky's diversified professions often left him missing for days on end; but Josh was always grateful whenever Ricky emerged and wanted to get together to do something or work out at the gym. Josh liked being with Ricky because Ricky kept Josh feeling connected and more gay than not. Ricky was usually a good-time sort of guy, even out of bed.

On Tuesday, when Adam and Josh met for their weekly meeting, there was a brief exchange about the restaurant and Mark's apartment hunting. Adam asked if Josh could recommend a good gym for Mark. Adam had taken Mark to the health club in his apartment building and it hadn't passed muster. "Not enough free weights," Adam said. "He doesn't like relying on all those machines."

Josh told Adam that his gym had a good selection of free weights and equipment that Mark would probably like. Josh wrote the name of his gym on a slip of paper for Adam. Josh wanted to know more about Mark, though he did not feel comfortable asking Adam. No mention was made of Ricky or the movie, nor were any more details of Mark provided.

Two months later they met at the gym. Josh was working out and noticed Mark, but couldn't place where he had met him before. Ricky was home sick with a cold, or so he said; for all Josh knew, Ricky could be drugged and tied up in a Congressman's apartment, earning a few extra bucks.

Mark noticed Josh and remembered meeting him at the restaurant. They shook hands and reintroduced themselves. Mark told Josh about the apartment he had found and asked about shops in the neighborhood—what store had the best take-out meals (Mark didn't like to cook on weekdays) and what pharmacies stayed opened late (Mark was an insomniac). Mark had no doubt that he would have sex with Josh, maybe that night, maybe another time. He could always tell when a guy was interested in him. Josh had time to consider the pos- sibility of sleeping with Mark during his workout; as he worked on his upper body (cable crossovers, lateral raises, bench presses), Josh thought about the easiest ways of asking Mark out without pushing it into looking like a real date, per- haps suggesting that they could go see a movie or have din- ner one night after the gym—something to get to know Mark better, make sure he was into guys, into wanting to date a man. At the back of Josh's mind was the fact that Mark was friends with Adam, and Adam wasn't gay, was he? There was nothing to confirm Mark's sexuality except the blatant chemical reaction Josh felt when they talked.

They finished their workouts at roughly the same time, though Josh did not notice Mark in the locker room and thought he must have left to shower at his apartment. When Josh walked into the lobby of the club, Mark was talking to the guy behind the reception desk. Their eyes met and Mark said to Josh, "Which way you walking? I'm going toward P Street."

They walked together in the direction of Josh's apartment, past the bookstore and the bagel shop and a couple of bars. The humidity was low and the traffic was light, and it gave the evening a distinct, easy quality. They talked some about the gym in short, brief grunts, their eyes flitting out toward the men they passed, measuring them up against themselves and each other. Mark said he liked the club's pool—it was at least long enough to do a good set of laps. Josh said he liked the new elliptical machines the club had recently purchased; he had stopped jogging last year because of continual leg pains.

They came to Mark's building first. Mark said, "Come up and see the apartment I found. It's got a great view."

Josh felt comfortable enough to respond, "Sure," thinking this was a way of getting closer to Mark and knowing him better.

Inside the door of his apartment, Mark made the first move. Mark always made the first move with a guy because he seldom found himself rejected. He clasped a hand at the back of Josh's neck and drew him into a kiss. Mark made the next move as well, pulling Josh closer and unraveling the ends of his shirt from his jeans. Josh did not resist, in spite of the suddenness. He was consumed by a raw attraction toward Mark, a desire to feel and taste and possess Mark's body. His hands found their way beneath Mark's shirt, then the shirt was off, and they stood rubbing their hands across each other's chest, as if warming themselves on a cold night. Mark stopped them, walked Josh through the room and into the next one, where there was a bed and a chair and a view of the city.

Josh did not look at the view. Mark again made the next move, pushing Josh into the bed and unbuckling his jeans. There was no negotiation, no questions about who would do what to whom. Their bodies collided, their mouths moved over chests and arms and legs and cocks. Their skins, used to sweating at the gym only minutes before, began to perspire again. Josh wrestled Mark down to the bed and they laughed and smiled, but Mark turned the tables, pinned Josh to the mattress, then lifted Josh's legs up to Mark's shoulders and slicked his ass with spit and lube.

Walking home, Josh tried to rationalize his behavior. It had been a long time since he had felt that spontaneously attracted to a man, but he had let Mark fuck him without using a condom, something he seldom let happen with a guy. He tried to find the moment he had allowed that to occur, the silent negotiation with Mark that it was all right for Mark to proceed bareback. It had happened so swiftly, so aggressively, so passionately that all Josh wanted was to feel Mark inside him. Had he considered suggesting a condom and rejected the idea even before it had happened? And why was he so concerned now, after the fact? They were both grown-ups. Adults who led worried and complicated lives. They knew the rules, the consequences of unprotected sex, the things that could happen when things happened this way.

✶✶✶✶✶✶

Adam and Mark were not army buddies; after all, there was several years' difference between them. Adam didn't like to acknowledge that Mark's friendship had begun at an adult bookstore in Houston. Adam had been attending a business conference; Mark had been on an assignment to analyze equipment being purchased as his company began its national expansion. Adam was something of a shy exhibitionist; he had the kind of a cock that some men proudly brag about (long, but not too long, and wider than you could believe it could be), though he was reluctant to show it off in a public way, preferring, instead, for it to be discovered like an extra bonus. Adam had even had his dick photographed, once paying a guy to take a picture of it. His wife had found the photo, tucked away in a drawer, and wanted explanations. Adam's account had not been too convincing, but it did something Adam had been trying to do in other ways for months: create the fissure in his marriage which would break further apart into a divorce.

Mark liked his guys to look like real guys. He considered himself to be a man's man; he liked the adventure of rock climbing and bungee jumping. His dislikes included cologne, drama queens, and shaved chests (but not shaved heads). Sexually, he could be as nasty as a guy wanted; he had no problem with barebacking, always pulling out before he came. His on-line profile read: No Stupid Questions. Stalkers or Fems need not apply—though he was often not as choosy as he sounded; many times Mark had landed in bed with a campy circuit boy and had had a better time than he expected. Mark had struck up a conversation with Adam over a rack of magazines, asking Adam if he knew of any sex clubs in the area (a standard pickup line for Mark—he was usually happy to hook up with whomever caught his attention in a store or whatever place they might end up in). Adam did not know where to go and was not comfortable with pursuing the suggestion of a sex club, but before he gave up on his own hope of hooking up with Mark, he offered to buy him a drink—back in his hotel room.

Mark accepted and Adam did not disappoint him; the size of Adam's cock played a major factor in Mark remembering him when his company sent him to Washington, again to analyze more equipment. A few months later Mark accepted his company's offer of a transfer to Washington because it made sense at the time; as they were expanding on the East Coast, Mark needed a new home base. And Mark was glad he had a buddy like Adam he could call on, someone serious and direct and not caught up in crap.

Josh called Mark to get together again. He had thought the chemistry was there for another time and he wanted to be certain he had not let down his guard for the wrong reason. Mark was not home when Josh left his message on the answering machine and listening to it the next day, Mark did not feel an immediate urge to respond. Josh was just another guy to him, a good time in bed, someone he might call on a rainy night to come over or to have a regular ongoing chat with at the gym. He didn't want a date with Josh. Or want him as a boyfriend. He was not really the sort of guy he even wanted as a friend. (He preferred a buddy like Adam—undemanding, out of sight, though always around for advice or willing to help out in a pinch.) And Josh had not left Mark a specific invitation to respond to—not a "Let's go to a concert on Tuesday night," or "How about a movie on Saturday?" The vagueness of Josh's message translated into Mark's disregard of it.

Josh patiently waited a day for Mark's response; then, he spent the next day hourly checking his home answering machine for messages. Josh's composure began to crumble. At first, he was worried that Mark was not calling him back because of his work relationship with Adam, even though Adam had not been mentioned beyond their initial handshake and introductory remarks at the gym. Mark did not seem the type of guy to Josh who would kiss and tell—and if so, what would be so embarrassing about what had happened?—that he had found Adam's friend hot and slept with him?

But the deeper conflict in Josh's mind was the issue of unsafe sex. It wasn't that Josh hadn't let it happen before, but when he did, it was usually after the third or fourth date with a guy and Josh always knew that his partner was negative. As he waited for Mark to call, Josh felt more used and abused. The order and routine of Josh's life seemed to falter: he skipped meeting Ricky at the gym, missed his volunteer night for HRC, and canceled his weekly meeting with Adam. At the back of Josh's mind was the fact that he had hoped he had reached the age where he could be considered more than just a trick—someone of intelligence and substance and values and worth—but that was exactly how he had treated Mark himself, hadn't he?—a quick fuck after the gym. Why should Josh expect to have been treated differently himself? They hadn't even had a conversation as Josh got dressed and left Mark's apartment. Josh had been as silent as Mark had, or was he already stunned by what he had allowed to happen and unable to articulate his emotions?

Josh did not confide in Ricky that he had slept with Mark, though they talked about sex the next time they got together for dinner after working out at the gym. Josh asked Ricky how safe he was with guys. Ricky, a bit surprised by the question, sighed and said, "Not as safe as I should be." Ricky explained that fewer and fewer guys wanted to use a condom, except for the closeted Republicans he slept with, who were all worried about passing something on to their wives.

"Hygiene is an occupational hazard," Ricky said. "Republicans included. I've had genital warts, amoebas, and urethritis—all within the last two years. Remember that cold I said I had? Well, that was no cold. It was lice. Some guy gave me head lice! And then said he got it from his kid!"

Josh left another message for Mark and waited another three days; when no response came, he turned to the Internet.

Desire, Lust, Passion, Sex

First, Josh did a Web search on Mark, then on his company. Then he did something unprofessional; at work, he ran background checks on Mark's credit, health, and employment history. Josh did not uncover anything that disturbed him, but even with this information, his hurt was not eased. He had hoped that by giving in to such a strong, emotional flash of lust he would have reaped a more profound benefit. Instead, he felt like a teenager again, spurned by the Big Man on Campus.

※※※※

Adam had found his best solution for meeting a guy for sex was through the Internet. After work, at home in his apartment, he would log on to his computer and enter chat rooms. He would talk dirty, or talk romantic (depending on his mood), sometimes sending out the picture of his cock. Adam was surprised that there were so many lonely men out there in Powertown; he'd always regarded D.C. as a city of fetishes and scandals, not as a series of desperate executives in hotel rooms, eager bureaucrats in bad marriages, or horny interns just back from the gym and hungry for someone new.

Ricky did not depersonalize sex; for him, it was a theatrical experience. With one man (a well-known comedian in town for a benefit), Ricky pretended to be a Czech immigrant looking for work as a handyman. He had the choppy diction and dropped vowels down perfectly, and by dropping his jaw slightly he could maintain a pouty and needy look. Ricky was also able to pull off a bisexual Brazilian and a Swiss airline steward. On-line he went by the profiles TuffButt, Studmuffin, or BttmBoi, which was the name under which he chatted one night with Adam. Adam lured him in by typing: "Enough inches to open your eyes and make you want to spread your thighs."

"We've met before somewhere," Adam said when Ricky arrived at his apartment. Adam could not immediately place where he knew Ricky from; Ricky had slicked his hair back and affected a deep Southern accent, pretending he was an all-American boy just in town from Alabama. Ricky knew at once he was going to sleep with Josh's boss. The moment, a few minutes later, when Ricky saw the size of Adam's dick, his first thought was: *Does Josh know about this? And if he does, why has he kept it a secret from me?*

Ricky did not explain how he knew Adam or reveal his own disguise. Instead, he immediately set about satisfying Adam as he had promised on-line. Adam, his heart pounding, his body sweating, was not disappointed. Adam saw right through Ricky's masquerade, but he asked Ricky to stay for dinner, asked him to come back again the following night, and then asked him out on a date. By the end of their first week, Adam felt he had found someone special: Ricky made Adam laugh, something few people had been able to do.

Ricky, too, felt something with Adam that he had not felt with other men. Adam was not needy or codependent; he didn't need to be flattered or coaxed into offering compliments, and wasn't jealous when Ricky mentioned and described his other sexual hook-ups. In fact, Adam loved knowing the details of what Ricky did in bed with other men. Adam did not shy away from talking about politics or religion, topics about which Ricky had strong opinions and which made him feel closer to Adam. (Ricky: "I could never walk into a church and pray, not after what they say about us." Adam: "The problem is with religion, not with faith.") Adam was also terrific at analyzing human behavior; he could reduce Ricky's tricks to just a few words: "So he was a tourist in town for a quick fuck," or, "It sounds to me like he was using you to get over another guy."

They began seeing each other twice a week, then Ricky began spending weekends at Adam's apartment. Ricky began to soften his party habits and lessen his extracurricular lifestyle; he turned down a request for a repeat performance from a Canadian lobbyist, ignored the request of a Congressman's aide looking to score some drugs for the weekend, and stayed in town instead of traveling with friends to a party in Manhattan. He cooked meals for Adam. They watched videos together. Ricky spent the night with Adam's arms wrapped around his waist, but he did so only with the knowledge that Adam knew he was not giving up seeing other men. "I've got expenses," Ricky said. "And a lifestyle to maintain." Once, Adam offered Ricky money. Ricky refused. "Nope," he said. "I don't want you to be one of those."

Sometime during their second month seeing each other, Adam remembered Ricky's connection to Josh. Adam did not confront Ricky on the issue, nor did he even bring up the fact that he had remembered it. Gossip is just gossip, Adam thought, even if word of this gets back to Josh—or had already gotten back to Josh, why should it matter? This affair had nothing to do with their workplace, their job performance. Adam was also certain that Josh would treat the news of it discreetly—Josh was not a troublemaker at work, why would he blabber this news now? Adam imagined Ricky and Josh sitting together at dinner at the restaurant where Adam first saw them together. "Guess what," Ricky would probably begin, arching his eyebrows and ready to reveal a secret. "Your boss has the thickest dick in town."

Which was exactly how it had happened.

$\wedge\!\wedge\!\wedge\!\wedge\!\wedge$

They were all Democrats by regards, if not by registration, concerned about discrimination and a balanced budget, affordable health insurance and civil rights. Josh went to the fund-raiser with Lisa, a friend from work who was a campaign volunteer and had asked him to attend. Adam was sent a personal invitation since he was a large contributor to the party.

Mark went because the Republicans were stalling a bill which would allow the private sector access to technology and equipment the military had developed. Ricky had not known that Adam would be there; he went as a guest of a Senator's intern, knowing there would be free food and drinks and plenty of single men to look at.

The fund-raiser was held in the lobby of a federal building; more than five hundred people were expected to attend. A local string quartet had been hired to perform for the occasion; some guests had arrived in black tie, attending the cocktail reception before a later event that would be held at the Kennedy Center. Ricky spotted Mark first, talking to a young blond man with a dark goatee. Ricky remembered immediately who Mark was and where he had seen him before. Ricky dismissed his first impulse to attempt to snare Mark for sex— there was Adam to think about, after all, and weren't Adam and Mark friends? Then, the more Ricky watched Mark, the more he regarded Mark's straight, proud posture, the long legs and flat waist and wide back and shoulders, the more Ricky reconsidered seducing this man, stealing him right out from under the blond-with-a-bad-goatee's nose.

Lisa noticed Adam before Josh did, talking to a lawyer who also worked at their firm. She led the two of them across the lobby and the reception, interrupting Adam and the lawyer to discuss a discrimination lawsuit filed by an ex-employee. Josh was in no mood to talk about business, uncomfortable with finding himself in a social situation with his boss. It wasn't that he disliked Adam; no, he now knew too much about him. He had accepted the news about his boss's sexuality and his affair with Ricky with quiet disbelief, but Ricky had not eased up on any of his details, describing each encounter with such a passion it sounded like a porn clip. Josh now preferred to keep his weekly meetings in Adam's office as brief as possible, positioning himself in such a way that their eyes did not have to meet. Josh stood beside Lisa and angled himself so that he could look away from the group, glancing out at the reception yet still pretending he was participating in Lisa's conversation, which was how he spotted Mark talking to a younger, blond-haired man with a goatee. Josh considered excusing himself and walking across the room to say hello to Mark; it had been five months since they had slept together, long enough time to pretend all wounds had been healed and the scars had turned into tougher skin. But then Josh saw Ricky approach Mark with a bounce in his step and the two men shake hands, the young, blond-haired man leaning in toward Ricky as if to catch the pronunciation of his name. Josh wondered if Ricky had slept with Mark, too, and if he had been lucky enough to get a second time or at least a call back. Of course Ricky would have a second chance, Josh thought, and found himself irritated and annoyed. Josh repositioned himself within his own small group, standing on the other side of Lisa so he would not have to witness Ricky and Mark talking to each other, which is how Adam shifted his stance and spotted Ricky on the other side of the room.

It took Adam a few seconds to realize that Ricky was talking to Mark, but he tried to keep his surprise and displeasure at this from being detected in his expression. Adam had not spoken to Mark in close to two months; Mark never called Adam unless he needed something—a recommendation for a physician or a dentist or a specific sort of store: "Where can I find a decent pair of hiking boots?" or "Where can I take my Jeep in for service?"—a habitual trait of Mark's which had come to annoy Adam. Adam had also not cared enough to keep in contact with Mark once Ricky became so entrenched in his after-work life. Watching the two of them across the room, Adam knew Ricky was putting the moves on Mark. Adam had seen all of Ricky's sexual personas; he understood Ricky's body language—the nervous ticks, the pouty lips, the flutter of his hands, as if he were trying to find the correct English word or pronunciation for something he wanted to say, using the stumbling speech to reach out and touch Mark's forearm or shoulder or chest. Adam knew he couldn't walk over to them and raise a stink; it was too risky, too public a place to create a scene without revealing too much of his private life. And how could he protest? How could he listen to Ricky's sexual conquests and deny him the opportunity of sleeping with Mark? Ricky would certainly label him a hypocrite. Adam imagined Ricky snapping his fingers in the air, a quick "like that" and turning on his toes, prancing out of the room in an overdramatic huff and ending their affair. Now, Adam realized he was more fond of Ricky than he had led himself to believe. Adam was not a man used to being denied what he wanted or had worked to achieve and he stood there, listening to Lisa's opinion on his firm's hiring freeze, the reception moving at a dizzying pace around him, and all at once felt defeated, jealous, and bitter.

Josh noticed Adam's behavior change: the complexion become pale, the eyes glaze over, the beads of sweat form above his lip and at his temples. The always composed, in-command ex-military man seemed to crumble before him. Slowly, Josh became aware of what was happening; Ricky's gossip and behavior was not forgotten chatter. What was Ricky doing with Mark if he was trying to keep something going with Adam? Josh considered sparing his boss from embarrassment and stopping his friend from making a mistake, walking over and interrupting Mark and Ricky's conversation and breaking things up with his presence, but he didn't. He stayed where he was. He wanted no part of this complication. Neither did Adam, for that matter; he excused himself, walked across the room to the bartender, and asked for a drink.

Desire, Lust, Passion, Sex

Adam remained out of sight, feeling like a fool, continuing to watch Ricky and Mark, glaring at them from behind a column and clusters of couples. How could he have become so careless with his affections? How could he have fallen so hard and so quickly for Ricky? Adam didn't find Ricky so funny now. This was nothing to laugh about. In fact, it felt strange to him to be this emotional; after all, he had been trained to be detached. When the speeches and presentations began, Adam rejoined Lisa and Josh and the company's lawyer and watched Ricky and Mark slip out of the lobby together. It was another crushing blow to Adam—yes, they were hooking up, there was no doubt in his mind now—Ricky would entertain Mark the way he had entertained Adam. Adam knew there would be no going back for the two of them now. Adam could not forgive Ricky even if Ricky hadn't known Adam was at the fund-raiser too. So Adam turned to Josh and Lisa and said, "This is getting quite dull. Let's go for a drink."

Across the street, in a small and dark bar, Lisa's presence kept the topic of Mark and Ricky out of the conversation. Josh did not feel sorry for Adam; Josh was too self-absorbed over his own misery about Mark and a lifetime of other unfortunate romances with men to be that considerate of Adam—instead, Josh quietly imagined Mark and Ricky becoming the kind of lovers he thought he might have become with Mark, which caused him to become sullen and depressed. Lisa, unaware of the psychological torture she had stumbled upon, excused herself after the first round of drinks. "I've got to drive home," she said. "I've got a three-year-old waiting for me."

Alone together, Adam and Josh continued to avoid the topic of Mark. And Ricky. They talked about work. (Josh: "Do you think the firm will relocate outside the Beltway?" Adam: "No, not yet, not enough tax incentives." Adam: "What is the sentiment in the office about the new dental plan?" Josh: "It should have been included years ago.") Then,

they recapped recent movies they had seen. (Josh, on a
Hollywood blockbuster: "It was too predictable." Adam, on
a thriller: "Too much blood spoils the effect.") Throughout
this, their thoughts had not left the events of the fund-
raiser. As Adam drank more and more he made a few
derogatory remarks about his wife, though his mood light-
ened a bit when Josh pressed him into talking about his
daughter and her new marriage.

After the third round of drinks they decided to call it
quits. Outside on the sidewalk, Adam realized he was too
drunk to walk back to his apartment and he clutched Josh's
arm and politely said, "Could you get us a cab? I've had a bit
more than I should."

Josh told the cab driver to make one stop: Adam's building. Josh felt certain he would be sober enough to walk home
from there; it was only a few blocks and the fresh air and
exercise would do his own sour mood good. At Adam's
apartment, after Adam had given Josh money for the cab,
Adam again clutched Josh's arm. "Don't go just yet," Adam
said. "Come up for a nightcap. I could use the company."

Josh knew he should decline, knew it was the proper and
businesslike thing to do. But at the back of his mind now was
Ricky's comment about Adam's dick, "as wide as a man's fist,"
haunting his tipsy curiosity. It wasn't that he expected Adam
to show him the goods and deliver them right then and
there; no, Josh's imagination was a much slower and romantic
one. Inebriated too, Josh momentarily considered Adam as a
potential boyfriend and a possible long-term relationship, and
the thought of stumbling on to such luck (and in Ricky's mis-
steps) made him suddenly happy and hopeful.

Upstairs in Adam's apartment, Adam showed Josh the view
from his balcony and fixed them both another round of drinks,
Josh's whiskey sour becoming more whiskey than mix. Adam
opened a bottle of wine and poured himself a glass. He turned

on the TV and left Josh alone for a few minutes while he went to wash his face and take a piss. In the bathroom mirror, Adam looked at himself and saw a man who was unhappy and aging too fast. Ricky was lost to him and Adam felt betrayed, but he didn't consider seducing Josh as a method of revenge. No, Josh had always been someone he wanted to know better. Josh was the better catch, wasn't he? The kind of guy who could be involved. The kind of man Adam wanted to know, now that he had gotten to know someone like Ricky better. Josh was a keeper, the kind of guy who would stick around.

Adam offered Josh another drink, even though he had not finished the one he had started. Josh declined, and stood up from the couch where he had been sitting and said, with a wobbly sort of indecisiveness, "I should be going. It's late."

Adam answered, "No, don't go," and he took a few steps toward Josh and placed his arms against the younger man's shoulders. Josh responded by closing his eyes and titling his head, as if he wanted to be kissed, which was how it began between them.

※※※※

The light in the bedroom was low enough for Adam to convince himself he did not know who he was with. Sobriety drifted up into his throat as he moved his fingers through Josh's hair, his hands grasping at the firmness of Josh's neck, then moving slower, lower, to the wide clutch of muscles at Josh's shoulders, delts, and triceps. Adam wanted to stop Josh and ask him how he kept in such good shape; Adam's own body had fallen apart when he was forty-four—first, the knees, then his teeth and eyes and waist. Adam realized his thoughts had canceled out Josh's anonymity and desire flushed through his chest like a deep breath of air.

Josh kept his awe in check, his hand wet and slick, stroking

Adam's cock. Even as he moved against Adam with hands and lips and tongue he felt flashes of regret, wondering: Should I be doing this? Is this the right thing to do? This is the man I work for, see every day at my job. But in every conflict he also felt advantage: the luck to be alive, to still find passion with a man, to grasp something like this in his fist—after all these years and with all these men—and still be amazed.

Above him, Adam felt embarrassed and old and over-weight and sad, even though his cock was firm and eager and youthful, enjoying Josh's attention. Regret moved into him and he thought about stopping them, though he knew they had already passed the point of no return. With most men Adam was usually the aggressor in bed, not content with simply lying back and letting himself be serviced or exploited. But he could not find that power now with Josh and he realized it was fear that kept him pinned in place. Fear of what Josh thought of him, fear that his whole life and career and personality would be reduced to a crude phrase such as "hung like a horse."

Josh worried that he was being too passive; through his mind flashed the thought: What if Adam tells Ricky I was bor-ing in bed? Or worse, what if he tells Mark in their next con-versation: "I understand why you never called him back." Josh knew he could not accommodate Adam's width in the way Ricky had, so he became more aggressive, cupping his hands around Adam's balls, squeezing and kneading and twisting them before slipping them into his mouth. He slipped a wet finger into Adam's ass, let it stay there for a moment, then moved in another finger. Adam's legs shifted on the mattress, lifted and bent as they moved further apart. Josh watched Adam's stom-ach lift and heave with a sigh and then the air work its way out of his chest. Adam reached down and stopped Josh's fingers, broke away from him and rolled over on the mattress so that he could reach the night stand beside the bed.

Josh followed Adam's body across the bed and he paused

above him as Adam rolled a condom over Josh's cock and wet it with lube. Josh could not see Adam's expression in the darkness, though his words, "Go ahead," landed deeply against his chest.

There was a moment of irony as Josh felt himself inside Adam's body, the phrase, "fucking your boss over" whimsically playing in his head. Josh felt the thought move from his forehead and break out into a smile on his face. The smile caught Adam's eyes, even in the dark, and Adam grinned, aware of what his partner was thinking. Adam leaned his head back and closed his eyes. Josh was nimble enough to curve his body and take Adam's cock into his mouth at the same time he was fucking him and this was what finally captured Adam's passion. Adam opened his eyes, his mouth, his body, his heart. He felt both attached and in pieces. He was empty and full.

ʌᴡᴡᴛ̇ʌ

Josh did not spend the night at Adam's and Adam did not ask him to stay over. Adam was out sick the next day, something he seldom allowed to happen, though Josh showed up with a hangover and stayed at his desk throughout the day, not even venturing to the cafeteria for lunch. Adam avoided Ricky's phone calls for almost a week, until he finally responded by e-mail, saying, "We should spend some time apart."

They stayed apart for another week, then another month, and then another month. Mark saw Ricky twice more—Ricky had lived up to his promise (and then some) the night they met at the fund-raiser and the next two times together Ricky had dropped the foreign ruse and showed up with an arsenal of toys to keep Mark entertained. Mark had enjoyed Ricky every time they were together in bed, but he was not the kind of guy he felt comfortable with as a friend— too campy, too loud, too outrageous and flamboyant.

Grown-ups

Ricky complained to Josh when Mark had not called him back after almost a week apart, but he got little sympathy from Josh, so he kept quiet about Adam, although that silence had hurt him more deeply. Ricky didn't understand why Adam had given up on him, why the older man had pushed him away after their becoming so intimate. And so he came to regard Adam as just another man with hang-ups, too mature and predictable to see his way beyond them.

More time passed and Ricky created four new screen names and as many personas. He entertained a Dutch sailor, a Texan rancher, and a diplomat from South Africa, but was sidelined by syphilis for longer than he expected. Mark seroconverted after a busy period at a private sex club. He took the news in stride, had his left forearm tattooed and his nipples pierced, and moved back to California when his company filed for bankruptcy protection.

Ricky and Mark never knew that Josh and Adam had got it on with each other. Josh and Adam never spoke of that night, either, in fact. Both kept it under wraps, out of their daily lives and away from their business careers. Josh was officially promoted to department head four months later, something he'd always thought Adam had a hand in (and which he did). A few years later Josh met a man at his gym and found himself unexpectedly in a relationship. Adam never came out on the job and stayed at the company till his second grandchild was born and then retired early. The last Josh heard from him, Adam had moved to Virginia Beach and had finally found a steady boyfriend—thirty years younger and nothing but trouble.

The Man
of My Dreams

The man of my dreams is a man I've never met, though I've studied his photographs in magazines and on the Internet and watched most of the videos he has made for a film company that specializes in hard-core pornography made to look like soft-core erotica. I won't reveal his true name, not that I know it, of course, but I won't reveal the name under which he performs and is photographed either, because if I were to do so, I fear my fascination with him would only lump me in with everyone else on the planet who lusts after him. I'll call him Carl for the sake of personifying him, to make him into something more than just a beautiful one-dimensional image. He resembles a lumberjack or cowboy in some of his photographs, or, rather, a lumberjack or cowboy as portrayed by an all-American pro halfback turned Hollywood actor: rugged, masculine, stereotypically handsome. He's far from stereotypical, however. His body is hairy, exquisitely so—to an extreme that is unbelievably magnetic to those who, like myself, are rendered dizzy by that quality. On his chest is a mass of thick chestnut fur. He sports a California tan, brown and buttery, and when he flexes his arms there is a faint ring of lighter skin beneath the joints of his shoulders—right before the skin disappears into the dark, straight thicket of hair under his arms.

Carl straddles two fantasy categories in which I've

searched high and low these last twenty years to find the ideal boyfriend—bodybuilder and bear. One resume I have uncovered for Carl lists him as a former Mr. Arizona title holder; another Web site reveals him with his impressive physique shaved and hairless except for a mustache and a beautiful helmet of slicked back black hair. (I must confess that as magnificent as it is, I have internally fought and fought with this second, hairless image of his body until I've transformed it into one belonging to someone else, someone who is not the beefy, hairy, mesmerizing Carl that I have come to love, but another Carl—a Karl, for instance. Karl in all his perfection seems so distant and godlike all oiled and muscled up, whereas Carl is burly and smiling and friendly, like a puppy you can't avoid wanting to pet and make your favored companion.)

My favorite photo of Carl is the one where he's tipping a creamy white Panama hat to the camera as if someone just off to the side of the photographer's lens were the object of his affection. He has no clothes on at all except for the hat. His eyes are large, liquid-black orbs, but his smile is bright and inviting, his head pitching back to laugh, dimples high and firm in his stubbly cheeks. His biceps peak in beautiful melon-like shapes as he reaches toward the hat and his shoulders taper to a washboard stomach covered by the brown velour of his body hair. His cock, long and weighty and semierect, hangs between legs so thick and well defined, the striations of muscle and hair resemble the bark of tree trunks. I have often imagined what it would be like if Carl were really my boyfriend, how I would bury my face in the mass of his chest hair as his arms enclosed me, my tongue swirling around his nipples, my fingers combing the dark, silky hair beneath his arms.

Tonight, I've pulled up a Web page that someone else has created as a shrine to Carl and I click on the small thumbnail prints and wait until the magic Pentium chip inside my computer translates them into larger images for me to study more closely on the monitor. I've poured myself a glass of wine and as I run down the photos one by one, I take a sip and then play with my cock, slipping it outside the fly of the plaid boxer shorts I am wearing, feeling it grow harder the harder I study Carl. Here's a man who would make me keep at it, I tell myself, a reason not to give up on wanting men.

The shameless truth is I've gotten myself in more emotional messes with men of Carl's type than any normal gay man should in one lifetime. This week alone I've broken up with a boyfriend of three years, had two blind dates, and met with another man via a chat room on the pretense that he was just going to give me a massage. If the truth be known, I'm disgusted with men: the massage easily turned into a session during which my asshole was oiled and kneaded more than any other body part, and the fat, stubby dick of the beefy masseur left my prostate so banged up that for two days afterwards I felt a constant desire to urinate. Each time I stood in front of the toilet waiting for my insides to sort themselves out I whacked my fist against the bathroom wall and cursed my unruly libido, vowing to curb it with a system of checks more rigorous than something NASA could devise. Why is it I can let a man so freely abuse me? Was this what I really needed? Was this what I wanted from a man? Every time I waited and waited for even a trickle of piss to form at the end of my cock, I told myself I was giving up men once and for all; this was the last straw. I didn't need all this physical pain and mental torment. But why was it that every man I met only wanted sex from me? And why was it I always believed that sex was the easiest path to love?

Now, sitting in front of my computer and stroking my cock, I realize I don't really want to be in love with Carl, only to make love to him, my erotic compass repaired and pointing full tilt toward the thought of engulfing his fleshy cock, slick and hard, within my bowels. Yet I know I would not like the person I would be if Carl were to say he loved me. Why is it that I have no strength or intelligence around men I find attractive? And why, just when I have vowed to chuck it all in, does my desire rejuvenate itself with a hard, greedy dick?

Tonight the wine has made me light-headed and Carl has made me more reflective than usual. As I think back, I notice that men with hairy chests or big arms have always been my undoing. Something about Carl—the stubble, the liquid eyes, the square jaw—reminds me of another man who *did* say he loved me. I'll call him Theo, to honor the privacy he was adamant about while we dated. It turned out he was a flaming gay man who couldn't get enough dick, but he presented himself as a closeted businessman. He lived somewhere in the suburbs; I was never to know that telephone number, or that of the law firm he worked for. I couldn't call him; he called me from his cell phone when he wanted to get together and showed up at my apartment with gifts of flowers, candy, or wine. But somehow what I saw in him when we got together was a man with whom I thought I might fall in love.

Theo wasn't quite as masculine as Carl, wasn't quite as perfectly constructed. The thing about Theo that was so magnetic was that all of his features were slightly exaggerated to a degree that made them terrifically sexy. His nose, for instance, was too big for his face, but when he went down on me, the tip of it, which bulbed out like an inverted pear, would rub its way through my pubic hair and tickle my groin. Theo also possessed a shorter and stockier build than Carl, but what made him so attractive was the greater contrast between his hair and skin: the pale complexion of his chest made the fine, fluttery cobalt-black hair that grew there look as if it had been sketched in with charcoal.

The Man of My Dreams

Theo had been born into a working-class Polish-Italian family, but made himself a success through investments in the stock market; this achievement created a cockiness and egotism in him that was difficult to overlook. He was close to fifty when I met him and close to bald, and the kinky sex we fell into right from the start should have warned me that he was nothing but trouble. Theo loved to be spanked, pissed on, restrained by ropes or handcuffs. At the time I met him I needed some adventure and change myself and this seemed one sort of change, but by the end of the first six months sex with Theo came to seem like a job. I was always having to *do* something to him when all I wanted was to enjoy him. Theo always felt that we needed to top our last sexual experience, that I must always find a different way of shocking him into reaching an orgasm. Our antics moved from my bedroom to the floor to the bathtub to the kitchen counter. Once, I passed out when Theo had gagged my mouth too tightly with his T-shirt.

The other problem was that after we had sex, after he had lowered his head and breathed coolly across my wet cock, or performed clever tricks with his tongue in my ass, we would always start arguing and break up. I felt that he should be out at his job and that he needed to give me some more regular day-to-day contact if this were to continue. He felt that I should make more money so that we could meet up in fancy hotel rooms at my expense. Soon the sex became part of this heated, volatile argument. It got to the point where I never knew if we'd be having makeup sex or breakup sex, both of which only heightened our intense sexual attraction. Soon it felt that every time we had sex it would be the last time. This went on for a year. In the end, I just couldn't do it anymore. I wanted a sex partner, a role which Theo filled successfully, but I wanted more. Even though Theo confessed he had a strong emotional need for me, he never made himself available to me for anything other than sex. It ended when I got Theo's phone number and discovered he had had another male lover for more than a decade.

〵〴ᾢᾢᾢᾢᾢ

I am nothing like the man of my dreams. I am short and pigeon-toed, prone to hiding behind my glasses, and have the physique of a matchstick; no amount of exercise seems capable of making my biceps peak or my pecs inflate. Genetics, however, has gifted me with a face, pretty and doll-like, that men do not dismiss. Living in the city for too many years has kept my complexion pale and my manners defensive, bitter, and reactive. I know I have a slightly effeminate way of pretending to flirt with a man who has caught my attention, talking too quickly on a random spree of senseless topics like a parrot chattering on and on.

If the truth be known, I must confess that I fall in love a thousand times a day. Images of men don't bounce off my retina; they soak into my cranium like maple syrup poured on top of waffles. As much as I hate men, I love and crave them even more. And my days are full of an endless supply of them: men on the subway on my way to work; men who arrive at the office with packages and mail; men seated nearby at the cafeteria at lunchtime; men at the gym, the grocery store, the pharmacy, the bookstore or the deli. Men, men, and more men.

Tonight I've strayed beyond the Internet shrine to Carl, pulling up other Web pages devoted to beautiful men. I want the perfection of a fantasy, a breather from the real-live-but-still-regular-jerks men I seem to attract in person. One of my blind dates this week was set up by a coworker of mine named Diane, an older, straight woman whose neighbor, she said, seemed to be going through the same difficulties with guys that I was. She described him as bright and attractive, more studious than athletic; but when we met he seemed depressed and overweight, though I carefully kept my opinion to myself. "I thought you would be taller," he said, after we slid into a booth at a diner and ordered coffee. The comment wounded more than I had expected it would and I felt defeated and unable to muster my usual chatty, lets-go-out-on-a-date persona, but that didn't matter since he only talked about himself, punctuating his monologue with a series of giggles.

Still, there was something appealing about him, something about the dark hair at his wrists, and I ended up following him back to his apartment. He was deliberately passive in bed, waiting for me to remove his clothing as if he expected to be worshipped simply for his youth. His body was weighty and unformed and in the pale light of his bedroom his wrists now looked more like glue sticks that had picked up lint. Nothing about him aroused me, so I scrambled to find an object for my erotic desire in my brain, remembering a man I had noticed earlier that day in the steam room at the gym, whose physique was beefy and hairy enough to excite me. I imagined my hands working at the thickly muscled body at the gym instead of the doughy slabs of flesh I was actually clutching. Below me, I felt my blind date's body break out in a damp sweat when I leaned down and took his cock in my mouth, rocking him back and forth as I lifted his ass off the bed and cupped it with my hands with a forceful passion that must have surprised him. In my mind I felt his cock grow larger than it actually was; I imagined the man in the steam room's dick hardening as I moved my mouth back and forth on the blind date's, and felt the heavy mist of the steam thickening my own skin as I forced the cock deeper into my mouth.

After a few minutes of this the blind date below me groaned and clutched awkwardly at my hair, then fumbled for my cock. I pulled back from him and he arched himself back against the mattress; I pumped his wet cock with my fist while my other hand began to search out his asshole. Just as I was massaging a finger into his rectum, he gasped and shot onto his stomach.

"You have great legs," he said after I lay down beside him, closed my eyes and successfully imagined my fist was the tattooed fist of the man in the steam room, jerking myself off. "Legs hardly ever show their age."

Tonight, sitting in front of the computer, I realize I don't have the strength to date anyone real right now, don't have the stamina to flirt or chitchat; my insecurities have been exposed and short-circuited like shoddy electrical wiring. I'm not interested in going through the machinations of negotiating sex with another guy. I can't even make it to the bar on my corner where I could sit on a stool and read the local rag. Instead, I've poured myself another glass of wine and found a home page on the Net where someone has distorted the features of professional bodybuilders into cartoonish superheroes; an artist has taken these men's photographs and airbrushed the biceps to the size of basketballs and inflated massive pectorals so tightly they could be used as flotation devices. I'm fascinated that the details the artist has exaggerated are exactly the ones I would magnify myself. I click on the images one by one, watching each set of biceps grow larger than the one before it, stroking myself as the trickery unfolds.

Fantasies, I think, as I continue to search for the man of my dreams. The perfect man. An image you don't have to communicate with, only regard and observe and worship from afar. If I could choose the perfect man I'd go for someone taller than me. I'd prefer a man older and hairier than myself, but the ideal lover could just as easily be younger or less furry. Mustache, beard, or smooth, clean-shaven face—I wouldn't care. I'd like my man to be muscular and masculine but not so butch he couldn't enjoy an outing to the theater. The man of my dreams would be smart, but not an intimidating or condescending genius; I would appreciate a man who could hold a decent conversation and ideally be able to talk as intelligently about the recurring characters in Armistead Maupin's books as he could about the meteorological effects of El Niño. He'd like every kind of music, even classical and country, and could sing along with a nostalgic Rodgers and Hart song without seeming like a sissy. He'd like cleaning up as much as he liked cooking gourmet meals, and he would know the right moment to suggest a romantic restaurant.

While I'm at it, while I'm creating the man of my myths, the man of my dreams would also have a sense of humor and a quick wit, full of ironic quips while watching TV. I'd like a man who believes that money is not important to happiness, or, rather, not so important that the desire for it overwhelms every other passion he possesses. The man of my dreams would have my picture in his wallet and on his desk at work, and he would introduce me to his friends as the man of his dreams.

"How come you don't have a boyfriend?" my blind date asked me as he escorted me to the door of his apartment.

Because everyone I meet is a jerk or a pig, I thought, though I only shrugged. They only use you and discard you. No one encourages, every one discourages you. Every perfect man I meet is somehow the imperfect one to love.

〰〰〰

These are the things I disliked about Russell: He was self-absorbed, self-focused, and self-involved. He could talk for hours about himself, but not pause for a second to ask anything about me. He didn't wear cologne sparingly, chewed on toothpicks all the time in order not to smoke, and wore fitted shirts which accented his narrow shoulders and wider waist instead of looking stylish. He was cheap, deceptive, and passive-aggressive; he would always let me pick out the movies we would watch so that he could freely complain that each was the worst of his long moviegoing life.

But Russell also had a great set of arms, broad and firmly muscular, and a hairy chest like the underbelly of a Labrador. He had a handsome face and a sexy swagger and he gave the best blow jobs I've had thus far in my life; my dick fit perfectly into his mouth as his jaws unhinged and his cheeks hollowed out to accommodate me. He knew when to take it slow and deliberate, knew when to cup and knead my balls with his palm, knew when to turn the flame up a little higher till I would beg for him to stop or suffer the consequences.

You might say that I fell in love with Russell because of the way his mouth treated my dick, but there were other reasons why I kept coming back. Russell had a distinctive streak of incredulity, overrating every experience as if it should be photographed and placed in a scrapbook. Walking to the park, for instance, he would stop in front of a store window and say, "fabulous," about the shade of a towel or a pattern of china, then turn and utter the same remark as he noticed a vintage car that had stopped at a red light. Russell always noticed the minute details of life, like the way an old green shirt I wore matched the shade of my eyes or the fact that I was wearing a new pair of shoes. I always looked at the necessary steps I had to take: if I could buy a cheaper pair of shoes this week, then next week I could afford to buy a new shirt. It was apparent to both of us that we saw the world in different ways. And Russell could be impatient if he didn't get his way; he would call me at the last moment to get together and then be annoyed if I wasn't around to meet him.

Something about Russell did unleash a boyish streak in me. Waiting in line to buy tickets for a movie we would lean our shoulders into each other; back at his apartment we would dance together to the radio. The thing I loved about Russell was that he was an incredible romantic; he was always dimming lights and changing music and reaching out to hold my hand. When I slept over at his apartment, I always woke up with his body protectively curled around mine.

But Russell didn't seem to expect love from me. What he wanted was his independence. In my mind that meant Russell was free to treat any man's cock the same way he treated mine, and because of that notion, I was wildly jealous all the time we dated. Once when I knew Russell was blowing me off to see another guy, I called his answering machine and told him I had lots of plans and wouldn't be available to spend any time over the rest of the weekend with him. It was fine for him to fool around on me but he certainly didn't want anyone to do the same thing to him. When he called back he told me how much he wanted to see me, how much he enjoyed the time we spent together. And when I showed up to spend the weekend with him he told me how much he had missed me. But the thing that I disliked most about Russell was that he made it so easy for me to cheat on him, when all I wanted was not to have to. In the three years that I dated him, I registered for a dating service, took out a personal ad to find another boyfriend, and harassed every person I knew to take me to parties so that I might find someone I could get along with better than Russell.

Russell came close to being the man of my dreams, but only through many compromises. I tolerated more of his bad boy behavior because he could, when he felt like it, make me feel so special and desirable at a time when I wasn't getting that from any other guy. For a while we even pretended to be in a relationship. But Russell never really wanted us to be significant others, never wanted us to live together, never even wanted to commit himself in advance to spending a

Desire, Lust, Passion, Sex

Saturday night with me in case he got a better offer.

This, then, was what happened to end it: One night I ran into Russell when he was out on a date with someone else. I was turning a corner and there he was, or, rather, there they were, approaching in the opposite direction. There was no way we could have avoided one another and what happened was that Russell and I stopped at the same time as if some celestial viewer had freeze-framed the movie. Suddenly there was a triangle of scrutiny: Russell checking out my expression, my realization that Russell's date was a younger and thinner model of myself, and the date's realization that Russell was not the person he had perceived him to be. By the time I got home he'd left three messages on my answering machine. In order, they went like this: "Give me a call," "Call me when you want to talk," and "It doesn't have to end like this."

I felt really wounded by Russell, but, like I mentioned before, Russell's mischievous conduct had encouraged my own. The night I ran into Russell and his date I had been on my way to see the masseur I hooked up with on the Internet. By the time I got home, my ass was so sore I had no desire to ever talk to another man for the rest of my life.

᭡᭡᭡

Men. They enter and exit like cars on a highway, moving so fast I'm unable to reassemble all the individual details of color and size. It's surprising how much time and attention it all demands, when the actual sex only accounts for a small part of my day. This week my other blind date lasted a grand total of two seconds. His name was Brad, or at least that's what I think it was. He was tall with deep-set eyes and a fair complexion. I can't remember if he was blond or not, or if he was a natural blond; I remember nothing about the color of his pubic hair or underarms. We met on a phone line one night, talking for about an hour before agreeing to hook up the next day. It went like this: I walked into his apartment, he shook my hand and that was the end of it, or the end of the date at least. Because the next thing that happened was, we started to kiss. We stood in the middle of the room of his apartment kissing and feeling each other up, then we moved to his couch, where we sat beside each other and continued to make out like teenagers. Then Brad started moving his lips around my neck, then around my ear; then we rearranged our positions so that he was lying on top of me. Soon enough our clothes were off and my legs were up over his shoulders. I reached up and played with his damp hair, brushing the colorless strands out of his eyes, and grasped my hand at the back of his neck to pull him deeper inside me. And then I was stroking my cock, slick with spit and lube and sweat, and thinking, *I'm close, I'm close, I'm close, so close.*

Afterwards, when I was back on the street, I realized that the whole experience had taken less than thirty minutes, including the time spent redressing and waiting for the elevator and the two seconds it took for the date to become a quick trick. And once again I was cursing myself and my situation, upset that I'd let a potential date swirl immediately into sex. Why, why, why was sex so important? I thought. And why, why, why did its casual occurrence make me feel so incomplete?

✶✶✶✶✶

Tonight, in front of the computer, I'm slowly masturbating and keeping myself hard while I surf for a man I could believe might be more perfect than Carl. Occasionally, as I wait for images to download, I allow my mind to wander away from the screen to other things: don't forget to do the laundry tomorrow; is there any credit left on the VISA card, should I

Desire, Lust, Passion, Sex

try to meet someone for dinner?

Men. Men. Men. They're all over the Web, amateurs and professionals posed before a camera with a desire to be found seductive. It's foolish when you deconstruct the notion: What is it that we don't have that our lives must be reduced to this? But the smaller truth is, of course, that desire makes the body feel younger and no man ever attempts to ignore that. Tonight, I've found a few guys who send tremors to my cock as I roam between muscle sites and hairy men galleries, but in the end I keep returning to study Carl, the apex of both extremes. Looking at him, memorizing his chest and arms and the patterns of hair across his body, I feel my cock fatten. I settle on a picture of him leaning against the open tailgate of a blue pickup truck, wearing a denim cap and the shredded threads of a flannel shirt. In this photograph he has a mustache, thick and dark and bushy like the end of a paintbrush. His only other clothing is a set of work boots and thick, gray socks. The man of my dreams, I think. Here at last. The perfect man: he doesn't talk to me, can't cause any trouble, won't dump me for another guy.

In the photo, Carl's cock, a fleshy tube, tilts down against his right thigh. My cock rises as I look at it, but I refuse to touch it, waiting for it to rise harder and grow firmer on its own. Soon I'm practically aching to touch myself again, but I continue to hold back. I'm sitting up straight on the edge of my seat, legs spread, the boxer shorts now discarded. Soon I'm studying my cock in my lap as much as I'm studying Carl on the monitor screen. A thick blood vessel travels the length of the shaft, disappearing short of the circumcision scar; a thin brown band separates the redder skin as it flares up into the head. The head itself is no wider than the shaft, but the spongy skin of the mushroom-shaped crown shifts again to a paler, pinker color. I tense all the muscles of my body to reduce the desire to stroke my cock, but as I relax them the desire to fondle myself does not pass. Instead, I stare at the monitor and compare the shape of Carl's cock to my own. His seems longer, thicker; he seems more tender, and not so needy. In my mind I imagine him reaching his hand to his dick, clamping his fist around the base, feeling the grainy wires of his pubic hair rub against his skin. He milks it from the base to the head, loosening his grasp as he reaches the end, and watches it grow harder and longer in his palm. He bounces it back and forth in his hand and I listen to the slapping sound it makes.

Then he begins to move his hips slightly as he strokes his cock with the quicker motion of a thumb and finger clutched around the shaft. He bounces it again and I feel my cock bouncing at the same time. His chest swells with a deep breath of air, his abdominal muscles rippling as he exhales. As he tugs and pulls and moves his other hand down to play with his balls, I feel myself growing flushed. I take a deep breath of air. Soon I can no longer resist myself, and I reach down and clutch my own cock. I shoot the moment my fingers touch the skin, a hot white spurt landing below my right nipple followed by a second dribble that wets my knuckles. Carl comes a second later, a long white jet that arches up before it lands on the ground.

On-screen I detect Carl's wry, knowing smile, and I imagine him asking me if I'd like to get together again. I shake my head and say I'm not interested in one guy tying me down all the time. His big brown eyes well up with tears and I can see the hurt on his face. "Sorry," I say, like every other man who's ever said the same thing to me. "It's best we see other people."

わいいいい

Theo once said I would be perfect if I stopped smoking, which I did, only to grow bitter because I still wasn't perfect enough to be his boyfriend, or, rather, perfect enough for him to give up his other boyfriend. Russell once said I was the best sex he had ever had, which meant that he wasn't going to stop looking for someone who could top me in the sack department. I once had a blind date who said I had perfect ears. He needn't have bothered to tell me that; I'd have slept with him anyway.

If I were to list my faults I'd say I was jealous and possessive and a little too romantically inclined to make it through life without being disappointed. I don't have much of a hairline left and in the last few weeks my waistline has gotten out of control as I turn more and more to food and booze. I have a tendency to be cranky when things don't go my way, and there are days when I wake up and find myself overwhelmed by everything I encounter. My own behavior with men has been hardly stellar. Since Theo treated me like a whore, I lifted money from his wallet; after spending time with Russell, I would stop off at a bar on the pretext of having a drink, but with the real desire to pick someone else up so I could knock him out of my mind. On my last blind date I wiped the remaining traces of lube and come and shit on the couch cushions when Brad went to get a towel. But my biggest flaw is that all it takes to get me aroused is the simple craving of another man. I suppose that makes me as big a pig and a jerk as every other guy I've met or dated or had sex with. What is it that my friends are always telling me? A hard dick shows no conscience.

Tonight, the computer has been turned off and the wine has successfully made me drowsy. I've washed my cock with warm, soapy water, dried it, and climbed into bed and turned out the lights. The first thing I think about is my vow to give up men and sex. But the computer has burned off a lot of my anxiety and a well-needed serenity washes over me like hopefulness. Of course I'm not giving up sex or men, I decide. And I'm certainly not giving up on the dream of meeting the man who's meant for me. Lying there in bed I create a sky full of thousands of stars above me, one for every man I've ever had sex with; closing my eyes, I make them all disappear. But before I fall asleep I imagine what it would be like sleeping next to Carl, how it would feel with his arms encircling me, or better yet, my arms enfolding him, or even better yet, wonder what it would be like to have him there night after night after night. As his image seeps over me, I feel my cock begin to harden with a pulsing ache and I twist myself so that I can rub it against the sheet. I fight off the urge to touch myself again, then fight off the dream of a man reaching out for me. If the man of my dreams is a man I've never met, I think next, how will I ever meet the man who dreams of someone like me?

Desire, Lust, Passion, Sex

Arnie had no interest in gambling his money away; he had no desire to spend time at the crap tables and slot machines. The whole noisy, raucous atmosphere of the casinos bothered him, which was why he had suggested Orlando as an alternative to Mitch—at least there was Disney World and Epcot and Universal to keep them occupied and away from each other's throats.

"There's been nothing but rain on the East Coast all summer," Mitch answered, and he nixed the alternative idea, Palm Springs, as well. "You'll just become obsessive again over some young guy and ruin the whole thing. We can see a show in Vegas and eat at a decent restaurant."

The whole purpose of a vacation was to be able to ogle, to stare at, to desire some young man, Arnie thought. Wasn't that the purpose of getting out of the house? Meeting someone so he could fantasize his way out of his miserable, unhappy relationship with Mitch? They had fought on the plane. (Mitch: Why do you always insist on having the window? Arnie: So I can sleep with my head to the side.) They had fought at the airport (Arnie: Why did you bring so much? It's only a weekend. Mitch: You told me to pack your laptop in my suitcase.) They had fought in the hotel room. (Mitch: Keep away from the minibar. You don't need it and I'm not going to

Desire, Lust, Passion, Sex

pay for it.) And the casino: (Arnie: What do you mean you're not gambling? I thought that's why you wanted to come here.)

At the pool, Arnie spread out his towel over a deck chair. He wore an oversized T-shirt over his baggy swim trunks. It was bright and hot, the temperature over a hundred degrees but manageable in the shade. He had no plans to swim. He wasn't about to take off his T-shirt and reveal his chubby waist and saggy chest. Mitch was lingering inside at the gift shop, worrying about whether he had brought strong enough sunscreen. Arnie spread Mitch's towel over the chair beside him, slanting it so he would have to squint in the heat. *Let him suffer,* Arnie thought. *Let him be as miserable as I am.*

The book Arnie had brought was useless, boring. He set it aside, looked back to the hotel to see if Mitch was coming or not. When Arnie turned back to pick up his book, he glanced over at the pool and noticed two young men swimming laps. They had stopped in the shallow end and were rising out of the water. The thinner one was pushing his hair back against his head. Arnie thought he was adorable; he must still be in his twenties. The young man treaded his way to the steps. He was wearing a black Speedo. As he stepped out of the pool and walked across the hot tiles to a deck chair and a waiting towel, Arnie studied the dark eyelashes, the pouty lips, the visible pelvic bones, the wet black hairs of his legs. The other man appeared to be about the same age, but stockier, beefy, like a football player: thick neck, muscular legs, a tattoo covering his right bicep and a pierced eyebrow.

The two young men dried themselves off and settled into their chairs. What luck, Arnie thought, they were only a chair away from him. From where he was seated Arnie could see the remaining water collecting into drips and puddles against the skin and hair of the thinner guy. Arnie had a brief doubt as to whether they were a couple or just friends. Then he noticed the rings and smiled at himself. This was sure to get

Desire, Lust, Passion, Sex

Mitch annoyed. Arnie had stumbled onto the youngest gay couple vacationing in Las Vegas.

When Mitch arrived at the pool, Arnie was already shamelessly flirting with Seth, the thinner, cuter one of the young couple. Mitch frowned while Arnie made the introductions, but warmed a bit when he shook Paul's hand and admired his tattoo. Arnie resumed his monologue about their trip to Hawaii last year. It was funny and self-deprecating, with Arnie winning the hula contest (because he had such a big waist to jiggle around) and Mitch cast as the antagonist because they had to leave the island early due to an emergency at the Baltimore hospital where he worked. Mitch settled in the sun and took off his shirt, which made Arnie frown. Mitch was in terrific shape for a man his age; he knew that Arnie felt it was unfair that they had aged differently. Mitch was an amateur bodybuilder with a broad chest and a full head of dyed black hair. Mitch had encouraged Arnie to go to the gym with him in the mornings, but Arnie liked to sleep as late as possible. After sixteen years together, Mitch resented that Arnie did not discipline himself. There were the chocolate binges, the pastry binges, the extra cocktails, and the second bottles of wine, followed by mornings of guilt and weeks of crash diets. Mitch no longer admired Arnie's body and he knew that it was another source of friction between them. But Mitch was also vain, and he was the first to admit it. Sitting in the chair that Arnie had aimed into the sun, he refused to put on his sunglasses, not wanting to hide his eyes while he talked to the young couple.

Arnie continued his questions: "Where are you from?" Paul: "Los Angeles." "Why did you come to Vegas?" Seth: "We found a deal on the Web." "Have you been here before?" Seth: "As a boy." Paul: "Never." By the time the young men decided to leave the pool, Arnie had invited the couple to join them for dinner at one of the better restaurants in the

Desire, Lust, Passion, Sex

hotel that evening.

Mitch was fine with the arrangement. Dinner with another couple would take the pressure off of being alone with Arnie tonight, though lately Arnie's habit of casting Mitch as the villain in the anecdotes that Arnie could unravel to a stranger had become increasingly annoying. Arnie knew that Mitch would not object to Seth and Paul joining them for dinner, even though it meant canceling the reservation they had made at another place on the strip. And Arnie had been certain that Mitch would find something alluring and attractive in the young men, too. What was there not to like? Mitch thought. Paul, the thuggish looking one, was perfectly suitable eye candy, and if Mitch wanted to push the game further by trying to woo one of the young men himself, he was sure it was fine with Arnie. After all this time, Arnie was not at all jealous of Mitch's intentions with other men. In fact, Arnie, watching the retreating young men gather up their towels and lotion, was probably already thinking: *Let Mitch find another guy who'll suck his dick. It's less work for me. I've seen it too many times already.*

In the hotel room, Arnie couldn't resist thinking about Seth. Arnie felt certain he could charm Seth with his wit and a quick friendship; he felt they were clicking by the pool, he could hear it in Seth's laugh. He fussed over his clothes, unpacking his suitcase and placing the shirts against the slacks on top of the bedspread, trying to decide what would make him look best. He wasn't about to wear a white shirt because he was bound to splatter it with food. The jeans were out of the question because they made his rear look as wide as an old farmhand's and the restaurant was too nice to dress that casual. He decided he would wear the floral print shirt he found in Australia that hid his waist and showed off his chest hair. It was colorful and festive, exactly how he wanted Seth to regard him.

Desire, Lust, Passion, Sex

Mitch walked into the bathroom to prevent provoking Arnie into an argument. He recognized Arnie's routine, the slow deliberation over the clothes. Mitch knew it was time to have another affair himself. It was the only way he could stomach staying with Arnie. Every time they had thought about splitting up it never worked out. There was too much between them: real estate, bank accounts, mutual friends, and memories. Mitch's last affair was more than two years ago. Cliff, a young bodybuilder at Mitch's gym, had unleashed a dangerous lust in Mitch. Mitch had stood over Arnie in the mornings, watching him still sleeping in bed, thinking, *I can leave you for good this time.* The stumbling block was Cliff, however; he was unwilling to give up his wife and nine-month-old son.

Now Mitch thought about Paul to keep from thinking about Cliff. Mitch imagined doing some of the things with Paul that he had done with Cliff: wrapping his legs around his face or burying his tongue in an armpit or wrestling with him until someone was on top and the other gave in. At the pool they had learned that Seth and Paul had only been together for ten months, four months living together, still enough time for Paul to want to fool around on the side, Mitch thought. They were too young to really be serious nesters, married men, monogamously clinging to each other; still young enough to want to sample whatever might be offered as a side dish. Mitch thought the young men's relationship wouldn't last, or if it did, they would end up like he and Arnie had. Mitch didn't want to sweep Paul off his feet, either. Just devour him, like a sweet and tasty dessert.

Back in the room, Mitch began to dress. He chose a dark, tight polo shirt that showed off his chest and arms. While he slipped it on, he dreamed of slipping off Paul's shirt and finding his nipples and the fine ridge of hair that covered his navel. Mitch sat on the edge of the bed and pulled on a pair of dark socks, shook out the wrinkles from a pair of tan dress slacks and stepped into them. He threaded a black belt between the pant loops and laced up his black shoes. Standing in front of the mirror, he knew he looked like a million bucks. He also knew the outfit would irritate Arnie. Arnie had noticed it and walked into the bathroom to avoid insulting him. From where Mitch stood in the room, in front of the mirror over the dresser, he could smell the cologne Arnie was spraying in the bathroom. Mitch walked to the bathroom door and said to him, "Not very subtle, are we?"

"It wouldn't hurt you to wear some every now and then," Arnie replied. "Your sweat stinks, too, you know?"

On the other side of the hotel, Seth said to Paul, "I think they'll be dressing up."

Paul had pulled out his jeans and a clean T-shirt to wear. "These are my good jeans. I didn't bring anything else," Paul said. "I didn't think we were going someplace fancy."

"Wear the white shirt then," Seth said. "The linen one. It's nicer."

While he was talking, Seth was fingering his underwear and thinking about wearing the pale blue shirt that he had bought to go clubbing last year, thin enough to take off and tuck through the belt loop of his jeans. Arnie would surely notice the shirt—it highlighted the pale color of Seth's blue eyes. But Seth wondered if Mitch would notice it too. Seth could see himself having a friendship with Arnie and an affair with Mitch, though Seth had no intention of even fooling around with anyone; Paul was enough to keep him interested and off the market. Seth took out his off-white chinos and a thin gray suede belt.

"You look nice," Paul said, smiling, and kissed Seth, when they were both dressed. Paul pressed his tongue into Seth's mouth and bit the corner of his lip to keep him from pulling away too quickly. They kissed each other deeper, blew warm, moist breaths against each other. Paul reached down and clutched Seth's crotch and felt his erection through the fabric of his pants. "Save that for later," Paul said and pulled his hand away.

Seth smiled back. He loved the way Paul made him feel, still, after ten months. No man had made him feel that way that long. Seth had no desire to ruin that; he was aware that Paul knew that neither Arnie nor Mitch were a threat to their relationship. Seth liked Arnie because he was witty and conversational. He knew that Arnie was white hot for him and he found that sweet and appealing, part of the reason why he had agreed to have dinner with the older couple. At the pool, Seth noticed Arnie taking in his body and at one point, even shifting his towel to his lap to cover a growing erection. Mitch, however, was one of the sexiest things Seth had ever seen: older, taller, well-built, successful. Seth had always had something of a daddy fetish, perhaps one of the reasons why he found Paul so attractive as well. Paul was taller and bigger than Seth, and Paul's face had a more mature look, another thing that kept Seth feeling boyish.

Seth and Paul showed up at the restaurant late. Paul hadn't waited till later; in the hotel room, he had stripped the shirt and pants off Seth and blown him till he came. Seth had pushed Paul against the bed and jerked him off. They both knew that this activity did not negate anything else happening later. Sometimes when they traveled they had sex two or three times in one day. Later it could be more involved and complicated. Lubes, dildos, maybe even a scene. Paul liked it that Seth was inventive. "Let's try that," Seth would say when they watched a porn video together and saw a position or setting he found hot. Paul was always willing to try whatever Seth wanted to do: handcuffs, bondage, mutual massage. Everything was okay as long as they were safe.

Paul had never liked the circuit scene. He felt out of place, clumsy (dancing like he had two left feet), and not a

part of the right sort of crowd. Seth had kept Paul from
going back to the sex clubs, where at least everyone seemed
on a level playing ground, but more than that, Paul kept Seth
away from them too. Seth had been a heartbreaker before
Paul came into his life, or at least that was how Seth told it
to him on their fifth date. They had clicked with each other
because of sex—Paul eager to please and Seth mischievous
enough to show off everything he had learned thus far.

At the restaurant, there was a good bustle and smiles
and laughs between the couples as they made their way to
the table, admiring the decor of the restaurant and one
another's outfits. The lighting was low, the music subtle, the
menu long and expensive, which sent Paul calculating how
much money he might need to take out of his wallet.

"That's a terrific shirt," Seth said to Arnie.

Arnie told a story of the store he bought it in in Sydney,
a short anecdote about a beautiful young salesman who did
not know how to use the sales register and overcharged Arnie
about a thousand dollars for the shirt. Arnie laughed and said
it took him months to get the store to refund the money
because he had signed the receipt without looking at the total.
(He was too busy admiring the young man.) Paul thought that
maybe he and Seth were out of their league with these older
men; their combined incomes were certainly not large enough
to sustain that kind of momentary loss of credit.

Everyone smiled and the conversation fell briefly into talk
about the desert air, dry throats, and thirst, until the waiter
arrived. They talked about wine choices, red or white, ordered
cocktails first, and Arnie flirted with the waiter, asking him
about the specialties of the house. The waiter laughed and
nodded with Arnie's choices because Arnie said he was watching his figure; he ordered a salad without dressing and grilled
salmon with vegetables and no cream sauce. Mitch ordered a
steak and the two young men ordered less expensive items.

Desire, Lust, Passion, Sex

Arnie tried to read Seth for signals and Seth tried to read Mitch for signals and Mitch wondered if Paul was thinking about him. The drinks arrived and Mitch and Paul fell into a conversation about the paltry exercise room at the hotel spa.

"A million rooms in this place and one tiny little exercise mat," Mitch said. "It's really shameful."

"Mitch's obsessive about his looks," Arnie said, sipping his martini. "It's a sign of getting old."

"Arnie wouldn't let me go to Palm Springs where I could show it off," Mitch said. "He's scared I might meet someone I like better than him. Huh, sweetie pie?"

They talked a few minutes about Palm Springs. Seth had been to a couple of circuit parties a few years before; Paul had once stayed at a clothing optional hotel. Mitch mentioned that a lot of the big hotels have small workout rooms. He was stuck on talking about keeping fit. "Even the major resort spas don't have a decent set of free weights," Mitch said. "That place in Utah we went to had nothing to speak of."

The salads arrived and the wine was uncorked. Seth asked what profession Mitch was in that allowed him to travel so much.

"He's living off my good name," Arnie said. Arnie explained that he was a corporate trainer, which meant he got to survey large hotels for potential meeting space and was the reason why they had traveled to a lot of places on promotional trips. Arnie told of some of their best and worst experiences. Best: Fiji, even though they left the airport just as a hurricane was arriving. Worst: Casablanca. They had become lost in a market and caught up in an angry crowd.

Mitch interrupted Arnie and asked Paul a question about the type of work he did, and Arnie realized he had been too self-absorbed and talking only about himself. He knew nothing about Seth, certainly less about him than Paul, after Paul announced that he was a bricklayer and Mitch bombarded him with questions about foundations and pointing and how a leveler was supposed to work.

Arnie sipped his wine and listened. Mitch explained that he was a staff surgeon at a teaching hospital in Maryland; he had done his residency in Atlanta and he named the medical school he had attended. Seth's eyes brightened as Mitch explained the staff hierarchy of the hospital and the medical school. When Arnie had heard enough and was convinced that Mitch was trying to steal the limelight, he asked Seth what kind of work he did.

Seth said he was a cartoonist. The admission came out with a boyish giggle, which made everyone at the table smile. Arnie leaned forward and grinned and fluttered his lashes and asked Seth to explain his profession with more details. Seth had gone to art school and had always had a passion for comic books since he was a boy. Superhero worship: Batman, Superman, the Hulk, Green Lantern. He had started out tracing the images in his school notebooks until he could draw them on his own. Since then he'd always drawn superheroes. He'd done some fashion work after art school—clothing sketches for a department store, that sort of thing, but his heart was really into comics and cartoons. Right now he was only doing detail work and inking for a strip, but he was certain, with time, he would be able to draw a storyline he had pitched. He was also hoping to get into animation.

Arnie imagined a thought bubble bursting above his head. *Oh my,* he thought. *He has no interest in me. He's interested in Mitch. He worships bodybuilders. Perfectly crafted men.* The entrees arrived and Arnie drank and ate in silence. He felt deflated and defeated, or, rather, inflated with fat and infuriated with fate. There was no one to blame for his overweight misery except his own miserable self. He had let his looks deteriorate on purpose, hoping for years it would drive Mitch away. Arnie had always believed that once Mitch left him, he could diet and find another, better lover. When the waiter reappeared, Arnie ordered dessert. He wanted something chocolate. Something sweet and sinful and sure to cause him to have a heart attack.

Mitch kept up the conversation. He was aware that Arnie had turned sour. He even tried to draw Arnie back into the conversation, throw him a few compliments by saying that the few freelance travel articles Arnie had written had been published in top-drawer magazines. Seth was the first of the young couple to sense that something was wrong with Arnie and that Mitch was trying hard to keep them entertained. Seth began to babble about the lousy meals he fixed for Paul—the oversalted broccoli, the limp spaghetti—then about how he had discovered a gourmet take-out counter at a nearby grocery store. The explanation of his incompetence made him embarrassed and uneasy. He shifted in his seat, felt flushed and sweaty from the wine. Paul noticed Seth's uneasiness and Arnie's silence. He switched the conversation to exercising, asking Mitch what were his best routines in the gym.

Arnie ordered an after-dinner drink while the others had coffee. For the first time in more than ten years, he wished for a cigarette. He tapped the table impatiently while Paul talked about a new ab machine he was using and the others lingered over their coffee. The waiter arrived with the bill and Mitch offered to treat the young couple. Arnie felt his face redden while the two young men protested and then graciously relented. Seth smiled, but not at all the kind of smile he had shown throughout the meal. His lips were tight, as if he were worried something else would be expected of them besides being dinner companions. Arnie liked watching him squirm. As much as Seth had enjoyed the flirting, it was accepted and returned without the intention of anything more serious occurring. Paul sensed his partner's tension and slipped his arm around Seth's shoulder as if to show their alignment against their potential adversaries: us against them, youth versus age.

They parted at the entrance to the casino, shaking hands. No mention was made of another time, nor were phone numbers or business cards exchanged. Arnie was ready to go upstairs to their room but Mitch wanted to watch a game of blackjack. He thought the stroll before going back to the room might do Arnie good. He encouraged Arnie to stick a few quarters in a slot machine, thinking it might deflect Arnie's thoughts from the discouraging dinner. Arnie was aware of what Mitch was doing and hated him more for it. In Arnie's mind, he was packing his suitcase and storming out of the room. While Mitch stood and watched the betting at a table, Arnie walked away and sat at a nearby bar, ordering another cocktail.

Seth and Paul wandered through the aisles of slot machines. They lingered a few seconds in front of a blinking one-arm bandit while Paul emptied his pockets of change. In the elevator a few minutes later, they had nothing to say to each other about dinner. It was already behind them. At the door to their room, Paul untucked Seth's shirt from his chinos. Inside, they fell against the bed and began kissing each other. Paul pushed his hands beneath Seth's shirt and rubbed his palms against Seth's chest. Seth's fingers found Paul's belt and fly and tugged at Paul's pants. They began something that lasted for hours, late into the night and on into the morning hours.

Downstairs, Mitch took a seat at the blackjack table. At one point he was up by two hundred and then down by five hundred. He left when he was down by one-fifty. Arnie was already in bed when Mitch entered the room; the television was on softly and Arnie was lying on his back snoring. Later that night, Mitch woke up and his throat felt dry. He rolled over and found Arnie's body and placed a hand against Arnie's hip; his lips pressed against Arnie's shoulder and he breathed in the warm moisture of the skin. Arnie was dreaming and had a nighttime erection. He turned over on his side, which was when Mitch's hand grazed against his cock. Mitch's own cock stirred at the thought of Arnie aroused by someone or something in his dreams. That started something between them, and it kept them going a little longer.

What Counts Most

Your discomfort mounts. It is too cold in the shade and too bright in the sun. On the street corner where you are waiting there is no in-between spot. You must either shiver or squint. You decide you look better shivering than squinting so you step into the shade and wait. While you are shivering in a neighborhood where you never like to be in the first place you are tormented by feeling overweight even though you have lost three pounds since last week. You try to look relaxed but feel your forehead tense into anxious ridges. You are waiting for a man who is impossibly handsome, possibly the most handsome man you have ever met in the city, even though you know he lives somewhere outside of it in a place that you have never been to. You are waiting to spend a weekend with this handsome man. His handsomeness makes you insecure about your own looks. Very insecure. You feel like you've gained weight just waiting for him to show up, even though you are certain your chattering teeth are burning up a few calories.

You are waiting on his route to the tunnel. Everyone who passes you on the sidewalk is able to regulate his body temperature except for you. A large, muscular man in a sleeveless T-shirt goes by eating an ice cream bar. A toothless homeless woman wrapped in a blanket pushes a shopping cart filled with empty plastic bottles. The smell of beer or urine or both surrounds you and the pile of garbage you are standing beside. A fly torments you while you shiver in the morning air. Minutes pass. You look out into the street, thinking you will recognize his car even though you have never seen it before. What possessed you to agree to spend the weekend with this guy? His handsomeness? Or just being around him, breathing in the possibility of such beauty?

You imagine him arriving to find you shivering, parking his car, warming you up by rubbing his hands along your shoulders, and drawing you into a deep, silky kiss. Then somewhere from behind his back he presents you with flowers. Or chocolates. Or chocolate flowers that are calorie-free, saying he has thought about nothing except you since the last time you were together.

A passing truck sends a gust of hot dust into your eyes. You step further back into the cold shade. Nothing like that will happen of course. This is not a romantic outing. You don't expect him to arrive with gifts. He may not even kiss you. The last time you saw him you lay side by side in a hotel bed without even touching. He would not kiss you. He would not let you kiss him. He would not touch your body. He would not let you touch his.

"I can't risk it," he said, and he stroked his big beautiful cock and you stroked your smaller, more imperfect one. His handsomeness made your orgasm easy even though he made you feel like a bag of festering germs. So why are you even bothering to see him again? When a car stops beside you your body surges with blood. You are again reminded that he is the most handsome man you have ever met in this city, even though he is not a resident of it. Of course you are going to see him again. Of course you will wait in the middle of nowhere for him to pick you up to take you out of the city to somewhere in the country for the weekend. Of course you won't do whatever he doesn't want you to do because, after all, being around someone so beautiful is nothing to take seriously.

ᴡᴡᴡ

In the car you feel your anxiety mounting. He is just as good-looking as he was the last time you saw him, even though you were dizzy from the aftermath of two martinis when you started talking with him. He might even be better looking now because your vision is not as blurry as it was when you were drinking. Yes, you decide, he is better looking than the last time you saw him. This makes you feel more inadequate. He is wearing a blue cotton button-down shirt that highlights his eyes. You wonder if he can tell by the T-shirt that you are wearing that your stomach is not flat enough to have ridges of muscle showing. Of course he can tell, you remind yourself, he's seen you without the T-shirt. He knows exactly how much weight you have and where you have it, except for the three missing pounds since last week. You wonder if he can tell you have lost three pounds.

"You got your hair cut," he says.

Yes, you think, he can tell you lost three pounds. Three pounds of hair is missing from your head since last week, since the cheap barber you go to went a little too crazy when you were crazy enough to ask him for a quick trim because you wanted to look perfect for the perfect man this weekend.

You don't ask him if he likes your haircut. You will not set yourself up for disappointment, even though you are desperate to receive a compliment from him because it would be a compliment from a truly handsome man. "It's shorter," you say.

"It makes you look younger," he says.

You are not certain if this is a compliment or not, but the sound of his voice makes you nod and smile. You watch him

Desire, Lust, Passion, Sex

drive around a circular ramp and merge into the traffic disappearing into the tunnel. You met this man at a bar last
week. His name is Jack and he is forty-six years old. It is no
joke to you that the digits of his age add up to the number
ten. He is a perfect man. An all-around ten. At least in the
looks department. He could be a movie star. Or a politician.
You are certain he is popular with everyone who knows him
for what he is: a very handsome man.

But this is also a handsome man with a few too many
flaws, though you do not let them bother you and you do not
subtract any digits from the total count of his overall appearance. One flaw is a wife named Colleen. In a less handsome
man this would knock him down a digit or two. Two other
flaws are a daughter named Annie and a son named Wes. He
could lose a few points for these two other things, as well,
though this married man named Jack with two kids does not
lose even a fraction of a point for having them. Another flaw
is that his family does not know he is not where he has told
them he will be and he is with someone they would not
approve of if they did know where he was. This gorgeous,
closeted married man named Jack does not lose any digits for
this, either, though if any other guy had lied to you or about
you and you had discovered the lie and the secret, his digits
would be turned into a negative number.

When the car emerges from the tunnel the sunlight
makes you squint. You realize you forgot to bring your sunglasses. Why didn't you remember to bring your sunglasses?
This perfect man will now be reduced to watching you squint
the entire day. This thought makes you break into a sweat.
You are twenty-nine years old and worried about the way
you look when you are squinting and how flat your stomach
appears when you are sitting in the bucket seat of a car. Your
stomach is not that imperfect, you remind yourself, even
though you can do nothing to prevent the squinting. Your

stomach might not be flat enough to see your ab muscles through the skin but you would also not lose any points for the way it looks, either. Your waist is the same size it was when you were in college. Your waist size is the same two digits as your age.

"I'm starving," Jack says. "You don't mind if I stop somewhere to get something to eat, do you?"

Of course you don't mind, noting he did not ask if you were hungry, too, but accepting because of the way he looks it is acceptable for him to be self-involved and not thinking of your hunger. Yes, you think, swirling in the irony of your own self-involved fantasy: He is hungry and does not lose any points for being self-involved because he is hungry for someone just like you.

~~~

He could lose a few points for the way he chews, too, because it forces you to look at the food in his mouth and not at his beautiful, gorgeous, handsome face. While he talks about his car with his mouth full of food, you look at the couple at the next table eating hamburgers and sharing a plate of french fries even though it is barely noon. They are incredibly overweight. Their buttons pull and their zippers strain. They are as extremely overweight as Jack is extremely handsome. But they chew their food with their mouths closed.

You try not to slip into a bad mood because you are looking at an overweight couple eat instead of the handsome man in front of you chew with his mouth open. You eat your frozen yogurt. The cold surge in your mouth creates an instant headache. You squint and grimace and groan. The bad mood has arrived. It is in full force inside your skull. You hope it does not destroy the weekend. You will try to keep it to yourself. You will try not to take your bad mood out on an extremely handsome self-involved closeted married man.

"What are you staring at?" he says, as if he is talking to a child. He has noticed you are no longer looking at him.

"I'm not," you answer. "I must have just been lost in thought."

"What were you thinking about?" he asks. He grins like he is running for election.

"Nothing," you answer. "I was thinking about nothing because this yogurt was giving me a headache."

He gives you another kind of grin, a shift of the lips, this one strained at the corners.

You realize that you are now on the path of ruining his weekend. You try to salvage the conversation by changing the direction back to him. "Where did you get that shirt?" you ask. "It goes good with your eyes."

The smile widens again; the first kind, the natural kind, is back. "I have them made for me," he says. "A tailor from Hong Kong does them. He comes to the city once a year and I order a new set of them."

"How many do you have?"

"A lot," he answers. "I change colors every year. I have a lot of white, some striped, even a pink one, though I don't wear that one much."

"Why not?"

"It feels obvious," he says.

Of course it does, you think. An extremely handsome man in a pink shirt. Even a set of kids will not deflect that.

"A few years ago I even had monograms put on the cuffs," he says.

"The pink one?"

"Of course not," he answers. "It was blue and white striped. You could barely detect the initials in the pattern. It was very subtle, like it wasn't even there unless you were expecting to find it."

What Counts Most

That certainly makes sense, you think, hiding something where no one will notice it.

〰〰〰

You squint for another hour. And then for another hour. The city gives way to suburbs which change to farm land. The yogurt gives you gas, which makes you silently grimace and squirm and squint some more. The land changes into hills. The highway crosses a river and goes around a mountain. The conversation in the car shifts from his tailored business suits to the house he designed back to his custom-built car (which is incredibly expensive and uncomfortable). For the last hour the radio has been on. Top 40 has now been replaced with country music.

When he parks at the lodge, you follow him up a set of wooden stairs, your head bowed to the ground to avoid the sun. In the lobby he continues to walk ahead of you, and you clasp your hands behind your back to complete the feeling that you are merely a geisha following three steps behind a great man.

At the counter you watch a sleepy-eyed clerk, not much older than you, drop his jaw when Jack's attractiveness begins to register with him. His expression becomes bug-eyed when Jack asks about a reservation. Jack gives the man two names you have never heard before—certainly not yours and definitely not his own. When Jack asked you to spend the weekend with him, he said a friend owed him a favor and could get a room in an out-of-the-way country lodge. He didn't tell you any other details about the friend, which makes you believe that he didn't tell the friend any details about you, either.

You notice that there is no credit card exchanged when the clerk blushes and looks for keys. No cash is exchanged between them, either. This has all been arranged days before, though unbeknownst to the clerk, Jack's handsomeness is completely unexpected. While you are waiting you realize you have not told anyone where you are going for the weekend or that you were spending it with an extremely attractive closeted married man. You wonder if that was wise. You wonder if you should have told someone where you were going and why you were doing it. Maybe someone could have talked you out of it.

As you follow Jack out of the lobby he says, "I hope you don't mind that we got two rooms. I'm a light sleeper."

You are so stunned that you cannot respond. You feel as if someone—a giant puppeteer above you—is nodding your head for you. You follow Jack down a corridor, around a corner, and into another hallway.

"You can have the room at the end of the hall," he says. "I'll take this one."

He hands you a key and unlocks the door where he has stopped. "I'm going to take a quick nap," he says. "All that sun and driving has made me a little edgy."

No sense in both of us being in a bad mood, you think, as you continue down the hall to your room.

༄༅༄

Your room does not surprise you. It is small and has a view of a parking lot. You try to decide if you are more disappointed in the size of the room, the lack of an interesting view, or the fact that you are alone, spending a weekend with a too handsome, too closeted, married man who has decided he wants to sleep in separate rooms. You grow angry when you realize that this has all been planned in advance. He has always planned that you would be in separate rooms. All you can think about is how to get out of this. Your weekend is destroyed. You are humiliated. You are not even young and attractive enough to share a room with. You open your wallet and try to calculate if you have enough money to call a cab to drive you back into the city. No such luck. You barely have enough for food.

Your headache grows wider. It moves from a point above your left eye to a larger point between both of your eyes to an even larger point somewhere near your hairline. You are in agony. Your head is hurting so much now you have to close your eyes.

In the bathroom while you are taking an aspirin you smell something strange. You breathe in the foul odor, breathe out, and breathe it in again, thinking it will not be there this time. No such luck. The stench is still there. You look at the glass you just drank from. It looks clean. You smell the water. Nothing. It smells okay. You stick your nose closer to the tub, then the sink, then the toilet. You decide your bathroom must be sitting on top of a septic tank. Your headache shifts to the other eye. You wobble into the room and lie down on the narrow single bed. Maybe a nap will make everything go away. Or maybe a nap will make things seem better.

༺༺ᛨ༻༻

The phone startles you. The room is dark even though the curtains are open. Hours have passed. Or at least it seems as if hours have passed. You fumble around the room for the light switch, find the knob for the lamp, and flick it on. The phone is so loud you think it might jump off the table if you do not answer it.

"I must have been really tired," Jack says when you answer the phone. "Let's get something to eat."

"Okay," you answer and hang up the phone. Your headache is gone, you realize, or at least it is temporarily hiding from you. You put on your shoes and ignore the smell from the bathroom. You meet Jack at the door to his room.

"The restaurant downstairs is supposed to be good," he says and locks the door behind him.

He leads the way. You follow three steps behind him with your arms behind your back. The nap has freshened your wit. Or deepened it. You have decided that if he can humiliate you with separate rooms you can at least mock his attractiveness by pretending to be his geisha.

In the dining room everyone stares at Jack. The bartender, the waitress, the busboy, the couple at the next table and the table after that one. You find great comfort in knowing that if something were to happen to you, if you were to be murdered in your sleep in the middle of this nowhere lodge, everyone would remember that he was here this weekend at this particular lodge, though you doubt that they would remember you, the way you looked, or the person you were. "Was he the scowling one?" the bartender might ask. "No, he was the one in the T-shirt with the not-so-flat stomach," the waitress would say. The busboy would probably pinpoint you as the dreamy-eyed guy who looked like he had a headache coming on. The couple at the table next to you would say, "Oh yes, he was the geisha, wasn't he? What was that all about anyway?"

There is a candle at the center of your table. A flower in a vase is near the left ledge, closest to the window. The mountain rises outside. It is very romantic but you will not succumb to this setup any further. You now pretend that Jack is not so good-looking. You pretend he is just a normal, average, ordinary gorgeous-looking guy in a beautiful hand-tailored blue shirt with a wife and two kids who know nothing about you. It does not surprise you that the conversation during dinner revolves around him. There is some discussion about his clothes. He talks briefly about how much money he makes at his job.

After dinner Jack suggests you go back upstairs for the night since he has no clue of how to find town or if there is even a town nearby. You think this is a smart idea because you do not wish to be any more lost with him than you already are. Following him through the corridor, around the corner, and through the other hallway you realize that you did not bring a book to read to fill up the upcoming empty hours. The reception on the TV is probably lousy in your stinky room. What are you going to do until you are ready to go back to sleep?

You don't even stop at his door when he pulls his key out to unlock his room. You continue down the hall feeling defeated. After a few steps you sense that something is amiss. You hear him, over your shoulder, say, in a strange and childish voice, "Don't you want to visit for a while?"

You turn and give him a surprised look. "Sure," you answer and follow him inside his room.

His room surprises you. No, it flabbergasts you. It is the size of a suite. A lavish suite. There is a couch and a fireplace. On the floor is a furry dead animal that has a nose and a mouth with a wide set of teeth.

"Damn," he says, standing in front of a huge, wooden-framed mirror. "I got stains all over my shirt."

"I'm sure they'll wash out," you say. You do not mention that he got them from chewing with his mouth open.

"Nope," he answers. "It's oil. From the salad, I guess. Or the sauce. The shirt is ruined. I'll just have to toss it out now."

"You're throwing the shirt away?"

"It'll never look the same," he says. "Those stains won't come out. Colleen tries and tries and she just can't get rid of them."

"But it's such a beautiful shirt," you say. "You just can't throw it out."

"You want it?" he asks.

He begins to unbutton the shirt. Blood surges through your body. Your mouth drops open. You can barely breathe. You cannot decide if you are more amazed that he is willing to give you the shirt off his back or that he is standing there undressing before you.

When the shirt is off he tosses it to you. Your hands lift to catch it, as if the puppeteer is back, deciding what motions he will allow you to make. Your eyes follow Jack as he moves shirtless through the room. He crosses to his suitcase, unlocks it, then sits on a stool and begins to untie his shoes.

"I've got a surprise for you," he says.

You sit on the arm of the couch, or, rather, the puppeteer makes you fold your legs so that the arm of the couch can support your weight that is three pounds less than it was a few days ago.

"A surprise?" you ask. You think someone is also now throwing his voice into your body. The puppeteer is also speaking. You have no idea who you are anymore.

Jack unzips his pants and steps out of them, folding the legs of the pants carefully over the edge of a chair. He is now down to a set of boxers and a pair of socks. He leans against the chair and removes the socks.

"What kind of surprise?" you ask.

Jack opens the suitcase and waves you over to it. "I want you to help me," he says.

You walk across the room, barely missing stepping inside the mouth of the furry dead animal on the floor. You look into the open suitcase and see three, no, four dildos of varying sizes. There is a long, skinny one. A short stubby one with a handle, that looks more like a short plug. There is one about the size and shape of Jack's dick, as you recall the size and shape of it from the last time you were together. And another one that is much bigger. Much, much bigger than any normal or, as it goes, large dick should be.

"I've never done anything like this before," he says. "I want you to help me get used to it."

"Where did you get these?" you ask him.

What Counts Most

"In the city," he says. "Not far from the place where I met you."

٨٨٨٨٨٨٨

The suitcase yields more surprises: a bottle of wine, a corkscrew, plastic gloves, and a bottle of lubricant. Jack opens the wine, pours himself a glass in a cup he finds in the bathroom, and stretches towels on top of the bed so the sheets will not be ruined. "Have a glass," he says to you. "You should be relaxed too."

You wonder if he can tell that you are tense, or if he can tell that one specific part of your body is very, very tense and the rest of you is sweating. While he arranges the dildos on the bed you pour yourself a glass of wine and realize that you are part of a plan that a gorgeous, closeted, married man has been hatching probably long before he ever met you. "Take your shoes off and stay a while," he says, and adds a little laugh. His grin is from ear to ear. "Get comfortable," he says and laughs again.

You take off your shoes and then your pants. You keep your socks and T-shirt and underwear on, the T-shirt hiding the growing tense part of your body that is growing more and more tense as you watch Jack move around the room wearing only a pair of boxers.

The boxers come off next. He lies on the bed on top of the towels. He is flat on his back. His dick is not entirely hard but not entirely soft, either. You wish you had a camera so you could capture the perfect look of the perfect man stretched out in a perfect pose, but you know a camera is not necessary. This is a sight you will not soon forget. He tells you to put on the plastic gloves. He says he can't take any chances. He doesn't mention the wife and kids though you know he is thinking of them because he believes that you are a bag of festering germs ready to attack him.

Desire, Lust, Passion, Sex

You snap the gloves on.

You lather your fingers up with lubricant and then lubricate his asshole. He looks down at you at the end of the bed, as if you were a doctor examining his body. You, of course, *are* examining his body. Every inch and curve and glorious muscle of it. You watch him breathe. You tell him to breathe. You tell him to relax. You watch him relax. Your finger goes in and out of his rectum. When he is comfortable, you put another finger inside him. When he is ready, you lubricate the long, thin dildo.

While you push the dildo in and out he fondles his dick and balls. He grows harder. He closes his eyes. You imagine that he has decided that you are no longer here. Someone else is doing this to him—*his* fantasy man. His perfect man is penetrating him, giving him the pleasure he so desperately desires. He strokes and kneads while you push the dildo in and out. Your mind wanders from one part of his body to the next. You fight off your own urges to fondle yourself, stroke yourself, substitute yourself for the dildo that is in your hand pumping in and out of his ass.

After a while, he allows you to use the larger dildo, not the giant, too-big-for-any-kind-of-purpose one but the one that is the perfect imitation of his own cock. His head is pinned against the bed; his eyes are closed. Sweat gathers at his collarbone. His nipples are large and moist. As you move the larger dildo in and out of his ass you fill your free hand with more lubricant. You rub this onto his cock and his body shudders to accept your touch. His eyes look down again at you briefly and blink in your presence, noting you are still wearing the plastic gloves.

As you move your hands in and out, up and down, he shudders again and comes.

What Counts Most

If he were any less handsome he would have lost a lot of points by now. He would lose points for falling asleep after you pulled the dildo out. He would lose a lot more points for not helping you clean up.

While you are in the bathroom washing his dildos you realize there is no stench at all in this room. His bathroom is large and perfect, just like his room. His bathroom is not on top of a septic tank. Maybe this was all arranged beforehand. Maybe the sleepy-eyed clerk is in on this. Maybe the sleepy-eyed clerk expected him to call room service so that he could show up at the door and offer some kind of service. *Go ahead*, you think. *This one is all yours. He didn't even care if I took off my clothes. Go ahead, take what you can. Give what you've got to give. He's all yours if you want him.*

While you're putting your jeans on you have another glass of wine and then finish the glass that he started. He is still sleeping. He looks like the kind of guy you would only someday hope to look at like this in a room like this one. You consider staying and just watching him sleep, but when you realize that he is snoring you decide to go back to your own room. You gather up the stained blue shirt and the bottle of wine and softly close the door behind you.

Back in your room you realize the wine has started to have an effect on you. Your mind moves from one image to the next. They are all of him. They are all of him on the bed with one of your hands grasping a dildo and the other hand grasping the real thing. You are a part of the picture but not entirely seen. It is his ass, his cock, his dildo that mesmerizes you.

When you are undressed you realize that the pleasure has been all his tonight. You never came. You never had an orgasm. He never even cared that you didn't come. Any other man would lose a big chunk of points for this (and most usually do), but this man, you realize, has given you something that you cannot quite shake from your head. You sort through the images in your mind of his ass, his cock, his dildos, and your hands and find the one you need. Blood surges through you once more. This heightened sense makes you realize that the stench of the bathroom has now invaded your room. You take the beautiful blue stained shirt and press it against your nose. You come easily, overwhelmed by the sense of being near something that has been so near to him for such a long time.

ᴬᴬᴬᴬᴬ

In the morning it is raining. When you meet him for breakfast in the lodge restaurant you agree to drive back early. You have no desire to traipse around the mountain in the rain and mud, and you would rather be in your tiny apartment in the city by yourself than alone in a tiny, smelly room in the country.

You are fully prepared to sit in silence for the entire drive back to the city. While he is just as handsome today as he was the day before this miserable, rainy one, you have no desire to open a channel of communication with him. He begins the drive with the radio on, but since he is in a bright, chipper mood, despite the rain, he wants to talk, so he turns the music down low.

"Have you been with a lot of married men?" he asks you.

His question startles you and you struggle with your thoughts before you supply him with an answer. You are not sure if he means if you knew the men before him were married when you had sex with them or if you consciously had sex with them because they were married. You realize the answer, "Yes," would work in both cases. "A few," you tell him, though you do not provide him with any more details. You try to calculate the number of married men you have slept with and lose count because you keep remembering a few you are certain were separated at the time. You decide the best way out of this miserable internal counting game is to turn the topic of conversation back to him.

"When did you know you were gay?" you ask.

The question frightens him. You can tell this by the way he grins.

"I mean, were you already married? Or did you know it before and hope that being married would make it disappear?"

He clearly does not want to answer you. He pretends to look at the traffic on the road, the way the rain is falling. He slows down the car, grips the steering wheel with both hands. "I could never do what you do," he says.

His answer is vague and you struggle with whether he has insulted you or not. Something in the next few seconds makes you realize that he would never admit to being gay. It is no surprise when the next sentence out of his mouth is, "I could never leave my wife. Or my kids."

The rain continues. The windshield wipers flip back and forth. You decide you are enjoying his discomfort. For the first time this weekend you feel in control of the situation. "But which do you prefer?" you ask him. "Sex with guys or sex with women?"

"It's not that black or white with me," he says.

"What do you mean?" you ask him. "You have a mistress too?"

When he doesn't answer you realize that of course he does. Of course this too handsome gorgeous man takes everything that comes his way. Even his next answer, "I see a few women, too," doesn't surprise you, though it disappoints you. Terribly, terribly disappoints you.

The balance has again shifted into his lap. Of course he sees women. Of course that explains everything. He has sex with women and you are a bag of festering germs who sleeps in a separate bed. You try not to feel insulted when he says, "It really depends on the person. I know it's really shallow but I'm attracted to the way a person looks, not whether it is a guy or a girl. I can just tell by the way someone looks who's worth spending time with and who's not. Or at least I hope I can tell. That's why I thought we would get along."

You are not sure if he has insulted you again. But his tone, like that of a parent scolding a child, makes you feel lousy. You look out at the rain, then press your forehead against the window. The conversation is over. The music grows louder. You feel a headache begin. Someone, someone above you—yes, that giant puppeteer is back and in the miserable gray sky above—wants you to find out one more thing. He will not let you close your eyes until you know it. "Have you ever had a boyfriend before?" you ask. Your voice bounces against the window and slices through the music.

His answer is low, soft, and you have no idea what he is saying. You have no desire to ask him to repeat it. Instead, you look out at the rain and then close your eyes. You realize you are very, very sleepy. When you wake sometime later the suburbs are growing more dense, the buildings are taller; the highway stretches around another and into another. The radio blinks on and off when you enter the tunnel.

When the car stops at the point where he picked you up the day before, he asks, "You have an umbrella?"

"Somewhere," you answer.

"I can call you in a few days," he says. "We could get together again."

Before you open the door you take another look at him. Yes, he is right, you can tell things about a person by the way they look. You can tell exactly who and what they are. Or are not. And what they could mean to you. "Okay," you answer and before you know it you are on the sidewalk facing a new set of choices. Do you look for your umbrella buried in your bag or do you just walk in the rain?

No contest, you decide. You start walking.

Buddies

There was a time a few years ago when my life was less than idyllic. I had just moved back to Manhattan and was rock-bottom poor. Everything seemed to cost much more than what I had in my wallet or could earn in a week at the job where I worked as a publicist. I was depressed because I felt I did not have enough time to write down all the stories that were swirling around in my head. And I was desperate to find a boyfriend; I saw this as one easy way that I could bring a ray of light into all that was unhappy and unfocused in my life. I fantasized that if I found a boyfriend I could give up my job. Together my new boyfriend and I could open up a bookstore or run our own off-off Broadway theater company, or we could move in together and I could leave behind the sixth-floor walk-up apartment that did not even have enough electricity on some days for me to boot up my computer and write. And I reasoned that if I had a boyfriend, I would no longer feel that desire to write. Instead I could be content playing the happy homemaker. I could shop for groceries and plan dinner parties and worry about mildew settling into the bathroom carpet. And I could channel my energies into making my boyfriend happy.

But as it happened I was making my way through a string of blind dates and quick-sex tricks. I complained to my friends that I had trouble meeting a man who wanted a relationship with me for more than a few hours. Even though I could not afford to date anyone I asked every friend I had if they could set me up with someone who might be serious about getting involved in something long-term. I met a few guys this way but no one lasted any longer than the ones I could find on my own in a bar or on a phone line. So I complained more and more until one day a coworker dropped a piece of paper on my desk with a name and phone number.

"Call him," Chris said. "He wants to meet you."

His name was Dennis, or so I shall call him, and he was a fortysomething Republican lobbyist who lived in Washington, D.C., and came to New York frequently on business trips. Chris had worked for Dennis as a student intern and they still kept in touch, meeting for drinks at one of the Madison Avenue hotels where Dennis stayed when he was in town. Chris had told me that Dennis was in a long-term relationship that was drying up and he was looking to meet someone new. I didn't have any expectations when Dennis and I spoke on the phone and arranged to meet for drinks a few days later. I didn't possess enough confidence in either my appearance or personality to imagine that I could be the potential wedge to finally break up two warring lovers.

Dennis was short, barely five-feet-four in his socks, and a good four inches shorter than myself. He had a beautiful body; his boyhood dream had been that he'd become a professional bodybuilder and he had used this passion to create an impressive physique of oversized muscles on his short frame. Dennis had grown up on Philadelphia's Main Line and was sent off to military school and an Ivy League college. He seemed, as Chris had painted him, an ideal candidate for a husband hunter such as me—a well-bred, athletic, preppy, and professional catch.

We met in one of those mirror-lined hotel bars in the West 50s—the kind frequented by straight, married men in town for conventions or meetings and on the prowl for babes and New York experiences. Dennis and I chatted a bit after our introductions, to make sure neither of us was too off-the-rocker for the other, and then he invited me upstairs to his room.

In the room, we undressed separately and awkwardly; there seemed to be only a little passion generated between us. Dennis was somewhat embarrassed to reveal such a smooth, pumped-up physique and I was even more self-conscious to reveal my hairy, boyish one. Sex was very vanilla that night. Dennis didn't want us to kiss on the lips and after a few minutes of clutching and groping, we ended up jerking each other off. Five minutes later I was politely escorted out of the room, and the door closed behind me. Dennis was no different from the other guys I was meeting. I stood out in the hall waiting for the elevator to arrive, feeling cheap and disgusted about our hasty transaction—not that Dennis had paid for it, or that I hadn't been paid for it before, but that it seemed so impersonal and not at all what I had wanted or needed. After all, we had been set up by a friend. This was supposed to be a date, not a trick. We hadn't even had dinner or finished a drink together. And since it wasn't the hottest or most fulfilling sexual encounter I had ever had—or had even had *that week*—I wasn't too upset with the likelihood that I would never see Dennis again.

So I was surprised, truly surprised, when Dennis called me ten days later and asked if he could come over to my apartment between meetings while he was in the city. I agreed, but cordially warned him not to expect things in my home to be, well, on the level of a Main Line estate, a D.C.

Desire, Lust, Passion, Sex

duplex, or even a renovated Times Square hotel.

What he liked about my apartment—I found out some time later—was the seediness of it: the lack of ventilation between the rooms, the cracked linoleum floors, the flickering electric current, the bed frame that sagged at the end because one of the support boards had broken and I had not been able to afford to repair it. Dennis loved my poverty because he could instill my life with a bohemian glow I did not wish to acknowledge. Instead, I saw myself as a writer struggling to make it in Manhattan by living in an overpriced tenement apartment. I never had enough money to afford even the lunchtime special at the corner Chinese restaurant.

I was, of course, embarrassed by my poverty and surroundings, embarrassed that Dennis had to call me from the corner so that I could go down five flights to open the front door of my building for him. I was embarrassed for someone to find that I had stopped cleaning my apartment because I felt my time could be better spent doing anything else. And I was embarrassed to lead him into my overheated bedroom; an air conditioner was a luxury I couldn't even consider.

It was a blistering early summer afternoon when Dennis first walked into my apartment. The temperature had reached over one hundred degrees that day and the air, inside and out, was thick with humidity. Dennis wore what I would soon come to call his uniform: a dark business suit, white shirt, red power tie, black suspenders, and black patent-leather wing-tipped shoes from Brooks Brothers. In the bedroom, the sounds of taxi horns and squealing truck brakes from the impatient traffic on Ninth Avenue drifting through my open window made it impossible for us to begin a conversation. So we undressed as we had done the first time at his hotel room, separately and on opposite ends of my bed. But before our clothes had hit the floor—or, rather, before mine had hit the floor and Dennis's had been folded and gently placed on the only chair I owned—our bodies were covered with a thin film of perspiration. By the time we had finished, the sheets were drenched with sweat and crumpled as if they'd survived a tumble over Niagara Falls, and Dennis, so eager and aggressive during this second encounter, shook his muscles out as if he had just run a marathon.

Marathon running was, in fact, what now kept Dennis in such great shape, along with a two-hours-a-day three-times-a-week gym regimen. If it weren't for the gray in his full head of short, black hair, he might have been mistaken for a young man in his late twenties; his skin was tight and devoid of body fat and wrinkles. But there was something asymmetrical about him that all his exercise had not perfected, a little slope at the shoulders, one eyebrow lower than the other, and a cock which curved to the left like the base of the McDonald's arches and captured the cedary fragrance of his groin.

Dennis left that afternoon with an air of contentment I still had not achieved from our encounters. I was angry at myself for falling into such an easy sexual trap, and in the back of my mind an alarm was going off: Don't waste your time on him if he isn't lover material. I did not have any further expectations of a relationship from Dennis and so I was surprised, once again, when he called and asked to see me a few days later.

There was no fixed pattern to Dennis's comings and goings. Sometimes I'd see him twice a week, sometimes not for a month or two. A typical afternoon get-together would find me rushing home from work to unlock the front door for him and escort him upstairs. Dennis would arrive equipped with a cold six-pack and a box of condoms, and he would chug and talk while I put out the lube and towels and found a few dirty magazines or porno tapes in case we wanted them. Unlike some of my other gay friends, I felt that fuck buddying was a less than ideal relationship; intimacy and romance have always been bigger turn-ons for me. Those few minutes' worth of conversation with Dennis at my kitchen table before we headed back to my bedroom were an important aspect of what kept me interested in him. Little details of who he was casually surfaced without my having to force any direct questions on him—enough information, in fact, to convince me that Dennis was not the ideal catch I had imagined him to be and I might best content myself with our sexual explorations and nothing more. For one thing, we differed in our degree of openness about being gay. Dennis wasn't out at work, wasn't even out to his parents or the circle of straight friends he maintained in Washington. He loved for me to use this fact in our sex play; for a while we went through a phase where I verbally taunted him for being a Closeted-White-Republican-Faggot while I spanked him and he pleaded for tolerance. One thing that worked about our relationship was that we were willing to sexually experiment with each other in ways that we had not attempted with other men.

But our conversations were also how I found out that Dennis's long-term relationship had finally dissolved and he was casually involved with a new boyfriend in Washington, though the details of his affair were often slim or mentioned offhandedly. Instead, Dennis loved to tell me all about his recent vacations; New York was often a pause on the way home from Burma or Peru or Tahiti, and he would arrive with tales of the sexual situations in which he found himself in these foreign locales, from his trips to bathhouses to hiring the local "talent." These stories convinced me that Dennis was sexually experienced in ways I had only imagined for myself. Not all of our discussions revolved around sex, how-

Buddies

ever; now and then I would mention something I had written or published or try to explain to Dennis why writing a novel was such slow going, or why I had given up a permanent job and become a temporary office worker so that I could have the mental freedom to write. But I never talked to him about my most recent dates or my ongoing search for a lover, which must have been why it came as such a surprise to him when I confessed one winter afternoon that I had started dating someone seriously and that maybe we should take a hiatus from our activities.

"Who is this guy and what does he mean to you?" he asked me, alarmed, his face drawn tight. I had waited till he was dressing to leave to explain that this would be our last get-together.

"A boyfriend," I answered.

"A serious boyfriend?"

"Maybe," I said. "Maybe not."

"You don't need to get yourself into a half-assed relationship. You deserve better than that."

I was surprised by his tone of voice; a touch of intimacy had crept in where there was never one before. "Unfortunately no one is offering me that," I said.

There was a moment of silence between us as Dennis buttoned his pants and drew the suspenders over his shoulders. My apartment was cold that day, and we'd had to stay close to each other beneath the comforter to stay warm. Already there was a history of more than six months between us. He rubbed his hands briskly together to keep them warm and I thought, for a brief moment, that he might try to offer his own open relationships as a model for mine. But he didn't pursue that path. With the same tone of concern, he said, "You should complain to your landlord about the lack of heat in this place."

"I'll add it to my list of grievances."

"Do you want me to call him? I could probably pull some strings."

"He has to turn it on eventually," I said. "It's the law. Every year he gets a little later."

"You should let me help you."

"I can take care of myself."

He looked around my bedroom, then pitched his head back and looked at the ceiling. I thought he was going to make a bitter, condescending remark about the place—the lopsided floor and the cracks that traveled up the wall to where he rested his eyes. Instead he asked, "How long have you been seeing him?"

"Almost three months."

"So there's no point in getting serious so soon," he said. "You've got plenty of time before you have to make that decision. I'll call you next week when I'm in town."

✶✶✶✶✶

We didn't stop seeing each other. My more serious boyfriend didn't stick around for a relationship. And I didn't confess this to Dennis. In the meantime Dennis had moved on to another new boyfriend and was soon juggling dates with two guys in Washington. On one level I resented the fact that Dennis and I never left my apartment together, never went out for dinner, never did the things that couples do together—go to the movies or to the theater, even though I couldn't afford to do any of those things with him—but on another level I was happy that our sexual sessions now ended with postcoital conversations and cuddling, even though this growing level of intimacy confused me. Something told me that I should not want to push Dennis into any other role than the one he had found in my life—while we were good sexual partners we might not be so good as boyfriends or lovers—and I should be happy with the status quo we had somehow arrived at and not attempt to define or change it.

And then one day during our third year of seeing each other—after we had both passed through many other sexual and romantic partners—Dennis lay in my bed complaining about a new guy he was dating named Michael, who was afraid of showing him any emotional commitment. Dennis said Michael wouldn't spend the night at his apartment. He was upset that Michael had disappeared on a business trip to Texas for eight days and hadn't bothered to call Dennis at all. I was able to realize the irony of this from many angles—an unfaithful lover complaining about an uncommitted one—and I asked Dennis if Michael was aware of our relationship.

"He knows I see a friend in New York," Dennis said.

"But we're not really just friends," I answered. "We've never seen each other outside of this room, except the night we first met at your hotel. I could tell Michael that you're afraid of emotional commitment, too. We've never even spent the night together. I don't think I've ever seen you for more than two hours at a time."

Dennis had found his way out of bed and was unfolding his pants from the back of the chair. I saw that he wanted to say something but was holding his thoughts back. "But then we're not boyfriends either, are we?" I said, letting him off the hook. "So that kind of behavior makes all of this behavior acceptable."

It was not the next time, or the time after that, but it was soon thereafter that Dennis asked me to meet him at his hotel room after a business dinner engagement had ended. "You can stay the night, too, if you want," he said.

The notion that Dennis might have thought about our relationship outside of my bedroom surprised me. "We'll see how it goes," I said, knowing that Dennis was an early riser and that he might change his mind once I got to his hotel room. Or that I might chicken out and not even show up.

At the hotel, Dennis and I lay in bed watching television after we had finished with sex. Sometime after midnight, when he was groggy, he rolled over and turned the lights out. I was wide awake beside him in bed, unable to sleep, aware that what we were doing was changing the meaning of us.

"Am I as good as your other lovers?" he asked. He had snuggled himself into my embrace, our arms floating around each other, his breath hitting the cleft of my neck in warm pulses.

I hated this comparative game, surprised that a man would put his ego to such a test. The truth, of course, was that I was much too much of a coward to hear how deeply someone else could feel for another person, particularly if the other person wasn't me. I had long ago erased my curiosity of what Dennis's life was like outside of our rendezvous—I felt I had fully accepted our being only sex partners and it would only have been painful for me to know more. The weight of his arms had pinned my own arms against my body and his hands had found mine where they rested near my stomach. He twisted our fingers together and kissed the back of my neck. I knew from the childish tone of his question that he wanted my affirmation.

"Yes," I lied, not mentioning that at that moment he was my *only* lover.

"Am I as big as they are?" he asked, again, a bit too sincerely for comfort.

"Bigger," I lied again, for Dennis was only of modest endowment, and no guy, regardless of his size, likes to hear that someone is more gifted than they are in that department—so I told him what he wanted to hear. That was what a lover should do, shouldn't he? *Any* lover, be he trick or timeless. And this was a role we were now playing. We were pretending to be lovers.

"Do they do anything I don't?" he asked next.

"What do you mean?"

"Treat you differently?"

"I think we're a little different together than what I've done with others."

He didn't pursue my path of reasoning. This was bedtime talk—talk that was supposed to be comforting and soothing, to make the worries and stress of a day disappear. "Is it working for you?" he asked.

"Yes," I answered honestly. "It's always nice to be with you."

"You should come visit me in Washington," he said.

This was another surprise. In the dark I was sure he could see the inside of my mind working. "I can't afford a trip right now," I answered.

"I can give you some money, if you want," he said. When he realized what he had offered me, though, he backtracked a bit. He pulled us closer together, rubbed his chin against my shoulder. "You can borrow it if you want. Pay me back when you can."

When I didn't answer him, he continued. "I just want to take some of the sleaziness out of this for a bit."

"But it's not just sleazy," I answered defensively. "I think you know that."

"Then there's no reason for you not to come to Washington."

"Maybe when it's warmer," I said. "I always think better when it's warm."

᚛᚛᚛᚛

I never visited Dennis in Washington. We never took a trip together. Dennis never sent me flowers, never celebrated my birthday. And I never gave him a present, never wished him Happy Valentine's Day or Merry Christmas.

Desire, Lust, Passion, Sex

And more years passed between us, as if in some fairy tale. I was published but never conquered my poverty. Dennis went to Vietnam, Italy, Ecuador and the Galapagos Islands. Chris, the friend who had set up our introductions, drifted into a forgotten memory. And then I met a man about whom I *did* become serious. For a while I didn't know how to explain Dennis's presence in my life to this guy, and then after another while I realized that things were likely to fall apart with him if I did. In bed Dennis would ask for details of my new lover and sometimes I would be vague and other times I wouldn't be. It was easy for me to describe a vacation to California with my boyfriend—the restaurants we went to in Los Angeles and the resort where we stayed in Palm Springs—but it took more effort to admit that I knew I was more serious about my boyfriend than he was about me. He was still seeing other men, still on the prowl for another boyfriend—a good friend had actually witnessed him picking someone up in a bar. I'd love to say that Dennis was supportive, that he helped me work things out, see things clearly about the different kinds of relationships gay men can have, but he wasn't that kind of talky, intuitive man, not that kind of friend or boyfriend, nor that kind of lover. Instead, Dennis became a diverting constant for me: entertaining, reflective, always coming back into town. And as it was, I had to do many foolish things to learn the error of my ways in that more serious and one-sided relationship, from snooping through appointments in my boyfriend's daybook to monitoring his movement in Internet chat rooms, things which out of context now seem appalling to admit. And I let that kind of behavior of mine stretch out longer than it should have. But there's a lot of truth in the saying that no one can change your life except yourself. And nothing is a better teacher than time and experience.

Four years later, this difficult, complicated, and now too

serious relationship finally came to an end. It was early September, a Friday night, and I'd had a disagreement with my aberrant boyfriend because I felt he was shutting me out of his life and growing distant. In the end, sex had little to do with our final break; our communications had grown stale and strained. We could not share our experiences, either together or apart, and the only thing we could agree on was that it was time to end things completely between us. Leaving my boyfriend's apartment, I had walked from the Upper East Side across town feeling both burned and burned-out. I had fallen in love and now I was out of love. When I got home an hour or so later there was a message from Dennis saying he was in town for the night before he caught a plane to Rio the next morning, and if I wanted to, I could visit him at his hotel that evening. My body was aching with disappointment and rejection and an odd sense of relief, and the last thing I wanted to do was attend to someone else's sexual needs. I felt like I didn't have a sexual pore in my body. But I also didn't want to be alone.

On the walk back across town to Dennis's hotel it occurred to me that ours was the longest relationship I could lay claim to thus far in my life, outside of my family and friends. We had been buddies by then for more than eight years. I tried to let the cool Manhattan evening work its romantic charm on me—the flashing lights of Times Square, the yellow blur of taxis on the street, the great starry ceiling of Grand Central. I wanted to convince myself that I loved Dennis, that my love for Dennis might replace the love I had just lost. But I knew that couldn't happen. Dennis was not to be that man. I had learned how to divorce emotional content from our sexual relationship, but I had not yet learned if such a thing could be easily restored.

And it wasn't something I really wanted to try with Dennis. I could see now how he had pushed and challenged and changed our relationship simply by being a steady, yet evolving presence over time, and how I had at times selfishly held myself back because I was scared of feeling something deeper for him. At his hotel room, Dennis knew me well enough to know that I was not in my best spirits. "Do you want to talk about it?" he asked, when I settled onto the bed beside his luggage. He was taking clothes out of his suitcase, folding and unfolding items with the precision and deliberation he always used.

"No," I answered. "Not really." I was done with trying to make something into something that it was not. Dennis knew instinctively that I was not shutting him out, that in time, if I needed to, I would open up and talk with him. He tossed me a brochure he found from the inner sleeve of his suitcase and said, "That's where I'm headed."

The brochure was of a luxury resort and full of photos of candlelit dining rooms, hotel suites with king-sized beds and bathrooms with marble sinks and oversized tubs. For a moment I imagined walking into such a place with Dennis and discovering it for the first time, as I had done with a history of boyfriends but never with Dennis. I knew Dennis would not be traveling alone on this trip; he seldom did now, even if it meant inviting one of his well-to-do ex-boyfriends to accompany him, but with this particular trip he had been elusive about any details up till now, and I knew I was better off not asking for any more. Still, I felt an odd moment of jealousy overwhelm me, and to fight off my despair I looked up at Dennis and asked, nonchalantly, "Want to take a bath together?"

It was something in all the years we had been seeing each other that we had never done together—we had occasionally showered together, using it as a prelude to or a cleanup from sex, but we had never soaked together in a tub nor used the tub as a toy, though we had often talked about wanting to do so.

Dennis smiled and said, "The tub is awfully small here. That means we'll have to be sort of intimate with each other."

I nodded and smiled and found the energy to get off the bed and run the water in the small bathtub of his hotel room. It was hardly as luxurious as the destination in Rio where he was headed, and his tiny, cramped New York City hotel bathroom had not a shred of romance to it. I was able to muffle a nearby closet light so that we would not have to bathe in the full brightness of the bathroom and found an FM classical music station on the radio. We sat in the tub in various awkward positions with cramped knees or splayed legs, our laughter bouncing against the white tiles of the room as we tried to adjust to accommodate each other. Dennis massaged my back; I washed his hair. Both of us had erections by the time the water turned cold, so we dried off and padded across the carpet and continued in bed. That night is still one of the most vivid memories I retain of Dennis; an unexpected buoyancy heightened everything—our skin, the air, the fabric, the music floating through the room. I saw the fact that Dennis and I could go on and on like this for as long as we needed each other. Dennis was capable of suspending my life; he could make me forget, even if only momentarily, many things: unhappiness with lovers, friends who had died, money and success that eluded me. And, after all this time between us, he could keep me aroused.

I stayed with Dennis that night and we slept embracing each other as if we were lovers. Before he left for the airport the next morning, we kissed each other lightly on the lips before we disappeared back into our other lives. I realized I had something enduring with him that I'd had with no other lover. I was his buddy—the guy he saw for sex in the city—and needed nothing else from him at all. I knew I would see him again, though I didn't know when and wasn't worried about how soon. "Love ya," he said before he left me for something else that morning.

I know he didn't mean it, at least not in the way I had been looking to find it for so many years, but it was nice to hear the phrase, nonetheless, especially from him. "Love ya," I answered back. I thought it had a nice sound to it, so I tried it again, even though he was now out of earshot. "Love ya," I repeated. "Hope to see ya soon."

Acknowledgments

Without an ongoing association with other authors, editors, publishers, and readers most of the stories in this collection would not exist, and I am indebted for the advice and attention each has given to my writing. My special thanks and appreciation go to Anne H. Wood and Brian Keesling, who have continually read my work and offered me valuable advice. Thanks and gratitude also go out to Richard Labonté, Sean Meriwether, Lawrence Schimel, Paul Willis, Greg Herren, Michael Lassell, Jim Marks, Aldo Alvarez, Bill Sullivan, Marti Hohmann, Susie Bright, Marilyn Jaye Lewis, Greg Wharton, Ian Philips, Jay Quinn, David Bergman, Christopher Navratil, Brian Bouldrey, Robert Drake, Terry Wolverton, Michael Ford, Lynne Barrett, David Olin Tullis, Charles Allen Wyman, Kirk Read, Michael Rowe, Scott Heim, Felice Picano, Christopher Bram, Felice Newman, Frédérique Delacoste, Daphne Young, Mark Sullivan, Wayne Hoffman, Tom Long, Catherine Ryan Hyde, Merle Daniels, Aaron Smith, David Groff, Charles Flowers, Hugh Coyle, Will Berger, and Wesley Gibson. Special thanks also go to Hermann Lademann, Arch Brown, Edward Iwanicki, and the New York Foundation for the Arts.

This collection of stories would also not have existed without the attention given to it by my editor, Kevin Bentley, and my publisher, Andrew McBeth. Kevin especially deserves praise for encouraging me to assemble my stories and for patiently wading through an accumulation of drafts and potential works to consider.

I've also been blessed with a supportive group of friends to whom I am always grateful: Martin Gould, Larry Dumont, Jon Marans, John Maresca, Joel Byrd, Deborah Collins, Jonathan Miller, Edward Bohan, and Andrew Beierle.

꙳ꙮ꙳

About the Author

Jameson Currier is the author of a novel, *Where the Rainbow Ends*, a previous collection of short stories, *Dancing on the Moon*, and wrote the script for the documentary film, *Living Proof*. His short fiction has appeared in many literary magazines and Web sites, including *Christopher Street*, *Blithe House Quarterly*, *Velvet Mafia*, *OutsiderInk*, *Absinthe Literary Review*, *Rainbow Curve*, *Harrington Gay Men's Fiction Quarterly*, and the anthologies *Men on Men 5*, *Best American Gay Fiction 3*, *Certain Voices*, *Boyfriends from Hell*, *Men Seeking Men*, *Mammoth Book of Gay Erotica*, *Best Gay Erotica*, *Best American Erotica*, *Quickies 3*, *Circa 2000*, *Rebel Yell*, and *Making Literature Matter*.